DEADLY
YELLOWSTONE

thalia press

Deadly Yellowstone Anthology Copyright © 2024 by Thalia Press

Individual authors retain their copyright © 2024

All rights reserved.

No part of this book may be reproduced in any form or by any electronic or mechanical means, including information storage and retrieval systems, without written permission from the author, except for the use of brief quotations in a book review.

DEADLY YELLOWSTONE

CONTRIBUTORS

David Bart
Celeste Berteau
Alyssa Bowen
Cheryl Fallin
Julie Fasciana
Karen Keeley
Kenzie Lappin
R.T. Lawton
Lise McClendon
Robert Mrazek
Sally Milliken
Katy Munger
Katie Thomas

CONTENTS

Foreword   vii

1. DEAD ZONE   1
   Karen Keeley

2. THE INTRUDERS   18
   Robert J. Mrazek

3. FOR THE LOVE OF ANSEL ADAMS   29
   Celeste Berteau

4. SOME DAYS YOU EAT THE BEAR   53
   Katy Munger

5. PREY FOR REVEREND MORGAN   72
   David Bart

6. LITTLE GLORIOUS LIFE   87
   Sally Milliken

7. THE DEAD BEAR AFFAIR   113
   Kenzie Lappin

8. YELLOW STONE   141
   R.T. Lawton

9. WHAT ROAMS AT NIGHT   153
   Alyssa Bowen

10. HONEYMOON TRIP   180
    Julie Fasciana

11. TERRACES   203
    Katie Thomas

12. HIGH WIDE AND HEINOUS   228
    Lise McClendon

13. YELLOWSTONE AWAKENING: 250
    A Legend Arises
    Cheryl Fallin

FOREWORD

The wonders of Yellowstone—the geysers and mudpots, the wildlife, the incredible landscape—have fascinated visitors for over 150 years. The hydrothermal features in the park number more than half the world's total. Before—and after—its early 19th-century discovery by mountain men, Native American tribes hunted and traversed the region for over 11,000 years. It was named America's first National Park in 1872, and visitation continues to grow today.

These stories are fictional, and bear no relation to real people or events. Some of them are amusing, some scary or mysterious, some fantastical. Yellowstone is like that: something for everyone. We hope you find a story or two that will take you back to Yellowstone, at least in your imagination.

Then come back soon. One trip to Yellowstone is never enough.

—*Lise McClendon, editor*

DEADLY YELLOWSTONE

I

DEAD ZONE

KAREN KEELEY

It began at Schanks Bar 'n Grill on Macleod, enjoying a beer, or what was meant for a beer, mine having long since gone stale. By my watch, it was well after midnight, and me with the knowledge I'd had one brew too many, my bladder about to burst, when Randy interjected into the conversation, "Did you know there's a dead zone in Yellowstone?" Like I knew the answer when all I wanted was that side-trip to the men's room.

"What's that?" I asked, elbows on the table, half yelling over the noise of the canned music, Keith Urban giving us a *Better Life,* him wanting to love somebody, what we all wanted.

"A dead zone in Yellowstone," said Randy, his delivery making it sound like some kind of limerick.

"Never heard of it." I toyed with my beer glass, feeling done in with the brew, the atmosphere, and the company. And besides, it was way past my bedtime.

"It's a kind of no-man's-land where someone can commit murder and get away with it," he said. "No jurisdictional boundaries."

"And I need to know this because—?" I was half way out of my chair, nature calling.

Randy told me to sit, asking, "Would I lie to you?"

Maybe not outright but I'd known him to embellish the truth or lie by omission, if it served his purpose. Nothing new there.

He'd always been bigger, faster, and smarter. The reason for the IT company he ran, and me? I was hired help. I booked the appointments, handled payroll, the Workers' Comp claims, made the phone calls regarding inventory and follow-up services. Randy and others took care of the tech support providing the hardware, the software, and the training. As a business, we'd started out small. When the economy boomed, oil prices skyrocketing, Randy took it as a window of opportunity to grow the business into something resembling a Fortune 500 Company which put coin in the bank and in our pockets. It also provided Randy the nice wife as an added perk, a lovely gal he took for granted, like me, like all of us who worked for him.

While I was navel gazing, Randy hollered over the noise of the music, "It's true. A guy out there in the dead zone, he murdered three people. Literally got away with it."

"The relevance being—?"

"Some documentary I saw on TV." He then stated, if it was a bogus documentary like that Blair Witch Project, the videographer made it look real. "There's still controversy around that film. The people were so terrified, their fear was palpable, whether they'd believed the curse or not. It was *too* real, if you get my drift."

"And the Blair Witch Project reminded you of the dead zone," I said.

Randy nodded, twirling the few ounces remaining in his glass.

Tonight he'd dressed in his signature look, cowboy boots with lighter overtones on the toes, Neiman Marcus dress slacks, an Arnold Palmer golf shirt and his leather jacket. He looked badass, ever the guy out on the town, searching for a good time. Me, not so much despite being similarly dressed, more milage on my boots than his, faded Levi's, a navy pullover from my college days. It was, after all, Calgary which meant colder temps once the sun went down no matter the time of year.

"Whether fiction or fact," he said, "the documentary I saw, the director supposedly spoke with the relatives of the three who were killed. Young guys, college students. They were camping in Yellowstone, something they did every year. The fellow who killed them, he came across their campsite, broke bread with them, played nice."

Randy drank the last of his beer, set the glass on the table. "He then went ever lovin' ape-shit, killing for no apparent reason. After the murders, he tracked down the nearest ranger station, told them what he'd done, made a full confession. The rangers didn't believe the story. Not until they checked it out, found the remains of those he'd killed. Pretty horrendous, I guess, but no one could arrest the guy on account no one lives in that section of the park, therefore, no crime. Not one single solitary citizen who could've been called for jury duty."

Okay, maybe it sounded plausible, but hell, my mind was centered on the men's room. This time, I didn't take no for an answer. I stood, telling Randy, "So there's a dead zone. What's that got to do with us?"

Randy smiled. Took on the look of the cat who ate the canary. "We're going there. Camping. Seventy-two hours to hike in. I've made the arrangements."

"You're crazy. We haven't camped in years."

Randy fiddled with the coaster accompanying his beer. "As my friend, *and* my business partner—"

We were now partners? When did that happen?

"Indulge me," he said. "It's my fortieth next week. I'm saying we should do something exciting."

"And you figure trekking seventy-two hours through the back country in Yellowstone would be exciting."

"Damn straight, buddy. Imagine the views. Like standing on top of the world. And whether the story is true or not, we'll find us our own dead zone."

I didn't like the sound of that.

Randy gave me the weekend to pack my hiking boots, a windbreaker, a pair of khakis, a couple of t-shirts. He took care of the rest of the gear and the provisions, including a lightweight tent, easy to assemble, according to him.

That Monday, the beginning of July, I handed the keys to Christine, Randy's intern, leaving her in charge of the business. She'd come on board a year ago; she too was a wiz at computers.

Some ten hours later, we entered Yellowstone at the Bechler Ranger Station, the trip south having proved uneventful. The plan was to follow the trailhead to Cascade Corner, our jumping off point. Upon arrival, Randy stood by his Ford Ranger, scratching an ear. "Whaddya think?" he said.

"Impressive," I replied, and it was. The ranger station, not large but certainly serviceable for the couple of working stiffs on site, offered signs out front pointing to the elevation, sixty-four hundred feet above sea-level, various trailheads, points of interest, and outhouse facilities. It was chilly but not cold. A thick band of lodgepole pine encroached on the parking area, the wind high up in the trees, branches swaying.

I spotted three vehicles in the lot, a couple of SUVs and a pickup belonging to the rangers. Bird song was in the air, along with mosquitoes. One took a juicy bite out of my neck. I slapped at it, turned my eyes skyward, a vibrant blue, not a cloud to be seen.

"We'll check in, be on our way," Randy told me.

When we first arrived, tires crunching on gravel, he'd backed in and parked near the trees at the periphery of the property. I half wondered what was in those trees, deadfall certainly, a chipmunk or two. Anything larger and I wasn't sure I'd keep my wits about me.

It took ten minutes to sign the register, to tell the rangers on site where we were headed.

"You got three days travel," said the guy at the desk. "And keep in mind, it is grizzly bear country, along with other wildlife. Keep a clean site. Keep your distance."

Randy smiled, cementing the deal. "No doubt about that. I've got a birthday to celebrate."

"Don't we all," countered the ranger with a melodious chuckle.

While Randy continued to make pleasantries with the guy at the desk, I wandered over to a display case filled with pamphlets, readjusting my backpack so it hung from one shoulder. A second ranger was speaking with a family of four, telling them that the animals had the right of way, to stay clear of them. He then got on about a group of tourists parked on a roadway, elk grazing nearby. One idiot, on crutches, made the dubious decision to march right on up to one of the animals, looking to take a selfie. Needless to say, the elk was not impressed. The guy hurried back to his vehicle much like a praying mantis hyped up on amphetamines as he churned his way across the meadow, the elk snorting, giving the fella the evil eye.

"We had another who figured he'd get up close and personal with a bison," said the ranger. "Him too, running for his life."

I leaned into Randy, telling him, "If we get lost, we're on our own."

"We're not getting lost. I've got the map and a satellite phone. We stick to the trails, easy-peasy. As to the animals, it'll be chipmunks and squirrels. Plenty of room for them and us."

I wasn't feeling at all confident about this trek into the wilderness despite Randy's assurance all would be 'easy-peasy'. I was now chowing down on a handful of cashew nuts, hoping to keep my sugar levels elevated while trying to lower my anxiety. I'd always been a prairie boy, growing up in Saskatoon, college in Regina, a career in Calgary. Long stretches of highway had been my area of expertise, navigating gentle curves in the road, the land flat and unassuming, able to see whatever was coming at me—18 wheelers with their B-trains, Greyhound buses, panel vans, not a tree for miles.

I drank from my water bottle. I dug out the can of bear spray and hung it on my belt, knowing I hadn't a clue how to use the damn thing. If a grizzly zeroed in for the attack, five hundred pounds of mean with its four-inch claws and a bite strong enough to crush a bowling ball, I'd literally lie down and die.

We returned to the vehicle. Randy unlocked the tool box in the cargo bed and took out a rifle. "I thought there were no firearms allowed," I told him.

"Discharging a firearm is illegal," Randy replied. "Possession is permitted. I'd rather be safer than sorry. No telling what wildlife we might run into no matter what they say."

"You said it would be chipmunks and squirrels."

"I lied," he said, tossing me a wink while hoisting his own pack onto his back.

He then locked the tool box and the vehicle itself. I figured when we returned in six, seven days' time, the damn thing would be covered in pine needles and sap from the nearby trees. It would be a bitch removing the sap, knowing, if memory served, it played havoc with the paint job. Randy wasn't gonna like that one little bit.

THE FIRST FULL DAY OF TRAVEL WENT PRETTY MUCH ACCORDING TO plan. We followed the beaten path over hill, over dale, getting into the rhythm of the hiking, taking breaks, chowing down on the beef jerky or the dried fruit and keeping ourselves hydrated. The only wildlife we encountered were the aforementioned squirrels and chipmunks, cheeky little devils not at all happy we'd intruded on their space. By the end of that day, I was thoroughly bushed.

On the second day, pulling myself from the tent, I didn't know if I had it in me to keep going. I was sore, stiff, grumpy and hungry. The weather had changed overnight, low cloud cover now giving us fog patches along the creek bed near our campsite in addition to a severe drop in the temperature, cold enough for me to see my breath. I dug out my old pullover. Christ, what the hell was I doing out here? Randy was in his element, heating water for coffee, going on about the joy of mother nature and getting back into the wilds. When the drizzle hit, it darkened my mood to downright intolerable. Each time I heard a rustling in the woods, my heart hammered in my chest, thinking of that grizzly, but nothing showed.

It was the middle of the third day, the weather cleared, blue sky above when we hiked through meadows and spied a few deer grazing. Twice we saw a fox in the distance which left me thinking, most of the larger animals were further up in the mountains given the time of year. Plenty of wildflowers with their intoxicating scent. Plenty of insects. As for the terrain, we kept on keeping on and shouldered our way through the trees and over boulders while picking annoying pebbles out of our hiking boots, all of it messing with my sensibilities, my knees and joints hollering for relief.

Randy, ever the taskmaster, groused yet again about me holding him back, always on my tail about dragging my feet while drinking bottled water or meandering off trail to take a shit. Each time we made camp, he put me in charge of the tent, working the poles in place, hammering in the tent pegs while he built the fire. This night, he started reminiscing about our Cub Scout days. "Remember knot making?" he said.

I nodded. "I was all thumbs, never could get the hang of it."

"Maybe our troop leader thought we'd join the navy." For some reason that brought a loud guffaw out of him. "Could you imagine—us, in the navy?"

"Never," I said. "I'm a flatlander through and through."

I meant it for a joke but Randy didn't respond. What was the point? There were some things he simply ignored, like twenty years back, the first time we ventured to Yellowstone, three of our group, including me, wanting to hit up Florida, babes 'n bikinis. But no, Randy was adamant we were headed into the wilderness famous for geysers, waterfalls, and fumaroles.

So, there we were, four frat buddies taking in Old Faithful, the paint pots and the hot springs followed by a hike to the top of what is known as Artist Point. Sure, we'd had fun, ready to kick up our heels, probably too much beer and too much dope while sitting around a smoky campfire, sticking to the tried and true, not wandering off the trails into some dead zone in the middle of nowhere. That time, we took a Coleman stove, propane bottles, coolers for the beer and the food. Not at all like this trip, traveling light, mostly nuts, dried apricots, apples and beef jerky, a few granola bars, a block of cheese.

IT WAS LATE ON OUR FOURTH DAY, OUR GOAL IN SIGHT, WHEN RANDY commanded yet again, "Quit clowning around. Put some effort into it."

My patience had long since run out. My lower spine felt like someone was stabbing me with a red-hot branding iron, my feet blistered, the shins in both legs hollering at me to stop, likely shin splints. The path before us was a steep grade, more rock than dirt.

"It's just up ahead," said Randy. "I can feel it."

"You've been telling me that for over an hour," I whined, thinking he sounded like the boy who cried wolf, why should I believe him?

"You doubt my veracity?" He was smiling as though all of it were a big joke.

By then, I was thoroughly pissed, doubting everything. Blood pounded in my ears, sweat on my brow, the sun beating down, and me without a hat. My face felt like sandpaper, four days since I'd last shaved.

"You think I should've brought Laura on this trip?" he asked.

"What's that?" I swatted at another annoying mosquito, them out in droves.

"Laura—should I have brought her with us?"

"Christ, no. She'd hate it." Why the hell was he bringing up Laura?

"And you know this how?"

"I think I know your wife. Now who's being a clown?"

Randy laughed. "Yeah, I would say you know my wife."

I didn't care for the tone. I'd caught up to him, stood by his shoulder. "What the devil are you on about now?"

He didn't bother with an answer. "Look," he said, and I did. And he was right, the valley stretched out before us, trees as far as the eyes could see, a lake in the distance, a couple of bald eagles flying high, having taken advantage of a thermal layer updraft, gliding on their six-foot wingspan, all the world below.

It was then the fight went out of me. "Christ, Randy. It's beautiful."

"It is that," he said, moving onto a bit of a ridge. He turned and took in the view, inhaled a deep breath, stretched his shoulders. He spread his arms wide like he was the goddamn savior greeting the sun.

I sat down, took a load off, my legs grateful for the break. My back, too. I knuckled the kinks out of my lower spine.

"What you got there?" he asked.

"A ladybug, landed on my arm." I was studying the little critter thinking how they were supposed to be the meaning of good luck and new beginnings.

I made mention of that and Randy said, "You think you need new beginnings?"

"We need something, out here in the middle of nowhere despite the view."

"Nowhere is where we've been most of our lives," he said.

"What's that supposed to mean?"

The ladybug took off, greener pastures elsewhere.

"Here we are turning forty," Randy interjected, "and what have we accomplished?" Even for him, he sounded maudlin, not a good look on him.

"You've got a thriving business," I told him. "And a lovely woman at your side."

"You think?"

"I don't think—I know." Christ, where was he headed with this?

Randy now grabbed a piece of buffalo grass, set it between his lips, talking out the side of his mouth. "The way I figure it, you and Laura, good friends, are you?"

What the hell? "Of course, we're good friends. You two, you've been together since college. So yeah, I know her pretty well. How could we not be friends?"

"And you," said Randy. "Never found the one, did you?"

"The one what?"

"A good woman. Someone to call your own."

"Just meant to be single, I guess."

"So, you figure you can take mine?" he said.

"Take your what?"

"My wife, dumbass."

I quickly bounced onto my blistered feet, and backed away, six, eight feet down the path. "You're crazy. I'm not taking your wife."

Randy swung the rifle from his shoulder. He aimed the damn thing at me, him standing there on that wee bit of a rise, looking like the lord of the manor house. "You don't think I don't know? This past year, you and her together. God only knows how many times."

"No times," I said. "You're talking gibberish."

"She told me. She went into graphic detail. Told me she wants a divorce."

I took another step back. "Whatever she told you, it's not true." I took another step away from him. "You know me. Christ, we've been best buds for years. You said so yourself."

"I thought we were." He waggled the rifle barrel at me.

"Where're you gonna run? Back to camp? You think I won't follow?"

Sure, he'd follow. But maybe I could dodge through the trees, hide. Yeah, right. And maybe pigs could fly.

"On your knees," he said.

I shook my head.

"Do it, or I end you now."

I knelt.

The next thing I knew, he was coming at me. He slammed me upside the head with the butt of the rifle. My world went dark. Any thoughts I had of him, or Laura, were gone.

When I eventually came to, I was on my stomach, lying maybe six or seven feet from the edge of the cliff, my hands tied behind my back. Pine needles were stuck to my lips, dirt in my mouth. My head was pounding, a doozy of a headache and no way of knowing if he'd split the skin on my scalp. Was I bleeding?

Randy sat beside me; the rifle cradled in his lap. He was again toying with a piece of buffalo grass, pulling it between his fingers. "Remember the skunk," he said. "Our trip to Yellowstone all them years ago. You were so certain it was going to spray the tent, it snuffling around outside, in the dark. Just a damn skunk and you were fit to be tied."

My response: "The only skunk I'm seeing is you."

He laughed. "Good one. Only you're the skunk, you goddamn weasel." He tossed the buffalo grass and stood, taking a step or two away from me. "You don't think I saw what you were doing? Skimming money out of the business accounts, thinking you'd make a monkey of me? I reckon you got nearly fifty thousand over the past couple of years, and then, to add insult to injury, there you go, stealing my wife."

I rolled backwards, managed to leverage myself into something of a squat, my weight on my legs, leaning forward, breathing deeply, dizziness prevailing. This was not the time for a muscle cramp.

"I didn't steal any money, and I certainly didn't steal your wife." I managed that much despite my labored breathing, my woozy head. Had we made it to the dead zone?

"The way I see it, I have two choices," he said. "I shoot you in both kneecaps, leave you here to die. Either starvation, dehydration, or the animals get you. Or I simply end it quick, a bullet to the head."

"Do I get a say in the matter?" The knots were tight, tighter than I realized. Every time I jerked my wrists, the binding cut off my circulation. I felt blood while trying to pull my hands free. Would the blood act as a lubricant? Or would the smell attract the animals? Not something I wanted to imagine. I kept struggling, twisting my body one way, then the other, using my shoulders for leverage, circulation be damned.

Randy didn't seem to notice or care. "Either way you die," he said. "One slow, one quick. It'll be such a sad story for Laura. She'll be devastated at first. But she'll get over it. You'll become nothing but a distant memory."

You wish, I was thinking, one hand almost free. Sure, I'd taken the money, and I'd taken Laura. She'd finally gotten tired of his drinking, his mood swings, his irascible view of the world, people there to be used and abused, puppets on a string.

As for me, I'd been on the receiving end of Randy's acerbic remarks more times than I cared to remember. I knew exactly what Laura had dealt with all these years. The extramarital affairs finally pushed her over the edge, especially when he blamed her, stating she was the problem. One thing led to another, me, the shoulder to cry on, and there we were, planning our escape, Europe maybe, or the Caribbean. The reason for the money. But even for all that, I wasn't about to fess up to any of it. Why hurry my death along? Keep him talking. Keep wiggling my fingers.

"You're wasting energy," he said. "You can't get loose. Gotta love Boy Scouts, you and me, best buds except for the fact, best buds don't stab each other in the back."

"I didn't do any stabbing." Not unless it was on a keyboard using the PC at my desk, pecking away on Excel spreadsheets and Word docs. I made mention of that.

My attempt at humor fell on deaf ears. "If not for me, you'd have no job."

"True," I said. "But you've done well over the years. Half a dozen high-end techs, all of them working full-time, out in the field, looking after the diagnostics."

"And you, cooking the books. Easy to pilfer the accounts, thinking I wouldn't know." He turned, taking in the view of the valley once more. "I caught on during the last audit. You made one huge mistake with that Acorn account. Nothing to do with the actual work."

"But a good name." Keep wiggling the fingers. "I cracked the nut."

"Some nut," he said, and then, "How you making out with those knots? I used a piece of tree branch as the anchor, the rope twisted and knotted, better than handcuffs."

Yeah, I could feel the branch. Every time I struggled; slivers of bark cut into my wrists. But I was making progress, slowly. I pushed my right thumb against the branch, the branch shoved into the small of my back, for leverage. I felt the thumb give, double-jointed in both thumbs, thank Christ. Randy knew I had that talent, maybe the reason for the constrictor knots.

The more I struggled, the more they tightened. He wasn't taking any chances.

My chance had been Laura. Get her away from him, into my arms. Freedom for the both of us. Randy walked away from me. He raised the rifle, having decided on the kneecaps by the look of him, any escape pretty much a pipe dream. If the end was coming, I'd at least go out with a bang—literally.

I sprang forward, leapt like a snarling leopard, hit Randy square in the chest, him too slow with the rifle. I was a goddamn juggernaut, a linebacker mowing down the competition on the fifty-yard line. Didn't matter I'd never played football.

Randy woofed out an enormous *oomph* as the air went out of him, his arms flung to his sides, trying to recapture his balance. He stepped back—once, twice, three times—slipping in the gravel, toppling away from me, toward the edge of the precipice. Our eyes locked for a brief heartbeat, his with surprise, mine with victory. He again windmilled his arms, a futile attempt to level the rifle at me, the weight of it just enough to topple him backward, one last desperate attempt to take me with him. A hand reaching out, grabbing at air.

Over he went. As for me, I'd freed my right hand, the right thumb taking the brunt of the brute force. It throbbed like hell, as did my head, felt like he'd cracked my skull. I felt blood trickle past my ear, my wrists scraped, the rope and the tree branch having dug into the skin.

I collapsed backward, landed hard on my butt, knocked my teeth together. That too, hurt like a bitch, set my ears ringing. My whole body quivered like a newborn elk calf, my legs useless, the lifesaving adrenaline gone.

I heard Randy scream. His body hit once, twice, then a third time before it landed. All went quiet. Just birdsong, butterflies and bumblebees, the drone of insects. If I'd been in a frame of mind to make a joke, I would've said, what's wrong with this picture?

Minutes passed. I crawled to the edge, and yes, his body lay far below. Not a twitch, not a quiver. And no candid camera in the bushes to have captured it all though my fear was palpable, my heart hammering in my chest.

When I finally made it back to camp, I cleaned up as best I could, the wound on the side of my skull sticky with blood, not knowing if I needed stitches, something that would have to wait for later. My wrists too, were in dire straits, lacerations and more blood. I oscillated between relief and horror, laughter and tears, trying to accept the fact Randy had truly been set on killing me. I sounded like some crazy person blubbering, unable to control myself, rooting through the first-aid kit, searching for bandages, alone in some godforsaken part of the park.

THE FOLLOWING MORNING, I USED THE SATELLITE PHONE, CONTACTED the authorities. I then broke camp after spending a harrowing night jumping at every sound, every shadow, feeding the fire, certain some animal was going to stumble on the campsite, finish the job Randy had started. I took only my belongings.

Later that day, a rescue team picked me up in a meadow two miles from where we'd camped. I told them I'd fallen, lost my footing on a downward grade, shale and loose rock, caught up in the emotional stress of it all, the reason for the gash on the side of my head, the state of my wrists and hands. The ranger who took my statement seemed satisfied, offered sympathies. The team then headed to the coordinates I'd given them, to recover Randy's body. Hours later, the mission successful, they returned, making no mention of any rifle.

Perhaps it fell farther down the side of the cliff, lost in the trees below, Randy having landed on a rocky ledge.

If anyone decided to make a movie about our adventure, I could've made it plausible, hyped up my fear, my disbelief. Such a terrible tragedy, my best bud tumbling over the edge. Hell, I could've played the game. I would've won a goddamn Oscar.

Just two buddies camping in Yellowstone as a way to celebrate a fortieth birthday. The authorities put it down to death by misadventure. Who was I to say anything different? My best friend with murder on his mind, a killing in the dead zone.

Only I got to him first.

KAREN KEELEY WRITES LITERARY, SPECULATIVE AND CRIME FICTION. Many of her short stories appear in various anthologies published by Sisters in Crime—Canada West; Outcast Press; Last Waltz Publishing; Wolfsinger Publications; Black Beacon Books; and others. She is a member of Sisters in Crime—Canada West and the Short Mystery Fiction Society (SMFS). A former Communications Analyst with the Yukon government, she is now retired, and makes her home in Calgary, Alberta where she divides her time between family, friends, the outdoors, and writing.

www.facebook.com/karen.keeley.77
www.karenmkeeley.blogspot.com

2

THE INTRUDERS
ROBERT J. MRAZEK

The weekend began at the United States House of Representatives on the private balcony off the Speaker's Lobby that overlooked Pennsylvania Avenue. They were waiting for the final roll call vote to be called on the House floor late that Thursday afternoon.

Lonny Swaggart, whose district cut a wide swath through the hills and valleys of the Great Smokies, sat in a cushioned deck chair next to his friend Chip Lauderdale, who represented a slowly sinking chunk of the Mississippi delta.

They were braving the cold wind without overcoats. Since the Pelosi era, smoking was no longer allowed in the cloakrooms and they were forced to go outside on the balcony to enjoy a good cigar.

"So what are you doing this weekend?" asked Lonny as wind-driven sleet hammered the leafless oaks and elms on the Capitol grounds.

"What do you think?" said Chip testily. "Kissing ass... kissing ass at a school parade, a golden wedding anniversary dinner, an Eagle Scout ceremony, charity benefits, church suppers, Legion visits, and a couple dozen stop bys."

An evangelical on his third marriage, the stocky Chip was fifty-five with liquid brown eyes, cherub cheeks, and a long perfected air of humble sincerity when he needed to employ it. In contrast, Lonny could have been called ruggedly handsome except for the lantern jaw that had led to his high school nickname— Cowcatcher. Six feet tall and muscled like a steer, he spent an hour every day in the House gym and bench-pressed three hundred pounds.

"I'm heading out to Yellowstone," said Lonny with the endearing grin that had earned him five terms. "Why don't you come with me?"

"Yellowstone as in Wyoming?" asked Chip, drawing on his hand-rolled panatela.

"Yeah," he said. "I've got one of the Interior Department Lear jets flying me out this evening. I'll be taking care of a little problem and having some fun while I'm at it. You're welcome to join me."

"So what's the problem?" asked Chip.

"You remember the escaped mental patient in Tallahassee who bought the AR-15 across the counter and shot the twenty-six fourth graders?"

"It's hard to keep track anymore," said Chip.

"Well, it was a moment of weakness on my part...that and I had been into the jar at lunch before the interview. I told the reporter that I was possibly open to tougher background checks."

Chip shook his head in sympathy.

"The NRA gauleiter in my district came down on me like I had raped Dolly Parton," said Lonny.

"Gotta be tough," agreed Chip.

"So it was my wife who came up with the answer. I'm

going up there to shoot a couple of those grey wolves they now let run free. Imagine the picture of me holding up one bloody head in each hand...my problem goes away."

"They allow hunting in Yellowstone?" asked Chip.

"No, but I asked for a fact finder visit to monitor the Bison counts. That allows me to use the Lear and write the whole trip off. We'll be staying at the lodge of a concessionaire in the park that's off limits to the public. Fully stocked. On Sunday, we'll swing over to a place just outside the park boundaries in snowmobiles and nail the wolves. The outfitter keeps them drugged and ready for trophy hunters."

"I'm not into camping anymore," said Chip, hurling the end of his cigar down onto the concrete path to the public entrance where a line of school children waited to enter.

"Forget camping," said Lonny. "Wait till you see the lodge. It's right on the edge of a bottomless lake with a stone fireplace you can walk into. The lake never freezes and even the winter fishing is supposedly incredible. We can be back for votes on Tuesday morning. I'll make sure you get a wolf too."

Chip Lauderdale lived for fishing. The wolf was a bonus.

Claude, the lodge caretaker, was waiting for them in a Ram 3500 pickup truck by the chained gate at the entrance to the private road leading to the lodge. Lonny and Chip looked like space explorers in their yellow helmets, goggles, and padded snow suits as they pulled their snowmobiles to a stop alongside his pickup.

"You Claude?" shouted Lonny through the open window of the truck.

The man nodded. To Chip, he resembled a bearded ferret in a cowboy hat and red spattered coveralls.

Without taking his cigarette from between his lips, he shouted back, "Everything's ready. I laid on the fire and the beds are made up. All the supplies you'll need are in the kitchen." Glancing up at the sky, he added, "Looks like snow on the way."

"Thanks for opening up for us," yelled Lonny.

Claude tossed his cigarette out into the snow and said, "You should also know...you got a critter...probably been there a spell."

"What kind of critter?" shouted Lonny, but Claude's window was already zipped up. Starting his truck, he put it in gear, and turned back toward West Yellowstone.

"What'd he say?" asked Chip.

"Some kind of critter," said Lonny, gunning his snowmobile up the plowed, single-lane roadway lined with vast evergreens. It ran close to a mile before they slowed to a stop in front of a spectacular log and timber lodge.

Grabbing their bags from the small cargo sled, they climbed the front staircase to the porch and took in the magnificent view across the luminescent, crystal-blue surface of the pristine lake. Aside from the lodge and a small log outbuilding, there was no other sign of human habitation as far as they could see.

"Wow," said Lonny. Chip was speechless.

The lodge had been built in the late 19th century for one of the timber barons, and rose three gabled stories atop a dramatic cliff overlooking the lake. As a bitter and frigid wind began roiling the surface of the lake, they retreated inside.

The kitchen and pantry were crammed to the roof with enough provisions to feed the appropriations committee, along with ten cases of spirits, wine, and Coors beer.

Lonny was extracting a bottle of Stolichnaya from the pantry when he caught a whiff of something foul. It was coming from an open doorway at the back of the room.

Glancing inside, he looked down into the darkness. Turning on the light switch at the top of the stairs, he saw what appeared to be a shallow stone-covered basement inside the four foundation walls of the lodge. A large section of the bottom stair appeared to be missing. Before he could explore the damage, Chip shouted from the living room. "Jesus Christ. Take a look at this."

When Lonny got there, he was standing near one of the panoramic living room windows holding a glass of George Dickel sour mash in one hand and pointing through the window with the other. Lonny followed his finger.

The outer edge of the broad wooden staircase leading up to the side porch hung crookedly from the building. He could see what looked like dozens of bite marks on it, not only on the staircase and railings, but on the plank deck of the porch too.

Putting their parkas back on, they went outside and walked around to the side porch. The base of the vertical beams supporting it showed the same bite marks. One beam was almost eaten through.

"Be careful if you use those stairs," Lonny warned Chip. "Stay close to the house side."

Lonny saw that the lodge walls rested on the stone foundation that ran all the way around the house. One of the wooden hatches leading into the crawl space had also been eaten away. He poked his head into the opening and sniffed the air. It was the same odor he had smelled from the pantry.

"Something's living down there," he said staring into the darkness.

"Don't go in," cautioned Chip.

Lonny wished he had the Bazooka green Glock 19 he loved to carry in its black, diamond-studded holster during weekend stop bys in the district. The stupid FAA regulations had required both of them to leave their guns in Washington before they boarded the Interior Department plane.

Picking up a brick, he hurled it into the darkness. Nothing moved or made a sound.

"You hit anything?" asked Chip.

"I don't know."

"Well, let's eat. I'm starving."

After dinner, Lonny found a sack of rat poison in one of the closets and spread it around the hatch opening to the crawl space and the foot of the stairs below the pantry. They spent almost an hour trying to find the key to the lock on the big black gun safe in the library, but finally gave up.

Fortified with vodka and sour mash, they went to bed early. Lonny was nearly deaf, and never slept with his hearing aids. Chip couldn't see anything without his glasses but his hearing was fine. At around three the next morning, he woke up to a rhythmic gnawing sound, like someone was cracking and chewing gigantic walnuts underneath the house. It didn't stop and he had trouble getting back to sleep.

"What do you think it was?" asked Lonny as they cooked steak and eggs for breakfast the next morning on the commercial Garland stove.

"I don't know," said Chip, "maybe it's a beaver."

After breakfast, they got back on their snowmobiles. Using the map left for them by the Yellowstone staff, they headed over to the ranger station near the protected grounds of the bison herd.

"Thanks for coming all this way to see us," said the ranger superintendent when they arrived. "The bison count may not seem important to many of your colleagues but it's the canary in the coal mine," he said earnestly. "My staff will give you a full assessment of where we are right now. It's not a rosy picture."

Lonny was about to tell him that he liked his bison burgers rare but thought better of it. An hour later, the ranger was describing a bold plan for artificially inseminating some of the females when Chip found himself nodding off. He awoke to another ranger droning on about a recent outbreak of mycoplasma pneumonia. At least this one was attractive and female with an ample rack. He stayed awake by imagining what she looked like without her ranger blouse.

When it was finally over, they snowmobiled back to the lodge and spent the next three hours catching cutthroat trout from the lodge's amphibious ARGO. Back inside the lodge, Lonny reinvigorated the fire and they sat down to warm themselves with a fresh round of drinks.

"The outfitter will be here in the morning," said Lonny. "Then the fun really begins."

That's when Chip heard the same gnawing and crunching noise that had kept him awake the night before.

"Can you hear that?" he asked Lonny.

Lonny used his cell phone app to turn up his hearing aids.

"Loud and clear," he responded. "It's coming from the crawl space below us."

"Now what?" asked Chip.

"I've got an idea," said Lonny.

The idea began with a six-foot long broomstick pole after Lonny sawed off the broom. Next, he removed a razor-sharp Swedish carving knife from the blade set in the kitchen. Using duct tape, he wrapped the knife handle to one end of the broomstick and secured it with three layers of tape.

Grabbing a half dozen cleaning rags from under the sink, he wrapped each one around one of the first edition bird books in the lodge library. At the foot of the stairs from the pantry into the crawl space, he doused the weighted rags with charcoal lighter fluid, lit them with his cigar lighter, and hurled them as far as he could into the darkness.

"Go around to the other side of the house and keep watch

by that open hatch," he told Chip as oily smoke began curling up the stairs.

Lonny kept watch at the pantry door. A few minutes later, he heard an excited shout.

"I see it," yelled Chip. "It's heading for the woods."

Shuffling on his bad knees, Lonny came around the corner of the house to see the animal scuttling toward the small log outbuilding near the plowed parking area.

It was a porcupine. He had encountered plenty of them over the years in the Great Smokies but this was the biggest one he had ever seen. It was moving sluggishly and appeared to be carrying something under its stomach.

He cornered the animal between the lodge and the shed. When he plunged the makeshift spear into its needle-carpeted shoulder, the porcupine screamed loudly in pain. It attempted to lift its unwounded paw to ward off Lonny's attack, but he drove home the knife again and again into its chest.

"Take that, you big bastard," he cried out exultantly, his lantern jaw extended in triumph.

In its death throes, the porcupine finally crumpled to its side. Lonny made a last thrust with the spear into its back as Chip arrived to help.

"It was a female," he said.

"How do you know," asked Lonny.

"Look," he said pointing at the small balls of fur next to the porcupine's belly. "She was about to deliver the babies."

Lonny was unrepentant.

"That thing was eating the lodge," he said. "And it's taxpayer property."

It took them ten minutes to drag the carcass to the edge of the plateau and push it over the cliff. Chip heard the reassuring thud when it hit the rocks a hundred feet below.

They were celebrating on the porch with tumblers of Jameson's when Lonny noticed the snow front approaching that Claude the caretaker had predicted. It was moving toward them from across the lake. As they watched, it slowly rolled up toward the plateau. A few moments later, big snowflakes blotted out their view of the lake.

That's when Lonny glanced down at the shale ledge in front of the porch.

"I can't believe it," he said.

"What?" asked Chip.

"Look at that thing," said Lonny pointing down at it.

It was another porcupine, even bigger than the one he had killed. This one was the size of King, the Newfoundland he had owned before it bit one of his constituents at the annual Swaggart-day picnic and he decided to put it down.

This porcupine ran at least one hundred fifty pounds and it was covered with quills the size of knitting needles. The amazing thing was that it wasn't trying to hide. It just sat there on its hind legs staring up at them on the porch through the swirling snow.

Gulping the rest of his whiskey, Lonny shuffled back to the kitchen and grabbed the still blood-smeared spear from behind the pantry door before storming outside to do battle again.

"Be careful," called out Chip from the porch. "That thing is a monster."

The wind-driven snow was smarting his eyes as Lonny arrived at the ledge near the cliff. Through the swirling curtain, he watched as the porcupine turned and began scuttling away toward the edge of the plateau.

Lonny quickly caught up to it.

"Take that," he screamed as he drove the blade into the porcupine's massive posterior. But before he could strike again, it disappeared into the dense white veil surrounding them.

He stood and waited, turning around every ten seconds as snow fell heavily around him. He thought he heard something scurrying behind him and moved to meet the threat, but he saw nothing there beyond the white shroud. He realized he could no longer see the house and became slightly disoriented.

"Chip, where are you?" he shouted.

Chip's voice came back from above and behind him. "Back up here."

Deciding to abandon the hunt, Lonny had turned in that direction when something huge loomed up ahead of him. He felt sudden barbs of pain in his knees and was forced to lurch back away from it, driving the end of the spear into the ground so he wouldn't fall.

But there was no ground beneath the end of the spear. He was falling through the immense white void, the air rushing past his face as he gathered speed.

Chip heard the loud thud from all the way up on the porch.

"You get him?" he shouted.

There was only silence over the growl of the wind.

"Lonny," he cried out again and again until he realized he couldn't answer. Then it occurred to him that he might be lying injured at the base of the cliff.

The dense, wind-driven snow was churning wildly across the porch as he found the keys to his snowmobile in his parka pocket and headed down the stairs of the side porch to get aboard.

Too late, he remembered Lonny's warning about staying away from the damaged section. A step beneath him gave way and he fell straight down headfirst, only catching himself by using his arms to break the fall.

Above him, he felt a shooting pain in his left leg. When he

tried to move it, he realized his ankle was caught between two of the partially eaten support beams. Looking up, he saw his ankle jutting out from the rest of his leg at an unnatural angle. His glasses were gone too, somehow lost in the fall. Without them he was practically blind.

He smelled it before he heard it. A dark mass emerged from the snow. It had an earthy smell, rank with decay. Now he could hear the thing breathing, deep rasping grunts, as it came closer. The dark blur blotted out the remaining light from the driving snow.

"Please," he begged.

ROBERT J. MRAZEK IS THE AUTHOR OF TWELVE BOOKS, EARNING THE Michael Shaara Prize for Civil War fiction, the W.Y. Boyd Prize for fiction from the American Library Association, and Best Book (American History) from the Washington Post. A former five term congressman, he wrote numerous pieces of landmark legislation including the Amerasian Homecoming Act that brought 19,000 children fathered by Americans during the Vietnam War to the U.S., the law that saved the Manassas Civil War battlefield from being bulldozed into a shopping center, and the landmark Tongass Timber Reform Act which protected 3,000,000 acres of old-growth forest in Southeast Alaska.

3
FOR THE LOVE OF ANSEL ADAMS
CELESTE BERTEAU

Because of Ansel Adams I tripped over a dead man's foot.

Everyone who knew me knew I had a thing for Ansel Adams. I had a print, well, a poster, of *Moonrise Hernandez* hanging in my office and there was no doubt in my mind his work had inspired me to become a museum photography curator. It may have also inspired me, at the age of fifty-four, to pull myself up by my mid-western roots and move to the West.

In 1941 Adams was commissioned by the National Park Service to document the country's national parks through photography. It was my love of these photographs which led me to the crazy Wyoming escapade. And to the dead man.

It was early November when I told my neighbors Marian and Alice about my plan to take a road trip to Wyoming to see an exhibition of Adams' national park photos. The day was overcast, a rarity in Taos, and snow clouds shrouded the top of Pueblo Peak. Chamisa bushes swayed in clumps on either side of the street, and a few brave Russian sage stragglers kept them company. We'd gathered for drinks in Marian's kitchen, which on most days had the best mountain view.

"I got into photography because of Ansel Adams," I told them. "My father gave me a book of his National Park photos when I was fifteen. I can't miss this show."

The women exchanged glances, Alice winked, and before I'd taken a breath, Marian, in her booming Texas drawl, blurted, "We wanna go with you, girlfriend!"

I shouldn't have been surprised. Those two, despite being in their mid-seventies, possessed a thirst for adventure like no one else I'd ever encountered. Excluding myself of course.

"Where exactly is the exhibit?" Marian said. She pushed her lanky five-foot-nine frame back from the sturdy oak table and stood. She waited for my answer before crossing the kitchen to grab a stack of red, yellow, and green striped cocktail napkins. Her secret signature fragrance wafted behind her, and her pink cowboy boots clicked her way across the tile floor.

"At Yellowstone National Park," I said. "I'll be going in June, so we have time to plan if you really want to join me. I'd love it."

I took another ample sip of one of Marian's heavenly Manhattans, a cocktail I had taken up upon moving from Chicago to New Mexico. And taken up because I had moved to a cozy little neighborhood in Taos. And luckily, my house was directly across the street from Marian and catty corner from her best friend Alice. On a sunny morning seven months later, at the end of lilac season, the three of us headed north in my perpetually dusty Subaru.

I'd had no trouble arranging time off from the New Mexico Museum of Art, where I worked. An exhibit of Ansel Adams photographs could be considered work-related, and I'd proposed to our museum board that we mount a show of his work. After all, he'd spent a lot of time in New Mexico. His famous *Moonrise Hernandez*, the image that hung in my office, had been shot not far from Santa Fe.

Neither Alice nor Marian had ever been to Yellowstone. I had, but it had been forty years before, when I was fifteen, and besides bison, all I could remember was Old Faithful and the Old Faithful Inn. The image of the lodge's vaulted ceiling in the lobby, supported by massive log beams that crisscrossed between several floors of balconies had taken up residence in my mind for all these years. The gigantic stone fireplace, too.

Because I worked for the Art Museum in Santa Fe and planned on writing an article about the Ansel Adams exhibit for a national art magazine, the hotel granted me a two-room suite in the Lake Yellowstone Hotel in case my "assistant" would be traveling with me. Happily, my assistants turned out to be Alice and Marian. And my initial disappointment over not being able to stay at the Old Faithful Inn was quickly assuaged when I recalled one of my favorites of Adams' National Park photos was an image of Yellowstone Lake with Mount Sheridan in the background. I'd never seen that photo in person and the thought that I'd soon be seeing the photo from the very place he shot it thrilled me as much as if I'd taken the photograph myself.

At four o'clock on a misty June afternoon we passed through the East Entrance of Yellowstone.

"I feel like a kid at Christmas," Alice said. Her smile was huge. "The smell of these pine trees is amazing." She held out her arms as if to embrace the landscape.

"Let's take a selfie to document our arrival," I said. "Those amazing rock formations will be a perfect background."

Marian fought with the breeze to tuck a few bottle-blond

curls under her pink Dallas Cowboys baseball cap. I, on the other hand, released my straight shoulder-length auburn locks from their ever-present tortoise shell clip and let them fly.

"Ansel," I yelled, as I tapped the camera icon on my phone.

I took my time driving to the hotel. Traffic was light, and our heads swiveled from the left to the front, to the right, and back again, like owls looking for mice.

"You know girls, there could be one hundred bison standing fifty feet away and we wouldn't be able to see them because of this mist," Alice said.

"Maybe we couldn't see one hundred," I said, "but if you two will look to the left you'll see one."

"Oh my God," Alice cried. "Don't let him move until I get a picture."

I lowered my window and yelled, "Fido! Stay!"

We all laughed and took pictures of the noble creature's magnificent head, which appeared to be floating in the mist.

The sky had brightened when we stopped at the Fishing Bridge Visitor Center, a quintessential national park structure, built around 1930. Its sloped roof was perfectly designed to accommodate Yellowstone's heavy snowfalls, and the rustic stone and wood structure seemed not to have been built by man but created by nature herself. As we entered the building, we were treated to a view of the lake through perfectly positioned windows across the wide room that served as an information center and museum. It would have been an ideal place for the Adams exhibit, but I had no doubt the Old Faithful Visitor Center where the show was hanging would be just as lovely.

A carpet of orange and yellow wildflowers had tested the spring temperatures and were beginning to bloom around the building. I squatted to tie the lace of my hiking boot, thinking about how when I was fifteen, I'd vowed to return. There was something about Yellowstone, above all the other parks and places I'd visited, that moved me emotionally. In a good way. In the way great works of art moved me. Maybe I'd lived here in a past life. Maybe it didn't matter. But the cool thing was, when I straightened from tying my lace, a rainbow stretched across the lake, clearly visible in the full, late afternoon sunlight.

As a weekend photographer, I'm fully aware a photo can never truly do justice to its subject. At least where landscapes are concerned. And that goes for historic hotels too. I'd viewed pictures of the Lake Yellowstone Hotel, of course, but I wasn't prepared for its grandeur. The monumental building was the pale-yellow hue of chamisa blooms, and soaring white columns framed the entrance. This was nothing like the rustic charm of the Old Faithful Inn, but the moment I crossed the threshold of the "Lake" I had no regrets.

"Oh, my stars," Alice said. "Will you look at this place. I didn't figure it to be *this* posh."

"Holy smokes," Marian said. "That fireplace is as big as my bathroom. Let's get drinks in that gorgeous bar and take them to the sunroom."

DRINKS IN THE SPACIOUS SUNROOM BEFORE DINNER HAD BEEN A splendid idea. The blue water of the lake shimmered in the pre-sunset light, and that view combined with soft piano music was all we needed to unwind after two days of car travel. And then of course, there were the Manhattans.

We planned on calling it a night at a reasonable hour, so I had made a reservation for dinner in the hotel dining room for seven o'clock. The plan was to rise early the next morning and drive the forty miles to the Old Faithful area and see the Ansel Adams exhibit right off the bat. Once I crossed that off my list, we'd take our time exploring the many park attractions. The park had comped me two nights at the Lake, and we'd decided to go all out and spring for two more nights on our own. Having finally arrived in Yellowstone was a dream come true and I was imbued with a feeling of contentment.

Unfortunately, it was short lived.

"What's the matter, Cat?" Marian asked. "You see a grizzly in the bar?" She and Alice had just finished the last of their drinks when someone in the bar caught my attention.

"Maybe," I said. "I'm not sure."

"What?" Alice twisted in her armchair to face the bar.

The man had just carried a cocktail to a small table in the corner of the bar that faced the sunroom. He removed his black cowboy hat and placed it on the chair next to his and immediately began typing on his phone. Still wears all black, I thought. And if he was who I thought he was, he'd aged considerably in the five years since I'd seen him. That must be what happens when everyone you know hates you.

"His name is Devon Duncan," I said. We'd been seated in the luxurious dining room, where I'd purposely chosen to sit with my back to the door. While Marian perused the wine list, I filled my companions in on 'The Grizzly's' background. It was a perfect nickname for the guy.

"I knew him professionally in Chicago. He owns a photography gallery in Oklahoma City and would attend auctions in Chicago to look for inventory."

"He looks artsy," Alice said.

"He looks sexy." Marian never held back.

"Yeah, well, he's also an asshole," I said. "Just ask anyone who's done business with him or worked for him."

"What does he do that's so bad?" Alice asked.

"For starters, he's so rich he can outbid any museum at auction, then he resells the pieces to even richer collectors for five times what he paid for them, causing the values of the photographs to be grossly inflated. So the next time an Ansel Adams photograph, for example, comes up at auction, most museums don't have a chance of adding it to their collection. That's not illegal, but there's a lot more. Basically, he's a crook."

"Rich, you say," Marian said. She craned her neck obviously hoping to catch another look at him.

"Don't you even think about it," I said, shaking a finger at her. "Order us some wine, will you. I need more alcohol."

There was a lot more I could say about Devon Duncan's business practices, some of which involved selling counterfeit Edward S. Curtis photos, and a lot that involved him sexually harassing his female employees. But I wanted to enjoy my dinner. Still, I wondered what he was doing at Yellowstone. The Ansel Adams exhibit was not a selling show, and all the works were on loan from various institutions throughout the country. Tomorrow I'd be interviewing the curator of the exhibit for my article. Maybe something would come up about him then. In the meantime, I wouldn't let my curiosity spoil my return to Yellowstone.

I'd just taken the first bite of a lovely poached pear and gorgonzola salad, when two feet kicked me under the table. Oh no, I thought. Please no.

But yes, here he was. The Grizzly was standing next to my chair, cowboy hat in hand. His shiny black boots glowed in the warm light of the art deco chandeliers.

"Catherine Newcomb, I thought I recognized you," he said. "What a totally unexpected pleasure, darlin'." He extended his turquoise adorned right hand, which I shook while I thought, I am NOT your darlin'. I was relieved he knew better than to kiss my cheek.

I made the introductions and was pleased Marian behaved

herself. She was a great tease when it came to men, but she had no tolerance for bad behavior. She engaged Alice in a conversation about their coquilles St-Jacques and they both totally ignored him.

"I haven't seen you in Chicago for a while," he said.

"I moved to New Mexico," I said.

"Moved west for a man?" His lips curled in a Snidely Whiplash smile.

I was pretty sure my eyes rolled. "It was for the weather," I said. "What brings you out here, Devon? The Adams photos aren't for sale."

"Adams photos? I didn't know. I'm on vacation." He smoothed his graying black hair that was pulled into a tight ponytail. A new look. "Yes, ma'am, I'm here to soak in some hot water and maybe take a picture of a buffalo."

It's bison, I thought. My next thought was—he's full of shit.

He turned to Marian and Alice. "A pleasure meeting you ladies. Y'all have a good time and be careful. I hear Yellowstone can be a dangerous place."

He walked away down the center carpet to his table, where another man sat waiting. The ponytail swung across his back as if in time to his swagger.

"Do you know the other guy?" Marian said. "He reminds me of Truman Capote, but I can tell he's taller."

"Truman Capote!" Alice almost snorted with laughter. She glanced quickly at the other table. Her expression had changed from amusement to surprise. "You're right," she said.

The guy did bear a resemblance to the long-dead and often hated author. Small tortoise-shell glasses, sandy hair, pastel bow tie. Devon Duncan's back was to me, and I took my time studying his companion.

"There is something familiar about him, but I don't think I

know him," I said. I took a drink of the very nice Fumé Blanc Marian had ordered and continued to ponder who the Truman Capote guy might be. I pondered until dessert was served. Then I gave up.

MY APPOINTMENT WITH LINDA MANN, THE CURATOR OF THE ADAMS exhibit, was scheduled for eight o'clock. The drive to the Old Faithful Visitor Center was long, so we decided to leave the hotel at six o'clock to allow time for stopping to take pictures. We'd have breakfast at the Old Faithful Inn after my interview. Mount Sheridan reached for the heavens to our south, with the lake providing a foreground any painter or photographer would kill for.

"Just look at those mountains, ladies," Alice stood in awe before she scooted into the back seat of my Outback. "Our New Mexico mountains are spectacular too, but these are more majestic."

"Don't let the New Mexico Tourist Commission hear you say that," I said. "But I have to agree with you. And Wyoming has much more diverse wildlife."

"So coyotes, big-horn sheep, elk, and rattlesnakes aren't enough for you?" Marian said. She flipped her visor down and used the mirror to touch up her peony pink lipstick. "Now you want to see moose, wolves, bison, and grizzlies walking down Lilac Lane?"

I laughed, but the word "grizzlies" put me in mind again of Devon Duncan. He had to be up to something. 'Here on vacation,' my foot.

I had to put him out of my mind, at least for the next two hours. I was in paradise and that Okie grizzly wasn't going to ruin it for me.

Linda Mann was a delightful woman, probably mid-forties with curly blond hair pinned up in a sloppy bun on top of her head. It worked in a bohemian kind of way. As we viewed the Adams photographs, we shared our stories about how we came to love his work, photography in general, and Yellowstone. They were practically parallel. While I'd grown up in Illinois, she hailed from Minnesota, and currently held a curatorial position at the Whitney Museum of the West in Cody.

"You have to stop on your drive back to New Mexico," she said. "Our museum is amazing. I guarantee you'll be impressed."

The interview went well. I started to leave, then turned to ask her one last question. "By the way, do you happen to know a photography dealer named Devon Duncan?"

"Yes, I know the scumbag." She stood and crossed her arms across her chest. "I assume he's not an associate of yours. You're too nice."

I laughed out loud. "Not an associate and not a friend. I ran into him at the Lake Hotel last night and he claimed to not know about your Adams exhibit."

Now it was Linda's turn to laugh. "He's been here three times in the last two days."

"He's up to something, all right. We should keep an eye on him."

"I'm all in," Linda said.

"Was anyone with him when you saw him here? He had dinner with a guy last night that seemed familiar to me, but I can't place him. Looks sort of like Truman Capote."

"Truman Capote! No, I'd remember someone like that. As far as I could see Duncan was alone."

I handed Linda one of my business cards. "Text or call me if you pick up on anything, and I'll do the same."

I still had thirty minutes before I was due to meet Marian

and Alice on the porch of the Old Faithful Inn, so I decided to spend some time alone with the Adams photos. I'd be coming back later with them and planned on giving them a full-blown presentation on Ansel's life and work.

Linda had created the temporary gallery space for this exhibit, and it was in one of two rooms in a separate structure from the Visitor Center but only about fifty feet from the main building. The two rooms in the gallery building were connected by a hallway with tile flooring, and the entrance door led into the first room, so I followed the hallway toward the exhibit space. I'd noticed Linda hadn't locked the door so it would be all mine. The gallery wasn't open to the public until noon, and I could take this opportunity to savor the incredible images my 'mentor' had created so many years ago.

I approached the gallery room and heard a sound like Marian's cowboy boots behind me. I turned but didn't see anyone. Weird. Maybe a maintenance person, I thought. Then I heard more footsteps in the gallery, moving quickly toward the open door and me. Before I reached the door an arm grabbed me from behind and covered my eyes, while a hand shoved a piece of fabric in my mouth. I recognized the sound of tape ripping as it wound around my wrists, and at the same time something was tied around my head, covering my eyes, relieving the unknown hand of its task. Just before I was shoved into what I later realized was a closet, a pinprick stung my inner elbow, and I was down for the count.

Chances were I wouldn't be guiding my friends around the Ansel Adams exhibit today. That was my first foggy thought as I came around. Whoever had attacked me most likely was new at it since they'd taped my wrists in front rather than behind my back. It was a simple task to pull the rag from my mouth before I tugged the blindfold up to my forehead. The tape was wrapped tightly around my wrists, but I had no doubt once I

39

started yelling, I'd be discovered. According to my Fitbit, I'd only been out about thirty minutes. A smell like pine mixed with antiseptic assaulted my nasal passages. I felt around in the dark, and discovered a broom and dustpan, and a bucket and mop.

"Hey," I yelled. "Help! I'm in the closet!" The gallery wouldn't open to the public for over two hours, but surely someone outside would hear me. Marian and Alice would think of looking for me here, since I hadn't shown up to the Old Faithful Inn at our appointed time. Then I had another thought. This was a closet. Why would it be locked? My eyes were now accustomed to the dim light, and I reached up for the doorknob. I used it to help pull myself off the floor, stood up, and turned the knob.

Alice, Marian, and Linda Mann were walking out of Linda's office as I approached it.

"Oh my God," Alice cried. She ran to me.

My cheeks were wet with tears that had suddenly begun to gush when the thought of what had just happened. I had been drugged, for God's sake. Obviously, not dangerously. But still.

Marian wasted no time in gently removing the tape from my wrists. "Christ on a cracker, girlfriend. What the hell happened?"

Alice had already pulled a tissue from her bag and was dabbing at my cheeks.

After I was seated in Linda's office with a bottle of water in my trembling hands, and a cold, wet, paper towel on my forehead, I filled them in. Linda had already called the park rangers, and someone was on the way to take my statement. They would call in a report to the Park Service Investigations Branch.

Linda sat in front of me, her right leg crossed over her left knee. The right leg was bouncing and swinging like a whirligig.

I'd be nervous too if someone had been assaulted, bound, and drugged in my museum.

"I heard boots clicking on the floor behind me just before I was grabbed," I said. "And I think I know who was wearing them."

I told the ranger my theory of the boots belonging to Devon Duncan, and he chuckled. "I'm sorry, ma'am, but this is Wyoming. Cowboy boots are the preferred footwear for most folks in this state."

"All I see around here are shoes like mine," I said. I pointed to my new Danner hiking boots. "He was with a guy at dinner last night at the Lake Hotel," I added. "I can describe him."

The ranger shrugged. "I'll let you know. Can you walk back to the other building? I need you to show me where you were when they grabbed you. Had to be more than one, sounds like. Maybe they dropped something. Left a clue."

I nodded and so did Linda. "We need to get over there now," she said. "We shouldn't have waited this long." Her office was cool but sweat had broken out on her pale forehead.

I was fine to walk, but Alice and Marian insisted on each taking an arm as we made our way along the flagstone path to the other building. Linda and the ranger hurried ahead of us. The whole thing was so bizarre. Why would someone attack me? Everyone had been very concerned about the sedative I'd been injected with, but I felt perfectly fine now. Whatever it had been, it had been short-acting. I was lucky. Whoever had attacked me obviously had no intention of doing me serious harm.

When we got to the gallery Linda was pointing to an empty space on the wall. "Oh, my God. This can't have happened."

The missing photograph was not an image of anywhere in Yellowstone, but one of a Saguaro cactus from the Saguaro National Monument. I recalled its beauty as rather stark, but also one of the most textural photos I'd ever seen. So, this was what my attacker was after and I'd stumbled right into the theft in action. The perpetrators hadn't expected anyone to be in the building at that time. Obviously, they'd known the gallery didn't open until noon, and the other room was not being used.

A stolen Ansel Adams photograph worth at least half a million dollars, and Devon Duncan in the neighborhood. I couldn't be convinced there wasn't a connection.

The ranger was on the phone. The chief ranger at park headquarters in Mammoth was on alert, as was the Highway Patrol. They would put out a BOLO based on Devon's description, but that's all they had to work with until they could research where his car rental originated. If he had rented a car at all. He may have traveled with his accomplice.

"Ask that ranger if we can go now," Marian said. "We need to get out there and find that sorry son of a bitch. Right, ladies?"

"Aw, jeez, here we go," Alice said. "I bet she's packing."

The ranger said we could leave and told me he'd keep me posted. "By the way," he said. "Looks like they got in through the back door. Picked the lock. Simple as that."

Linda had just hung up a phone call. It occurred to me she seemed well versed in law enforcement lingo, both in her exchanges with the ranger and on the phone call. I'm so sorry," I told her, as I gave her a hug. "I'll call you later."

"Thanks," she said. "Shit can happen anywhere, I guess. Even in paradise." She was cool as a cucumber.

I WAS STARVING. ALICE HAD GIVEN ME AN ENERGY BAR FROM HER

purse back in Linda's office, and it saved my life. An exaggeration, but an apt one.

"Hey ladies," I said. "Let's see if there's a trail behind the building that might lead to the Inn. I am so ready for breakfast. Or lunch. Anything."

"I'm ready for a bloody Mary," Marian said. "A double."

The door the ranger had referred to was wide open, swaying in the breeze on its hinges. No doubt law enforcement would be dusting it for prints soon, along with the doorknobs and other surfaces in the building. I wondered if they'd bother with checking the exterior of the building, knowing the thieves had to be long gone. But they could have dropped something as they fled. Especially since one of them had been carrying an approximately 27 by 35-inch framed photograph. They must have had a vehicle parked nearby. Maybe it left tire tracks. Of course, the rangers would be right behind us, but it wouldn't hurt to poke around on our way to the Inn.

There wasn't a trail per se, but the ankle-high grass, interspersed with Indian paintbrush, that grew behind the building was beaten down in a narrow line that led toward a stand of aspen trees about one-hundred feet away.

"Let's go," I pointed toward the trees. "There could be a clue in this grass. And I bet they parked on the other side of those trees."

Nothing of interest was apparent in the grass and I was faint with hunger. I picked up my pace with the idea we could always come back and dig around more after lunch. Alice and Marian were about ten feet behind me when I fell.

Marian reached me first. "Cat, you okay?" she said.

"Yes, I'm fine," I said. "I tripped on a root or something."

Marian and Alice gave me a hand up, and we examined what had caused my fall. It wasn't a root. It was a shiny, black cowboy boot. A boot that contained the foot of a very dead Devon Duncan.

Alice and I waited with the body while Marian sprinted to the building we'd just left.

The ranger was on his phone again as he approached the scene with Marian. "Well, I'll be damned," was all he said as he surveyed the long, black-clad body lying in the soft green grass among the red and yellow wildflowers. There was a lot of blood.

"Now do you want to hear about the other guy?" I said.

"Yes, ma'am, I do," the ranger answered. "Highway Patrol is on the way, and one of their officers will take your statement with me. County medical examiner is on the way too."

"Any way we can run right over yonder to the Old Faithful Inn for a sandwich while we wait?" Marian asked. "None of us had had a thing to eat and we've been up since five o'clock."

"If you can get back in forty-five minutes that should be okay."

"Thank you, Gerald," Marian almost cooed. She'd read his name tag and taken it to heart. I was glad she had.

"In the meantime, Gerald," I said. "The man you may want to consider a suspect is about mid-forties, pale skin with dark blond hair. He wears round tortoiseshell glasses, and last night he was wearing a bow tie. Probably about five-eight, but when I saw him, he was sitting down."

"Sounds kind of nerdy," Gerald said.

I'd never tasted anything as good as the BLT at the Old Faithful Inn. Marian and Alice each had a patty melt and they said the same thing.

"We've got to come back later so you can see Old Faithful

erupt," Alice said. "We got here just in time this morning, and it wasn't even crowded."

"It was truly something," Marian agreed. "They say it'll probably go off again around three o'clock. We probably missed a couple of eruptions when we were fooling around with the dead grizzly guy."

"I'll be ready to head back to the Lake for a nap after the police finish with us," I said. "We can come back here tomorrow. I really want to see Old Faithful again. I can smell its sulfur from here."

"Us being so hungry got me to thinking about all the people in this world who are hungry all day every day," Alice said. "We can't complain about not having eaten for seven hours."

Marian and I nodded in agreement. Our mouths were too full to speak.

"When I was in high school, I went to West Virginia with a church group to work with Habitat for Humanity," Alice continued. "I was only there two weeks, but until then I had never imagined the poverty that existed in our country. That trip really opened my eyes."

I nodded again and took a french fry from my plate. *West Virginia*. Suddenly something was nagging at my memory. I'd never been to the state, but I knew of some good museums there. I knew of good museums all over the country, so that was no big deal. What was it?

Then, just like that, I had it. About twenty years ago a museum in West Virginia was expanding its photography collection at a record pace. The photography curator was a young guy who'd come from a privileged family somewhere out West. He seemed to have an in with dealers willing to turn over important works at extraordinarily low values. Finally, the head curator of the museum became suspicious. The "original" photographs the young guy acquired for the museum were original, they just weren't legitimate. Somebody printed the Paul Strand photo, the Diane Arbus, the Dorthea Lange. It just wasn't Paul, Diana, or Dorthea. I couldn't remember all the details, but I'd read about the scam in a professional publication after he'd been arrested. I thought how the crooked curator had given my profession a bad name. And a photograph of the curator accompanied the article. It had been a long time since I'd seen it, but how many people look like Truman Capote?

"I know who the guy is." I still held the french fry mid-air.

"Damn, girl," Marian said. "Spill."

"I'm trying to remember his name. Give me a minute to connect to Wi-Fi, and I'll find out."

It took about three minutes for me to find everything I was looking for. And then some.

"Will y'all pay the bill?" I said. "I need to talk to Gerald."

"You gotta be kidding me," Gerald said when I shared my information with him. Two Highway Patrol officers had arrived, and an agent from the National Park Service Investigative Services Branch was en route. Devon Duncan had been shot at close range in the back of the head. Obviously, a silencer had been employed.

"The former governor's son?" Gerald went on. "Lady, are you sure?"

"Yes sir, I am. And it's my guess Theodore Roosevelt Johnson is hightailing it to the family compound outside of Jackson." I could tell the Highway Patrol guys were wondering who the heck I was. They didn't actually scratch their heads, but they may as well have. "He probably has a buyer lined up for that Adams photograph, and will either meet him or her there, or hop on the family jet and go to them."

"Okay fellas," Gerald turned to State officers. "If he's outside the park, it's all yours."

The older of the patrolmen nodded. "I'll get a copter down to Jackson Hole right away. We'll put a BOLO out on Johnson too." He jammed on his hat. "I bet his daddy is rolling in his grave. He was a good governor and a good man."

Marian and Alice arrived just as the officers hurried away toward the parking lot. Gerald had posted two Rangers at the crime scene, and another two were at strategic sections of the trail that led to it. More tourists tripping over Devon Duncan's foot would be bad for park PR.

"This is crazy," Alice said.

"Look on the bright side, ladies," Marian said. "None of us is dead. Not yet anyway."

Gerald asked us to stick around the Old Faithful area where we'd be reachable if the Park Service Investigations agent would want to take an official statement. While we walked back to the Inn to browse the gift shop, I recounted all I knew about Theodore Roosevelt Johnson to Marian and Alice.

"I guess the year he spent in the slammer didn't teach him crime doesn't pay," Alice said.

"All I can figure is he and Devon were partners in the theft, and something went haywire," I said.

"Yeah," Marian said. "Theodore went haywire. Why would his parents name him that anyway?"

"A lot of people revere Teddy Roosevelt." Alice said. "Maybe more in the West than back east where he was from."

We all bought tee shirts, and Alice sprang for a gorgeous Pendleton blanket. "Let's take these to the car, then stop at Linda's office and see how she's doing," I said. "That agent should be getting here any time." Crowds of people pushed past us on their way to view Old Faithful's eruption.

"Good idea," Marian said. "I want to grab my backpack from the car. There's something in it that may come in handy."

Linda's office door was closed, but her voice was audible. "Damn it, Ted. You didn't have to kill the guy. And where's the photograph?"

A man's voice replied. "I could tell from our conversation last night he was going to be trouble. I couldn't take a chance."

At least he didn't talk like Truman Capote.

"You really think he'd have been a problem?"

"I know it, my dear. But I am afraid I've landed us in some deep shit, and now with that broad from New Mexico poking around it could be worse. She could figure out who I am. It's a good thing I had that knock-out shot with me earlier. I had a feeling someone might show up unexpectedly."

"So where is the photograph?" Linda said again. "And what happened to the guy who was supposed to pick you up after the heist?"

"Linda, my love, he's a druggie. Not dependable, those guys."

"And the photo?"

"Oh yes. Sorry. I can tell you it's very close. Practically under your nose. But don't worry. It's wrapped in a blanket so it won't get dirty."

"Okay. So now what?"

"So, now it's up to you to get me out of here."

"Ted, you don't need that gun in here. Put it down."

"I can't help but be a little suspicious of you. You suspected Duncan and I would be interested in lifting an Adams photo. I wonder why you thought that."

"Because I knew of your reputation. Listen, you can trust

me. We stand to make a bundle now that Duncan's out of the picture."

"You're wrong. *I* stand to make a bundle."

"What are you planning now?" Linda made no effort to keep her voice down now.

I backed away from the door, and my friends followed suit.

"Go get Gerald," I told them in a hushed voice when we reached the turn in the hallway.

"No, you go," Marian whispered. She was reaching into her backpack. "I'll wait."

Alice's eyes reminded me of Betty Boop's when Marian pulled her pistol from the backpack.

"Go get Gerald, Alice," I said. "I'll stay with Marian."

Alice trotted down the hall. The insanity would soon be over. This side of the building seemed completely empty. The Visitor Center was far enough away that Linda was pretty much assured of complete privacy.

Linda. I never would have taken her for a crook.

Marian and I tiptoed back to Linda's office.

"You're going to give me your car keys," Ted said. "I know your car is right outside the door. I'm going to wear my sunglasses and this lovely Yellowstone ball cap you conveniently keep in your office. All the rangers are hanging out with our friend Devon, and I'll be driving in the other direction."

"Okay then. Here are the keys. Good luck getting out of the park."

"Thank you. I have my ways. But before I go, I have to kill you."

At that I flung open the door.

He started to turn at the sound of the door opening, but I dove for his knees before he realized what was happening. He fell and dropped his gun. Marian jabbed her pistol into his neck, and seconds later, Linda pointed her much larger gun at his head.

None of us had stopped talking on the hour-long drive back to the hotel. We didn't remember to look for wildlife. The adrenaline was surging. The only time a silence fell was if we paused for a swig of water all at the same time. That happened once. When we reached the hotel, we were all ready for something stronger.

We sat in the sunroom. Had it only been twenty-four hours since I'd spotted the late Devon Duncan in the bar? It seemed like a week ago at least.

"This would be a story to tell our grandkids if any of us had kids," Alice said.

We had learned earlier from Linda that she was a former FBI agent who had worked in the stolen art division. She'd lived in Denver then but had since married and moved to Cody. She was "semi-retired," she said. When the bureau asked her to help with their investigation of Ted Johnson, she jumped at it. She was indeed an assistant curator at the museum in Cody, and her immediate supervisor was aware of her background and fully supportive of her going undercover at Yellowstone.

"Ted Johnson has been on the Bureau's radar since he got out of prison," she had told us, after Johnson had been escorted out of Yellowstone in handcuffs. "We suspect him in several art thefts since his release. This exhibit was planned by the National Park Service; we didn't mount it to lure him. But once we got wind of it, and knowing this was his home turf, I was called in. He and Devon started sniffing around last week."

She took a large drink from her water bottle. "Sorry I couldn't tell you when you asked about Truman Capote."

All four of us released a much-needed laugh, and she continued.

"And I especially felt bad after you were attacked. I had no idea you were going back to the gallery. Anyway, when they showed up earlier this week I told them I knew who they were, and if they had any museum or gallery clients who'd be interested in a "real" Ansel Adams photo, I could help them. For a third of the profit. They not only took the bait, they swallowed it."

"I have to say, when I saw you with that gun, I thought you might aim it at Marian and me," I said.

"It was locked in my desk drawer," Linda said. "He totally caught me by surprise showing up at my office." She paused to take a drink of spring water. Her eyes wandered to the towering pine trees, and she pinned up a few errant strands of her blond curls. "I'd like to think I could have gotten to the gun before he shot me, but I'm not so sure. I'm thinking you ladies saved my life."

I leaned over and hugged her, and Alice and Marian joined in a group hug.

"Too bad about Devon," I said. "He was a jerk, but still."

"I agree," Linda said. "That Teddy Roosevelt is nobody's hero."

OVER DINNER WE DISCUSSED WHETHER TO STAY AT YELLOWSTONE two more nights as planned or get out early before we found another body, even if I hadn't seen Old Faithful erupt.

"I would sure like to see those Ansel Adams photos one more time," I said. "And you need to see them properly too! Since the Saguaro photo was found stashed under the building it will be hanging with the others."

"And we still have to see a bear," Alice said. "And moose. And if we drive north, maybe even a wolf."

Marian extended her arm to propose a toast. "I vote we stay. They make a damn good Manhattan here."

A RESIDENT OF TAOS, NEW MEXICO, **CELESTE BERTEAU** WAS BORN and raised on the Lake Michigan shore in southern Michigan. Throughout her youth she was fascinated with her Cajun father's culture, and after attending college in Michigan, she moved to New Orleans where she resided for thirty-nine years before relocating to the high desert in 2018.

Celeste has had over twenty travel and art articles published, as well as five essays published in various collections. Her short story *Red Next To Yellow* was published in the anthology *Something in the Water, Twenty Louisiana Stories*, and she has had numerous book reviews published in the New Orleans *Advocate/Times-Picayune* newspaper. Her first mystery novel, *Murder in the Black Pearl*, is in its final revision stage. Maybe!

4

SOME DAYS YOU EAT THE BEAR

KATY MUNGER

"I'm not mentioning their tanning product without another fifteen grand on the table. You should have seen the comments when I recommended their blusher. Half my followers said it made them look like clowns. Their products are Shein cheap and I'm not pushing them without more money upfront."

Alexa cut the call off before her agent could reply then gave a dramatic sigh, kicking the back of the driver's seat as she screamed, "Move! This is bullshit! Move now!"

"Does it look like I can move right now?" Daphne asked, gritting her teeth as she wondered what it would be like to have someone hand her $15,000 just to mention their product online. And if there was a moral contradiction in insisting a product was crap, but saying you were willing to overlook that fact for more money, Daphne was not going to point it out to Alexa. She knew it was no use. She had known Alexa for over twenty years, ever since they had started kindergarten together and Alexa had snatched Daphne's set of colored markers out of her hands and proclaimed them hers, saying that since she was better at drawing, she deserved them more. Daphne, who had gotten the markers from her parents for her birthday, had said nothing. And that's the way it had pretty much gone for the last two decades. Alexa took and Daphne gave, each passing year only strengthening the dynamic.

Daphne—an introvert at heart, socially awkward, and so disguised by poor fashion choices that no one, not even her own parents, had recognized the beauty beneath—had always willingly taken the proverbial back seat to what Alexa wanted. Somehow, despite a degree in media studies from USC, Daphne had ended up as Alexa's chauffeur, cameraman, and sidekick—the latter a label that Alexa often used to describe Daphne, as if serving her every whim was some sort of great honor. Yet Daphne had never been able to quit the friendship. It was as if the reflected glory she enjoyed as Alexa's friend had drained away all of her confidence over the years, leaving Daphne so crippled by a lack of self-esteem that she had never managed to find her feet as an adult.

Daphne sometimes wondered why Alexa was the star and she was invisible. If you took away the cosmetic surgery, layers of makeup and pricey veneers, the skimpy clothing and hair extensions, not to mention the monthly trips to the salon for touch-ups of her artificially blonde hair, the truth was that Alexa would probably look a whole lot like Daphne did. Which meant that the only difference between them was that Daphne did not possess an ounce of self-worth, while Alexa sailed through life supremely confident that she was entitled to the worship of the lesser mortals who lived vicariously her, devouring her daily social media posts like a religion.

Daphne hated herself for not having recognized the truth sooner and for allowing Alexa to behave as she did, trampling over other people's feelings, throwing tantrums when she did not get her own way, sucking up all the attention in every room she entered by any means possible.

Daphne had known how selfish Alexa was for almost twenty-five years, yet here she was, struggling to make a living by completing surveys and picking up underpaid copywriting gigs online. Meanwhile Alexa racked up a couple million more followers on her TikTok account every six months, courtesy of staged experiences like appreciating Yellowstone's breathtaking natural beauty—none of which Alexa saw or cared about, except as the perfect backdrop for her Daisy Duke denim shorts and retro Ellie Mae plaid shirt tied high above her flat and well-tanned stomach. Alexa had paired this outfit with a pair of three-inch wedges that made about as much sense for a trip to Yellowstone as asking a dog to walk around the park on stilts.

"This is unacceptable!" Alexa suddenly screamed from the back seat. Her patience threshold was on par with a two-year-old's. "Find a way around this. Now."

Daphne gritted her teeth. She had warned Alexa that West Yellowstone was the most popular entrance into the park and would be bumper-to-bumper for miles until the gate officially opened. But Alexa had not listened, instead insisting they get there early so they could get the photo shoot over with and go. Apparently, there was some hot guy waiting for her back at the lodge where they were staying.

There was always a hot guy waiting for Alexa somewhere, though she never managed to keep a man for more than two weeks, usually announcing to her 4.7 million followers that she had dumped her latest "situationship" because she would not stand for being disrespected. She deserved to be treated at all times like the princess she clearly was.

"There *is* no way around it," Daphne told Alexa grimly. "As soon as they open the gates, traffic will start moving."

"That is completely unacceptable," Alexa declared. Clutching her iPhone, she hopped from the car and began teetering through traffic on her ridiculous shoes, drawing interested looks from every male in the vicinity and incredulous stares from their female companions, who no doubt had more sense than to go traipsing around a national park dressed like a failed country singer who had turned to walking the streets for trick money.

Daphne watched from the driver's seat as Alexa filmed herself talking into her phone's camera, ranting about the wait to enter the park, adopting an outraged attitude guaranteed to draw on-line attention.

But whatever Alexa said to the ranger manning the entrance gates, it did not work. Daphne watched with satisfaction as Alexa was turned away by a plump woman in a green and grey ranger uniform. Even from fifty feet away, Daphne could tell by the ranger's posture that she had met plenty of Alexas in her job and had no intention of giving this one any more attention than she had to.

Alexa was steaming by the time she got back to the car. "I'm going to get her badge number and report her," she said with satisfaction as she climbed back into the Escalade. "She can kiss her job good-bye. Remind me to look at the footage when we get back to the lodge."

"They're park rangers, not cops," Daphne said patiently. "They don't have badges or badge numbers."

"Whatever. I've got video proof of her rudeness and I'm going to report her."

Daphne sighed. Never mind that Alexa pulled in half a million each year for her TikTok and Instagram posts while the ranger made less than a tenth of that. Alexa lived to humiliate others online.

To think that Daphne had once been one of the millions of

girls who worshipped Alexa and longed to be just like her. To think that she had once thought herself lucky that Alexa had anointed her as her own personal servant. How could she ever have been so stupid?

Daphne's epiphany about Alexa had been years in the making, but it had come to a head a month before on St. John's, when they had run into an old classmate while Alexa was doing a swimsuit shoot for a cheap Chinese clothing outlet. Despite Daphne's protests, Alexa had commandeered whole swaths of the island's pristine beaches, insisting that the other tourists move out of her camera range and sunbathe elsewhere. Their old classmate had been one of the many dispossessed beachgoers, but instead of resenting it he had excitedly re-introduced himself to Alexa, so overcome by her celebrity that he stammered when he explained he had known her back in high school.

The guy had been nobody special then, and Daphne knew damn well that Alexa had no recollection of him—but to Daphne? He had been her hero. He had stood up for her not once, but three separate times, during those awful middle school years when she had been mercilessly bullied about her frizzy hair and weight. Daphne had loved him from afar then and all through high school, though he had never made the slightest sign of recognizing her after ninth grade.

Yet that day on St. John's, he *had* recognized her—and seemed delighted to see her, at least for the half hour it took for the photo shoot to finish and for Alexa to realize that Daphne was actually interested in him. After that, it took about fifteen seconds for Alexa to draw all the attention back to her, where it had apparently stayed throughout the entire day and long into the night since she had disappeared with him right after dinner, not returning to the penthouse suite she shared with Daphne until well after midnight, shoes and panties in hand, her hair and clothing disheveled. Daphne had pretended to be asleep but had no such defense at breakfast, where she'd been forced to endure Alexa's complaints about his lack of sexual prowess as well as a prolonged monologue about how there was not a man on the planet who did not desire her.

Something had died in Daphne that day. Something that had needed to die. She had been filled with a self-loathing that left her in despair, followed by a dawning realization that her feelings meant nothing to Alexa, that no one meant anything to Alexa except for Alexa, and that she, Daphne, would never have a life until she broke free of her so-called best friend.

What was she doing throwing away her talent on Alexa? Daphne began to ask herself. After all, she was a fantastic camera operator and an even better editor. She could be working at a network, or on blockbuster films, so why was she devoting all her time to someone who could barely remember her name after twenty-two years of knowing her?

That day on St. John's, as she had watched Alexa cut the classmate dead in the hotel's restaurant by pretending not to notice him at breakfast, Daphne had once again, hurried to make one of Alexa's victims feel better. She had wasted fifteen minutes of her life trying to repair the boy's ego that morning, while he'd been looking solely at Alexa, who was busy taking a selfie with a freshly-made latte for her first post of the day. He had barely heard Daphne's efforts to cheer him up and she had finally realized that she was, literally, wasting her life living it in Alexa's wake.

Yes, Daphne had decided that day, she was done. She just needed the right moment to leave. And she had to be smart about it. She had seen the nearly biblical vengeance Alexa was capable of unleashing more than once before and had no desire to suffer death by social media. But when would that moment ever come?

"It's about time," Alexa snapped from the back seat. Daphne was jolted back to the present, wondering if she had somehow telegraphed her thoughts. But Alexa was only referring to the traffic, which had finally started to move as cars began to snake their way into Yellowstone National Park.

"This better be worth it," Alexa snapped from the back seat as Daphne began to drive slowly through the park. Though they had not yet reached the mineral mudflats and geysers that made Yellowstone so famous, Daphne was still stunned by the miles of natural beauty surrounding them—the rolling grass-covered hills dotted with bison, the meandering streams that came together to create rivers, the meadows filled with wildflowers that bloomed in a riot of color, and the distant peaks of snow-topped mountains beneath azure skies. She had never seen anything like it. Even the air smelled fresher, as pristine as if mankind had never existed at all.

She glanced into the rearview mirror to see if Alexa had noticed, but her friend was staring intently at her phone, scrolling through her social media feeds and checking in on how many Likes and new followers she had racked up that morning. Daphne sighed as she watched a pair of hawks circling lazily in the sky, riding the wind currents just because they could. They were free, so very, very free.

So why wasn't she?

"Stop!" Alexa suddenly shouted. Daphne slammed on the brakes in alarm, causing a minivan stuffed with kids to nearly rear-end them. "Let's start there!"

Alexa was pointing to a field of iridescent blue-and-green

mudflats steaming on one side of the road, accessible only by a wooden walkway lined with handrails. A long parking lot fronted the area and Daphne quickly pulled into it. It was jam-packed and Daphne slowed, knowing that any minute Alexa's temper would explode over the inconvenience if they had to wait for a spot to clear.

"There's one!" Alexa screamed, pointing toward a red car pulling out at the other end of the lot.

"There are at least three other cars waiting to pull into that one spot and every one of them has been waiting longer than us," Daphne pointed out. "We need to wait our turn."

"Says who?" Alexa told her as she climbed out of the Escalade and marched down the gravel lot, spraying stones with every stomp of her heels. She reached the parking spot just as the red car finished pulling out. Planting herself firmly in front of the opening, Alexa crossed her arms and made it plain that she was not moving and that everyone else waiting was wasting their time.

Humiliated and feeling the eyes of other tourists on her, Daphne crept down the lot and grimly parked in the open spot, watching guiltily as a trio of old people watched her, mouths hanging open, then shook their heads in disgust and walked away.

"Grab the camera and follow me," Alexa ordered. "I have an idea."

Daphne retrieved the tripod and her high-end video camera from the front seat. By the time she caught up with Alexa, her friend had claimed a primo position in front of a multi-colored mineral spring that pulsated with color in the sunlight and bubbled with heat from far below the Earth's surface, sending plumes of steam into the air.

"How's this?" Alexa said, leaning against one railing and planting a long leg on the other in a provocative pose. With that single move, she had blocked the walkway for everyone else attempting to view or leave the attraction. "Start filming and I'll start talking," Alexa ordered. She unbuttoned her shirt a few more buttons, exposing breasts that Daphne knew had been augmented during their last year of high school.

"How's my hair look?" Alexa asked, tossing her head back so that her blonde extensions flowed behind her like a golden river.

Forced to ignore the grumblings of the other park visitors, Daphne scrambled to set the camera up quickly. She had barely finished affixing it to the tripod when she heard a voice behind her say firmly, "You can't do that."

A small, well-groomed man in a ranger's uniform stood behind them, arms crossed over his chest. "You can't block the walkway like that," he said in a tone of voice that made it plain he was in no mood to compromise.

"We won't be long," Alexa cooed in her sweetest voice, bending toward the ranger so that her shirt gaped open to reveal breasts spilling out over a black lace bra.

The ranger was unmoved and simply stood there, arms crossed, waiting.

"Fine," Alexa finally snapped. "Then we'll just get out of the way." She turned to the railing and started to swing a leg over it. The ranger darted forward and grabbed her arm, pulling her back.

"Don't you dare touch me!" Alexa shouted. "Get this on camera, Daphne! This is police brutality."

"He's not a cop," Daphne said grimly. "And we need to get out of here. He's right. This is rude."

Alexa looked at her with scorn. "You're never going to get anywhere, Daphne. Not until you grow a pair."

By now a crowd had started to gather. A family wearing matching Hawaiian shirts stopped as their bored teenagers gaped eagerly at the emerging spectacle, phones at the ready to capture the moment. A busload of Japanese tourists had arrived and were already snapping photos, while outraged hikers adjusted their heavy backpacks as they stared at Alexa with disapproval and waited to be let through.

Alexa ignored them and extended a well-manicured middle finger toward the ranger, shouting, "Why don't you leave me alone and go do your job for a change?" She looked up at Daphne. "Did you get that part on camera? I can say it again."

"OK, that's it," the ranger said grimly. "As much as I'm sure that everyone here would like to see you boiled alive in 160-degree water, I'm afraid it is my job to save you from yourself."

As Alexa stared at the ranger, wondering what the hell he was talking about, Daphne sighed and quickly dismantled the camera, then turned to head back to the car.

"Where are you going?" Alexa screamed after her. "I don't even have any usable footage yet."

Daphne kept going. There would be hell to pay when Alexa joined her back at the car, but she didn't care, especially when she saw the trio of old people who had witnessed their parking spot poaching earlier coming toward her, glaring at her with accusing eyes that made it plain that they damn sure remembered her face. Embarrassed, Daphne mumbled, "I'm sorry," as she squeezed past them. But she still kept going. She knew that without a camera trained on her, Alexa would not bother to stay. *What was the point of doing anything unless it was filmed?* was her motto. This was the only way to get her to leave.

Alexa began screaming the moment she climbed back into the back seat of the Escalade. "What the hell was that?" she shouted. "That guy had no power. You just folded. You have to be firm with these people."

These people? Daphne thought to herself. *You mean anyone other than yourself?* But she didn't dare say it aloud. She knew the time would come to leave Alexa, but she needed to do it right or Alexa would ruin her life.

"It was too crowded," Daphne explained instead. "All those people moving in the background would have distracted from you."

Alexa considered this for a moment, then nodded. If there was one thing that could get Alexa to change her mind, it was the possibility that she would not be the center of attention.

"Let's get out of here," Alexa ordered, sounding as if leaving was her idea. "We'll find another spot without some Nazi guarding it."

Daphne sighed and started the Escalade once again. It was going to be a very long day.

"Turn here!" Alexa suddenly shouted, nearly causing Daphne to swerve into a ditch.

"It says this road is for authorized vehicles only," Daphne explained, knowing that if they were ticketed it would not be Alexa paying the fine.

"Even better," Alexa declared confidently. "We won't run into any grubby tourists to ruin our shot."

Daphne said nothing but turned left onto a service road. The Escalade bumped its way over the hard-packed dirt surface, bouncing the camera equipment into the air each time they hit another pothole. "I don't think this really goes anywhere," Daphne said in a tight voice.

"Keep going!" Alexa ordered her. "I call the shots, not you."

A half mile later, the road abruptly ended in a magnificent wildflower meadow flanked by patches of forest on each side. The vista stretched before them, a grassy incline covered with a sea of lilies, lupine, poppies, larkspur, prairie smoke, trillium, wild hyacinth, and sunflowers.

"This is perfect," Alexa declared. "Stop the car."

"Like I have a choice," Daphne muttered as she slowed to a stop.

Alexa was out the door before Daphne could shut off the ignition. "Follow me!" she yelled over her shoulder as she began to skip across the meadow. "And don't forget to bring the mirror."

Daphne sighed again as she unloaded the equipment, struggling to carry the camera and tripod along with the body-length mirror they had picked up at a Dollar General near the airport. Alexa had gone through over a hundred mirrors in the years that Daphne had known her, buying them on location, then leaving them behind in her hotel room when they left, a regular Johnny Appleseed of unbridled narcissism.

Daphne propped the mirror against a tree along one edge of the meadow so that Alexa could smooth her hair and adjust her denim shorts by inching them up so that even more tanned skin was revealed. "I told you this was the spot," she said with a self-satisfied smile. "The light is perfect."

Finished primping, Alexa trampled through the wildflowers in bloom and found a patch of flattened grass to frame her slender body.

Daphne tightened the camera to the tripod and wondered briefly what had caused the indention in the grass. She glanced around her. She was no zoologist, but even she knew that Yellowstone was full of wild animals who could not read the signs posted everywhere for tourists. Animals that were probably far too familiar with humans to steer clear but were also quite capable of turning on them without warning.

Alexa was twirling in circles, arms outstretched, testing her balance. "How's this?" she called out to Daphne.

"You look like Julie Andrews in *The Sound of Music*," Daphne lied as she adjusted the camera settings. *If Julie Andrews had been trailer trash dressed like a truck stop whore*, she added to herself.

"Who the hell is Julie Andrews?" Alexa asked. "Is she an influencer? I've never even heard of her. She can't be as popular as me." She stopped and struck a pose for the camera, jutting out a hip and placing one hand on it as she leaned toward the camera and pursed her lips. "Let me know when you're ready."

"Rolling," Daphne called out.

Alexa stretched her arms out again and began to turn in circles, exclaiming rapturously, "This morning I'm here in beautiful Yellowstone. I'm surrounded by incredible natural beauty. My heart is full. It's almost like being in church." She stopped and peered into the camera, eyes wide. "Did you know that there are parks like this across America? Parks that cost next to nothing to enjoy? Why isn't the government spending its money on natural beauty like this instead of on handouts for the poor?"

"Cut!" Daphne yelled out, switching off the camera.

"What was that for?" Alexa demanded. "That was perfect. I'll let you know when it's time to stop filming."

"First of all," Daphne said patiently. "We've agreed that politics does not help you gain new Likes. In fact, it usually causes you to lose followers."

"I need to be more relevant," Alexa said airily. "Do you know how many people hate taxes? Not everyone can afford as good an accountant as I can. They want the government to spend their money on things that matter. Like places like this."

"OK, then," Daphne said through gritted teeth. "Would the fact that the government *already* spends its money on national parks stop you?" Alexa stared at her blankly and Daphne was forced to explain. "Alexa, national parks *are* owned by the government and the American people. Taxpayer money already supports the operations of the parks and funds the salaries of park employees. It's also taxpayer money that funds the building of the roads that go into and through the park."

Alexa looked confused. "What are you talking about?" she demanded.

"You can't advocate for the government to spend its money on national parks like it's some great new idea," Daphne suggested with a sigh. "The government is already spending its money on national parks."

"Oh, who cares?" Alexa said with a flip of her hair. "Politics is boring anyway. Let's start over." She stretched her arms out again, began to whirl, then stopped abruptly. "You won't believe what I'm seeing," she said in a loud whisper, as if confiding in her viewers. Suddenly, she darted toward the trees rimming the meadow. "Follow me!" she called back over her shoulder gaily.

She emerged from the woods a few seconds later cradling a black bear cub in her arms. She beamed a blindingly white smile at the camera and said with a giggle, "Look who I found! Can you believe it? This is just the cutest little thing I've ever seen."

Daphne froze in shock, fear flooding through her as she stared at her friend and the squirming cub clamped in her arms. It was no bigger than a medium-sized dog and seemed more confused than angry that a human had breezed in from nowhere, plucked it from the safety of the forest, and was now rocking it in her arms while making strange noises in its face.

"Who's a good boy?" Alexa cooed. "Aren't you just the cutest, sweetest thing ever?" She stared up at the camera and smiled. "I will remember this day forever. I have always wanted to hold a real, live baby bear. This is a dream come true for me."

Daphne began to signal frantically from behind the camera, afraid to make any noise. Surely even Alexa knew that you don't go around picking up baby bears, that if there was a cub than, somewhere nearby, there was also a mama bear. But if she said anything, Alexa would never let her forget that she had ruined once-in-a-lifetime footage. And more noise might attract the cub's mother.

I can't let that stop me from speaking up, Daphne thought. *This is too dangerous.* But before she could say anything, Alexa began to rock the bear cub in her arms as if it were a baby.

"The bear went over the mountain," Alexa sang loudly. "The bear went over the mountain, the bear went over the mountain to see what it could see. And what did that bear see?" She bounced the cub up and down as she sang, pausing every now and then to smile and wink at the camera.

Daphne could take it no longer. "I don't think this is safe," she called out.

"I know what I'm doing," Alexa snapped back. She glared at Daphne. "Check the time code. You're going to have to edit this out, you stupid bitch."

The little bear wiggled in her arms, either impatient to get away or anxious to hear the second verse. It began to emit a series of squeaks and squawks. "Oooh!" Alexa cried. "He's singing along!"

Daphne shook her head and zoomed in on the baby bear, then pulled back out to reveal the entire magnificent vista behind Alexa and the cub. She had to admit that her friend had been right. This was an incredibly beautiful spot, even for Yellowstone, a fairy tale picture of bucolic paradise. It was breathtakingly pristine. But as Daphne peered into her viewfinder, admiring the shot, she noticed a black shape emerging from the trees halfway up the slope. *Oh, shit. Oh, shit, shit, shit, shit, shit.*

"Alexa!" Daphne called out, trying not to panic. "Put the baby bear down gently and walk toward me. Don't ask questions. Just put the cub down and follow me back to the car."

But Alexa had launched into the second verse of her song and was now holding the tiny bear by its upper body, dangling it in the air like a baby, pausing only to rub her nose against the cub's forehead. "It smells like fresh flowers!" she called out gaily. "It's just like a fat, furry puppy!" She paused to grin at the camera. "Why is there never a marshmallow around when you need one?" she asked, hoping to coin a new viral catchphrase.

The black shadow on the hill above Alexa drew closer and Daphne could hear a low rumble, followed by snuffling that grew louder and louder as the mama bear spotted her cub. The massive creature paused, blew out a huge gust of air, pawed at the ground—then burst forward in an explosion of fury, head lowered, ears flattened in warning. She leapt through the wildflowers, galloping faster and faster until she was charging like a freight train at full speed. Its rumbling becoming a roar as it bore down on Alexa and the cub.

"Run!" Daphne screamed as she dashed frantically for the car. But even as she ran for safety, a thought popped into her head. *You don't have to outrun the bear. You just have to outrun the slowest person with you.*

By now, the bear was less than ten yards away from an oblivious Alexa who, intent on her performance, was now singing even louder and whirling the baby bear in a circle as it wailed in protest. "And what did that bear see?" Alexa belted out. "And what did that bear see?"

Daphne reached the Escalade and, hands shaking, pried open the door to the driver's seat. She climbed inside, slamming and locking the door behind her. She stared through the windshield, horrified, as the bear reached Alexa and reared up on its hind legs, then transformed its body into five-hundred pounds of airborne fury as it launched into the air. The infuriated sow hit Alexa from behind with all four paws, slamming her body into the ground and causing the baby bear to fly up in the air before it landed safely in a patch of wildflowers, where it rolled over then scampered away to safety.

Alexa was not so lucky. She began to scream as the mama bear climbed on top of her, pinning her body to the ground before throwing back her head and giving out a terrifying, primal bellow that announced the arrival of an apex predator, proclaiming to all creatures great and small that nothing else on this earth could stop her now. That she was queen of this forest.

It was as if time slowed, stretching every second of the bear's movements out for an eternity. The enraged creature shook its head back and forth in fury as thick ropes of saliva flew into the air, gleaming in the afternoon sunlight like strings of diamonds. Beneath her, Alexa began to scream, thrashing her arms and legs as she frantically tried to twist her way free.

Snorting, the mama bear sank her teeth deep into one of Alexa's legs and tore at the flesh, pausing only to snap at a flailing arm, casting chunks of muscle and blood into the air. Hopping off Alexa, the bear sank her jaws deep into her victim's body then tossed it effortlessly upward. Alexa hit the ground with a thud, her screams growing weaker. The bear roared to the sky before it attacked again, clamping her teeth around both sides of Alexa's head and shaking her body back-and-forth, as if Alexa was no bigger than a mouse and the bear a house cat intent on slaughtering its next meal as efficiently as possible.

Speechless, Daphne watched from the car, trying not to

panic, taking deep breaths, not knowing whether to cry or faint or pick up her cell phone to call for help.

That was when a thought that had been percolating somewhere deep inside her soul hit her: *the camera was still rolling.* The camera was still perfectly framing what was happening, recording every scratch and bite, every scream and roar of the struggle before it.

Daphne knew in a heartbeat that her moment had come. That now was her chance to take the spotlight. That if she sat tight and waited, just waited, she would have footage that millions and millions of people would flock to view. That she would be able to sell the rights to someone, somewhere, for a small fortune. That if she played her cards right, her life would change forever.

Alexa had ceased to scream. She had, in fact, stopped making any noise at all. The bear was ripping and tearing at her limp body now with ferocious focus, clawing and consuming the invader who had threatened her cub.

Daphne could not look away. *I'll call for help as soon as I get to a place with cell service,* she thought. *No one will know how long I waited to call.* Just a few moments more, she calculated, just a few moments more until the mama bear left. Then she could retrieve the camera and store it safely away in the back of the car, claiming they had not yet used it that day. The rangers would believe her, what was left of Alexa would be swiftly carried away to avoid horrifying the tourists, and she would pretend to be in shock. But all the while, hidden in the car, would be the footage, the precious footage that Daphne knew, with absolute certainty, would change her career—and her life —forever.

Yes, Daphne's moment had come at last. It was finally time for *her* to shine.

KATY MUNGER IS A NORTH CAROLINA-BASED MYSTERY AUTHOR AND editor who has written under several different pseudonyms. In addition to co-editing the neo-noir quarterly journal <u>Dark Yonder</u>, she is the author of the Dead Detective series; the Casey Jones crime fiction series; and the Hubbert & Lil mystery series. She has also contributed to numerous short story collections. Her books can be found on <u>Amazon</u> or ordered through Ingram Distributors by your local bookstore. Katy has also been a book reviewer for *The Washington Post* and served as North Carolina's 2016 Piedmont Laureate.

5

PREY FOR REVEREND MORGAN
DAVID BART

At the West Yellowstone vendor where they'd purchased their trail passes and rented the "sleds"—as snowmobiles were called around there—Morgan Adams read a poster about the reintroduction of wolves contributing to the restoration of aspen trees. Wolves cull the elk herds resulting in fewer elk to browse, allowing the aspen to spread. Apparently, for some to flourish, others must die.

Morgan and his wife Tonya rode on one sled, his best friend Rick on another, entering the park from the edge of town. After an hour, passing through newly-restored aspen groves, they left the network of groomed trails, Tonya driving. She'd downloaded the Yellowstone Park map onto her phone to locate this remote valley. Morgan had not been able to find his own cell before they left their home in Denver; odd, because he always knew where it was.

He stood in the deep snow, relieving himself behind a large cottonwood tree, gazing out over the stark winter landscape. He turned at the sound of the snowmobile revving up, Tonya shouting over the chattering racket of the machine: "See ya, wouldn't wanna be ya!" And off she went.

His best friend, Rick Saylor, on the other snowmobile, revved his motor, engaged the drive and headed after Morgan's wife, yelling over a shoulder: "You don't have a prayer, Rev." Cackled like a madman.

So, Morgan had been right; something *was* going on between them, an affair or something more sinister. And now they'd abandoned him in a place true to cliché: *the middle of nowhere*. Nearest traveled sled trail was probably a good five miles on the other side of that rise. The "Rev," as Rick had called him, was in doo-doo even deeper than the snow.

Of course, the not-so-good Reverend Morgan Adams was no longer any kind of minister, though people still called him Rev. A lot of those people, himself included, didn't think of him as "Rev" out of respect, but with mocking derision. He'd once been a TV star, hawking bestselling CDs and books, raking it in. But his addictions had brought him down, and so he'd ended up a fallen angel. But still very rich.

He trudged along in the tracks of the snowmobiles; it wasn't a groomed trail, so it was gonna be a long, tortuous hike back to something approximating civilization. If it was even possible to make it.

The two snowmobiles had disappeared into a ubiquitous stand of aspen at the top of the rise, the noise from the motors rapidly diminishing. Morgan figured the mutinous pair would follow the tracks back across a wide plateau to a designated park trail and then on to where they'd left Morgan's Escalade, in the vendor's parking lot at the edge of West Yellowstone. A good two hours by snowmobile. Maybe longer.

Morgan had no food, just two bottles of water, a book of matches normally used to light his illicit Cubans, which he hadn't brought anyway. No phone—which explained why he couldn't find it at home—Tonya had hidden the damn thing.

Scanning the valley, rim to rim, Morgan Adams easily concluded he was alone. Then he squinted, looking across the glaring snowfield.

Not completely alone. At the northern end of the valley, maybe a quarter mile away, a pack of gray wolves was chasing a herd of elk, sometimes called a gang (a little tidbit gleaned from his extensive reading.) Their labored breath from widely flared nostrils were visible in the icy air as tiny jets of fog. And despite his own precarious situation, he was fascinated by the ancient drama playing out across that cold expanse of snow. He'd always been interested in nature and how wildlife interacted to sustain an ecosystem. *Red in tooth and claw.* 'Course, now he was an unwitting player in the ancient drama. Without claws. Or any weapon. Morgan's role was prey.

The running creatures disappeared over a rise and now he was truly alone. He shivered; both from the cold and the existential threat of his predicament. He felt more helpless and lost than he'd ever experienced before.

Three days passed. Out of water, incredibly thirsty, he was tempted to eat snow for water but resisted the impulse, knowing it would not adequately rehydrate his body. In fact, it would do the opposite, because his body would have to produce energy in order to melt the icy crystals in his mouth. And that would also negatively impact his body temperature. So, with no pot to put the snow in to melt it over a fire, it might as well be sand.

Maybe just give up? Tonya and Rick weren't coming back for him. This hadn't been a practical joke. It was attempted murder. And if successful, he'd be the victim, like on one of the seemingly hundreds of crime shows on cable. *Episode 13: Morgan the Victim.*

The first day he'd followed the trail made by their sled tracks, but a storm blew in, turned into a howling blizzard, sweeping across the valley. He became disoriented; even more snow clung to trees and rocks, reconfiguring the landscape. And he had a low-grade fever, accompanied by brief bouts of delirium. No hallucinations yet; probably only a matter of time.

He needed to find some kind of shelter before nightfall . . . or die.

Violent shivers, teeth chattering, Morgan awakened from a phantasmagoric dream. impossible images, mind-blowing sensations way outside his normal range of perception. Though, oddly, the images were not all that disturbing; even having fangs seemed natural. He ran his tongue over his teeth: same boring canines and incisors. No fangs. The weirdest thing? It'd been the first dream he'd ever had in which he could smell things; musky odor of damp fur and the coppery smell of blood as it drained onto pristine snow.

At the same time, it'd felt familiar. He'd been truly alive; uplifted by an exhilarating sense of abandon—like being free for the first time. He'd been an animal in the dream, having the body and experiences of a wolf. Strange, but on balance it'd been amazing, and he still felt that way, despite his depleted physical condition.

Maybe it was what they call a lucid dream, where you know it's a dream *while* you're dreaming. But for all the clarity of sensation, he didn't think it was the dream that'd awakened him. Because in the dream he'd been oblivious to cold, being a wolf and all. It was more likely to have been the teeth-chattering cold that'd awakened him. A discomfort so profoundly chilling it'd overwhelmed his insulated clothing, permeated his flesh and seeped deeply into his bones. All the way to the marrow.

He'd somehow found an outcropping with a rock ledge overhung with a thick mantle of snow, well-sheltered from the wind. He'd read Jack London's "To Build a Fire" and so was careful to build his well back into the recess under the ledge, so that snow couldn't dump on it; though it did get a little smoky.

The fire had burned down to ashes while he slept. And blowing snow had filtered inside his snowsuit, melted from body heat, soaking the matches. Morgan stared at the remnants of his carefully constructed fire. Could the coals underneath still be smoldering? Morgan took off a glove, held his trembling bare hand over the ashes. Did seem less cold than . . . well, certainly warmer than everything around him, which was a vast ocean of glaring white snow, accented by touches of dark green from pine trees. He lowered his hand again. Could he trust the sensation of warmth? Our brains play tricks. On the other hand, what choice did he have? If he was going to survive, he *needed* the ashes to be holding at least *some* heat. There could—couldn't there?—be at least a thin bed of dimming embers under the insulating layer? It'd be a godsend at the very least, because he could get the fire going without much trouble, the energy from remaining coals would dry the fuel, eventually igniting it so he—

First find the hypothetical fuel. What's it called? Tinder. Dead twigs and dried grass hidden under a four-foot layer of snow.

As he dug down to gather the tinder Morgan thought of how Yellowstone was the very first National Park. He'd read that Ulysses S. Grant had—*ordained*—it? Was that the right word? Morgan loved the outdoors, admired the Buddhist concept of being "one with nature." Another president, Teddy

Roosevelt, had later been instrumental in saving Yellowstone from poachers and railroad companies eager to hack their way across the park. As President he went on to open other national parks around the country. A nature guy. Rough and ready.

Morgan had been tough once, but was now neither rough nor ready. His only redeeming quality was that prior to his fall from grace he'd helped people find solace in the existence of a deity, a force, or universal power, something larger than themselves. He'd provided guidance for thousands of parishioners. Then—to add, as they say, insult to injury—he'd lost his faith. This absence left him feeling hollow. So, he tried to fill that emptiness with gambling, booze, and even drugs.

Stop thinking, dammit! No time for self-pity. Get the fingers working—they felt like the frozen sticks and twigs he'd been gathering to resurrect the fire. All his digits were stiff and creaky, uncooperative when he tried to bend them. The gloves helped, maybe kept away frostbite, but blood must be oozing through his veins and arteries like molasses. Tip of his nose had gone from a stinging cold sensation to an alarming numbness. And though he no longer believed in a sure thing, without a fire, it was a stone-cold certainty he would perish.

And brethren—as though he was giving a sermon to his huge flock in the Denver mega-church he'd once pastored—*brethren, I have a larger question: what am I doing here?* Middle of a national park, dead of winter—the operative word being "dead." Is this retribution? Wrath visited on a sinner? Or is it just the betrayal of a wife and a—

A stark realization slammed into him like the avalanche he'd seen cascading off a high ridge yesterday. Tonya and his best friend Rick, dumping him out there in the vast and frozen park, perhaps had been his own doing. Maybe he deserved it.

A casual observer, somehow privy to his thoughts, might

concur: *your wife, your best friend, abandoning a minister? What the hell did you do to them?*

Morgan sighed, wincing as he rubbed his gloved hands together. He hadn't done anything to them, except accumulate so much wealth they couldn't resist a plan to get rid of him and take the money, the cars, the houses, all for themselves.

He'd thought it a great notion when Tonya suggested they ride snowmobiles into Yellowstone. They could invite his best friend to come along. Morgan had questioned whether Rick would enjoy it. Like Morgan's wife, Rick was pretty much a pampered city dweller. Neither he nor Tonya had ever camped out, didn't know squat about nature. Rick couldn't seem to make anything in his life work, except sometimes getting women to take care of him. He looked like Michael Douglas as Gordon Gekko; same slicked-back greasy hair. And the unctuous manner of a guy who could sell snow tires to a snake.

Morgan's morally-ambivalent wife preferred upscale hotels and exotic beaches to anything involving the outdoors, at least beyond a walk along the surf or a poolside tanning session. And she didn't work. Except on her mysterious novel, which she wouldn't let him see. Would jinx it, she claimed. He trespassed her laptop during one of her "night out with the girls" and there were only four pages, one of which was the title page: *My Life with a Sinful Preacher Man*. He'd tossed back four or five shots of vodka to erase that title from his mind. Not because the characterization was undeserved; he'd been the worst of hypocrites. He just didn't want to think about it.

But Tonya seemed really excited about coming up to Yellowstone with Morgan and his best friend, charming Rick. It made Morgan think of those stalwart folks who'd lived back a hundred and fifty years ago, hacking their way through whatever stuff one hacked through back then, seeking a new start, risking their own lives. The Native Americans, rightfully pissed at the intrusion, gave them a lot of trouble, often of an existential nature, and wild animals weren't big supporters of 'westward ho' either.

So, he figured, compared to what the pioneers had endured, the little inconvenience of enduring cold on loud machines would be a walk in the park for his wife and friend. But irony being his constant companion these last few years, the fact that they were undoubtedly warming themselves in front of a blazing fire, or warming off each other, while he was out in the cold, well, it seemed like something he should have expected.

Whatever. His situation was what it was. And like those people of old, he needed to buck up or freeze to death, die from dehydration, or maybe be mauled by a grizzly taking umbrage with the intrusion of yet another biped into its territory. And let's not forget about wolves, like the one he'd been in his dream. In these so-called modern times predators had become more aggressive as man encroached on their space.

Put like that, he knew he was probably going to die. But, dammit, not without a fight. Or something resembling a fight, like flailing wildly while shrieking and begging. He wasn't tough anymore. He was a former self-ordained minister, not a badass mountain man. His addictive habits had weakened him. He was no longer a man of the cloth; he was a man of sloth.

Though he did have a history of violence.

When Morgan was a kid, he'd robbed houses with his buddies. Took prescription drugs and cash, any liquor they could carry. Morgan was the leader; any of those boys who stepped out of line regarding their responsibilities to the gang, he'd beat the crap out of them. His dominance back then had been mysterious to him, his ability to control a bunch of tough youths. It came naturally though. Like a part of him was a wild man.

Then they got busted. Juvenile detention. Strict rules. Bibles handed out which you had to read, because you never knew when they'd spring a pop quiz. Morgan found much of the text incredibly boring, some of it interesting, meaningful, and some of it disturbing. Even to a juvenile delinquent. *Leviticus?* Scared the hell out of him.

He found enough inspiration in the Book to compel him to go to college and then seminary. Didn't finish. Too impatient, and he hated dogma. So, he started as a street preacher and when that took off, he opened his own church: *Essence of Life*. Word spread, people came in droves. Then local TV gigs.

Was it a calling? He later admitted to Tonya that aspects of the work hadn't ever been a good fit, except for his amazing ability to mesmerize an audience with his rafter-shaking oratory. Unfortunately, another talent soon emerged: constantly screwing up, drinking and gambling. In time, he'd been shunned by his flock.

THANKFULLY, THERE WERE STILL EMBERS UNDER THE ASHES AND HE finally got the fire going. Exhausted by the effort, he quickly fell asleep. Had the dream again about being a wolf. It was strange, but exhilarating; better than drugs or booze. It filled Morgan with a kind of primal energy.

Trotting along a snowy trail, his wolf perception a confusion of unwelcome thoughts regarding good and evil—which were not even remotely wolf ideologies—the icy path underfoot tamped down from pack traffic, and the occasional lynx or fox.

Wolf halted, wary of a large, crumpled object lying in a C-shape near a rock face beside the trail. He curled his lips to expose menacing white fangs. It was impossible: a part of him realized it was himself, lying there, in human form, curled next to the remnants of a fire, faint embers visible through glowing fissures in the bed of ashes. He ventured forward, compelled by an innate curiosity, wary of the dual sensibilities he was experiencing. Sniffed the unconscious biped. Wolf usually avoided people. With their traps and guns, they didn't play fair. In nature you kill to eat, or you're killed and eaten. Fair enough. Nature's way. But some men killed for sport.

He licked the slack face of the human lying there, hairs bristling on his neck as, again, he had the sense that he was looking at himself.

Wolf turned to leave, repelled by the stink of fear and desperation. He knew it was not the fear of dying, but that the man feared dying alone in the wilderness with nobody to mourn his passing. Concerned, even while asleep, with how he would *look* when his remains were discovered. If Wolf had been able to laugh, he would have. It was nonsense. You die alone. Appearance irrelevant. If you live, you die. Way it is.

Wolf took a last look at his human self and trotted on down the trail. After a while, Wolf stopped to nip accumulated ice out from between his toes. His paws were very cold, stung as circulation returned. Yeah, it's winter. Hot in summer. Cool spring for cubs. Real nice in autumn. And then winter again. Way it is.

His mate, the alpha female of their pack, rushed up to him, nuzzled against his neck, though it wasn't the time for coupling. Can't have tiny wolf pups appearing too soon. So, the pair renewed their bond by playfully cuddling, an age-old ritual, a prelude to the act that would further their species— but not until winter was winding down.

Morgan awakened and followed the wolf to this ridge. Magically bonded with a wolf? How Morgan's primate cognizance and Wolf's lupine sentience had melded was beyond either creature's comprehension. Together they looked down at the valley floor through both human eyes and wolf eyes—the view switching back and forth until melded into a combined perception, seeing through both sets of eyes simultaneously as raucous machines entered the snow-covered valley below, the two riders on the vehicles unmindful of, or not caring, that their intrusion disrupted the naturalness of a pristine wilderness.

Tonya and Rick had come back.

They were circling below on the wide expanse of snow, no doubt looking for a frozen body. To make sure the source of their hoped-for wealth, the former Reverend Morgan Adams, wouldn't survive to contest their claim. With hundreds of millions at stake you can't take chances. Of course, one thing they hadn't figured, despite knowing it was one of the harshest winters in Yellowstone in years, was the risk of their coming back with the sun so low in the western sky.

To the Wolf/Morgan mind the people below were not so much a threat as they were a nuisance. As a dual entity Morgan and Wolf tilted their heads back, opened their throats and howled—a primeval sound that elicited answering howls and yips that reverberated through the foothills and along the hard surfaces of frozen creeks, over boiling hot pools and fountain-like geysers. The eager cries were of pack obedience, coming to do their leader's bidding. As Morgan's gang had once followed *his* lead.

Morgan stood on his two legs, shivering, head spinning, as his four-legged doppelganger, the alpha wolf, jumped off the ridge to slide effortlessly down the long slope, leaving a plowed wake in the hillside. Wolf reached the flat snowy expanse below, quickly advancing on the terrified snowmobile riders, signaling his packmates to swarm forward, *en masse*, encircling what their leader had designated as interlopers.

Morgan felt an icy indifference toward the people who'd abandoned him to his fate. He was merely watching a primitive contest, one that had been waged for epochs, a wolf pack menacing creatures who'd violated their territory. He knew there'd never been a documented wolf attack on humans in Yellowstone. Very few anywhere in the United States. But this pack had a leader who might be part human, and that part, Morgan, had a grudge.

Tonya and Rick didn't know the statistics involving attacks; they just saw a large pack of snarling, howling wolves. They frantically turned in the opposite direction, glancing back at the pack as they headed west, away from their sled tracks leading back out of the valley, but now blocked by what they believed were ravenous killers. They thought they were heading toward safety, unaware that a deep chasm awaited.

Rick was ahead about ten yards, suddenly disappearing over the ridge, screaming as he plummeted toward the bottom of the gorge. Tonya tried to veer away, and managed to turn, but so abruptly that centrifugal force pulled her off the seat and she flew over the precipice, falling a hundred feet to join her partner-in-crime on the rocks below.

Shrieks of tearing, wrenched metal rose from the gorge, Rick's sled being ripped apart as it tumbled even farther, bouncing over jagged rocks, descending deeper into the chasm.

And then a deathly silence. Even the wolf pack had stopped howling, looking back toward Morgan as he made his way down the slope, trudging across the expanse of snow to the edge of the chasm.

The snow and rocks far below were splattered with red. The momentum of the falling bodies had buried Tonya and Rick deep under giant drifts of snow and he couldn't see them.

His wife's snowmobile, with no hand on the throttle, had come to a stop a few feet back from the ridge, and was still idling.

Morgan pulled off his gloves as he mounted the snowmobile, curling his fingers around the heated grips. After a few minutes he was able to flex them enough to open a water bottle from a holder on the console. He drank it all. Then he managed to engage the throttle, lurching forward to inscribe a long, wide arc in the snow, heading to where sled tracks marked the way up through the grove of stately aspen trees and back toward, if not salvation, at least safety.

MORGAN STOOD ON THE SLIGHTLY CANTED PORCH OF HIS REFURBISHED pioneer log cabin in the foothills outside Jackson Hole, Wyoming. He gazed at the Tetons through a rapidly gathering dusk. The jagged peaks, which had earlier been ablaze with crimson light, had now darkened into shades of approaching night.

Had it been a dream? Hallucination? Or perhaps a fear-fueled desperation manifesting as the self-reliance of a wild beast? Or something unknowable—universal intelligence perhaps, showing him, through the ancient ways of a wild creature, how he could make his way back to an authentic life.

And maybe it hadn't even happened, the bonding with a wolf. Didn't really matter. He was happy. Now a counselor of young homeless men and boys off the streets of different cities like Cheyenne, Helena, Boise, and Salt Lake City. He took them camping in groups, taught them outdoor survival skills and regaled them, sitting around a campfire, with fantastic tales of men and animals becoming one in spirit.

Morgan called the boys his pack. He gave them advice, always with humility, no preaching. When asked by one of them about the existence of a god or what it all meant, he'd tell them that it was a mystery. People had faith, which could be a source of comfort, but nobody knew those things for certain. What he did know was that no matter the adversity they encountered in their lives, they should never give up. Because inside each one of them was a spiritual entity that could help them, give them strength, if they'd listen.

He'd sold all his houses and expensive cars and moved into the small log cabin near a condo complex, not far from where an old gray wolf sometimes visited at sunset. It didn't howl or menace anyone's pets and never stayed very long. The wolf would just sit on a low rise and gaze down at the small log cabin by the winding creek. Bucky Dole, a trust-fund stoner in the condo complex, said he thought the old wolf was looking for a friend.

Morgan went back inside the cabin, sat at his modest desk to write a check to World Wildlife Fund. It was a huge amount that came to over ninety percent of his wealth. He slipped the generous check inside an envelope, the old type you had to lick. It left a residual taste on his tongue, an earthiness from the envelope's glue. And that sensation evoked images of the wild. His eyes misted as he listened to the howls from a pack of wolves somewhere out there in the wilderness. Hunting prey.

Morgan's prey, he now realized, had not been his wife and his best friend. Because of their fear and greed, they'd caused their own demise. His prey had been himself. He needed the old Morgan, the self-involved Morgan, to die, so that he could be reborn. And abide by that most important law: follow your true nature.

DAVID BART HAS PUBLISHED OVER THIRTY SHORT STORIES IN MAJOR crime publications, most notably *Strand Magazine, Ellery Queen Mystery Magazine, Alfred Hitchcock's Mystery Magazine, Mystery Tribune,* and *Mystery Magazine.* His work has also appeared in many anthologies, including the Anthony award-winning Mystery Writers of America anthology *Crime Hits Home,* edited by S.J. Rozan.

David lives in the mountains of New Mexico near ancient Anasazi Indian ruins. He enjoys hiking, rock climbing, and kayaking on the Rio Grande River. He has a wife and a cat, one named Linda, the other Ripley. Rumor has it he subordinates to both.

6

LITTLE GLORIOUS LIFE
SALLY MILLIKEN

"I wonder why Mary wanted us to come here?" Heather asked as she searched the map dominating one wall of the bar. "She gave me very specific instructions. July sixteen. The Mammoth Hotel Map Room Bar at 8 p.m."

Heather scanned the rest of room with its wood-paneled walls and floor to ceiling windows that she and her friends Jennifer, Alice, and Cathy had entered two minutes before. Red vinyl chairs were clustered around square black tables. A couple played checkers on a table pushed up against the large windows. *What were they missing?*

"Because a map of the U. S. this size made completely out of wood is unusual?" suggested Jennifer.

"True. But between the artifacts in the visitor center and the tour of the historic fort, we've seen many interesting things today." Heather dragged her fingers through her short spiky hair. She'd cut it recently because she was tired of it getting in the way while she worked at her bakery. Her only regret was that she hadn't done it sooner.

Alice's eyes were wide behind her red cat-eye glasses as she joined Heather to study the map. The white streak in her long dark hair glowed in the overhead light. That unusual streak made her notorious early in her career in the movie business. "And the geysers too, of course."

Heather nodded. "Of course. It's hard to believe we've only been in Yellowstone for a day."

Alice patted her shoulder. "Come on, let's find a seat. It's like the start of a bad joke—a baker, author, librarian, and washed-up actor walk into a bar…"

Heather chuckled as she followed Alice across the room, weaving around tables. Alice was not washed up and she knew it. They were all in their late fifties and enjoying a second chapter of life and career. Cathy had already pushed her way between two men at the bar, looking like the meat in a plaid lumberjack sandwich. As a romance novelist, she was in her element.

They'd eaten dinner at the hotel dining room and most of the families with young children had gone off to their rooms, leaving the hotel quieter. Heather had walked the boardwalks of the Mammoth Hot Springs during the day like every other tourist, dressed in t-shirts, shorts, and hats to protect themselves from the hot summer sun. She'd changed into jeans and pulled on a fleece before dinner after the temperature dropped.

Heather sat across from Alice at a table near the center of the room. "Mary must have had a reason. You know her. She had a reason for everything. It's just not clear yet."

"Well, right now it's as clear as the mudpots we saw today," said Jennifer as she joined them. She was the only one of them who proudly wore her hair in its natural gray color. With her black boots, sweater out of Vogue, dark eyeliner and mascara, Jennifer looked more artist than librarian. She enjoyed surprising people when she told them what she did for work.

Cathy appeared at the table with four pints. And wore a wide grin. "I know the reason," she said as she passed the drinks. "Rick asked if I was a friend of Mary Williams and when I said yes, he pulled this out from under the bar." Heather noticed that Cathy had a large manila envelope tucked under her arm. Cathy sighed as she settled into her seat. "Rick's the bartender." She smiled and waggled three fingers toward the man behind the long wood bar. "He's a big sweetheart of a bear."

He gave her a return grin and a salute.

Jennifer shook her head and grinned. "That tracks. You being you and us in Yellowstone and all."

"The bear or the sweetheart?" cracked Alice and reached for the envelope. "I think you've found your hero for your next novel."

Cathy giggled and flipped a strand of her long bleached blonde hair behind her shoulder. "I think I just might have." She stopped Alice from taking the envelope from her. "Nope. First, we toast."

Heather wrapped her fingers around the cold glass and lifted it. The other followed.

"To Mary," said Cathy.

"To Mary," they repeated and the clink of glasses was loud over the muffled conversations going on around them.

Jennifer took a sip. "God. I miss her."

Heather swallowed and nodded. "Me too. I wish she were here with us." Heather thought of the ashes in her suitcase upstairs. "I guess, in a way, she is." She couldn't help a chuckle.

"Jeesh, Heather, macabre sense of humor," said Jennifer and she laughed too. "Mary would approve."

Alice smiled and nodded. "She would."

The beer felt cool going down Heather's throat and she settled into her chair. She couldn't remember the last time she'd relaxed. Maybe that was why Mary wanted them to come here. She'd known they could all use a break. Besides, how could any of them say 'no' to spreading her ashes.

"Come on, Cathy, I can't take the suspense," Jennifer said. "What's in the envelope?"

Cathy leaned forward and was about to use a red fingernail to release the flap when two men sat at the game table next to them. With their full bushy beards, baseball caps, canvas work pants, and heavy boots they looked more local than many of the tourists they'd seen that day.

"Shot 'em right between the eyes," one said and they both cackled. "Come on. You go first."

Heather heard the clack of checkers as they lined up their pieces to play.

"God damn, it feels good to bag us as many as we want," the second man said.

Heather pulled her chair closer to their table and leaned in to whisper. "Did you hear that?"

Jennifer's eyes darted nervously around the bar. "Do you think he means they were hunting? I read that poaching has been a problem in Yellowstone."

"What should we do?" asked Alice.

Cathy took a sip and looked at each of them. "What can we do? We don't know for sure what they're talking about. Anyone know the hunting rules around here?"

Heather shook her head. "It's a national park, I assume you can't."

"I'll Google it later," said Cathy.

"I've got a better idea." Jennifer dug around in her huge purse. "It should say in the guide book I bought today at Yellowstone Forever." She pulled out an assortment of sunscreen tubes, a wallet, books, notepad, and pens and dropped them on the table. "Found it."

"While you look for that—" Heather patted the envelope. "How did Rick know?"

Cathy lifted a brow.

"Never mind," Heather said and laughed. "The time. The place. Four women in their prime with varying colors of hair." When she nodded toward Alice, she added, "And a movie star —Easy peasy."

"Pshh. No one recognizes me anymore." Alice dismissed the idea with a wave of her hand and leaned forward. "Besides, more people read Cathy's novels than watched my movies. Come on, then, open it up."

Cathy slid open the envelope and pulled out four smaller white envelopes. She laid them out in a line across the table.

Alice read the words out loud. "'Mammoth Hot Springs. Read this one first.'" Then "'Night Two. Old Faithful Inn. Night Three. Canyon Village. Night Four. Roosevelt Lodge.'"

"So, not only has Mary organized and paid for this trip, but she left messages for us for each night?" asked Jennifer.

"Apparently." Cathy opened the Mammoth envelope. "It's a letter. Here, Heather, you read it. You can read her handwriting better than me."

Heather smiled at the reference to their friend's messy penmanship, cleared her throat, and grasped the paper tightly in her hands. "Dear Heather, Alice, Cathy, and Jennifer. Welcome to Yellowstone National Park, my most favorite place in the world..." She continued to read Mary's words of love and admiration for the history of the park and the people who once lived in the area and the many animals who call the two-million acre park home as well as some of her favorite spots to visit. "Please enjoy this special place and know that I will be with you every step of the way. When you think of this trip, remember me in your hearts. Forever at peace and without pain. I love you, Mary."

Heather wiped a tear from her eyes. She wasn't the only one. "It ends with a poem called 'In the Yellowstone' by Harriet Monroe."

"I recognize that name. She was the founder of *Poetry* Magazine," Jennifer said. After a quick search on her phone, she added, "Yes. Still got it. She lived from 1860 to 1936. Go ahead, read it for us."

Heather cleared her throat and read,

> "*In the Yellowstone—*
> *Little pin-prick geysers, spitting and sputtering;*
> *Little foaming geysers, that spatter and cough;*
> *Bubbling geysers, that gurgle out of the calyx of*
> *morning glory pools.*'"

Jennifer checked the paper. "That's it?"

"There's a dot dot dot." Heather turned the page over. "I guess it continues. Must be in the next letter."

"It's an ellipsis," mumbled Cathy, ever the writer.

Heather read it again and when she was done, they sat in silence. Heather dragged her finger down her wet glass as she considered the words.

Jennifer interrupted her thoughts. "The images and personalities of the different types of geysers are amazing. I wonder if Mary was trying to tell us something?" As a librarian, she was used to leading book discussions. "That reminds me of the 'Women in Yellowstone' exhibit at the Heritage Center we visited today. Women had to have been seriously tough back then. Their heavy skirts and corsets alone would have made things a challenge."

They discussed their favorite parts of the exhibit. When Heather looked around, they were the last ones in the bar. Even the two men playing checkers were gone. She covered a yawn.

"Let's take a photo in front of the map," Cathy suggested.

"Great idea," agreed Heather.

Cathy was only too happy to ask bartender Rick but a woman wearing an 'I love Yellowstone' t-shirt, entered the bar with her husband and teenager at that moment and asked, "Would you like me to take a group shot?"

Cathy handed her the phone.

"Thank you," Alice said as they lined up.

When she was done, the woman gestured toward Alice. "Um. But are you Alice Darling? Would you mind if I take a photo with you?"

Alice laughed. "Oh, no dear, I'm not her. But how flattering. She's lovely, isn't she? And a terrific actor. I love her movies."

The woman laughed nervously and tugged at her shirt, "Oh, silly me. Sorry to bother you."

"No bother. How's your visit to Yellowstone so far?" Alice asked, then added. "We're having the best time."

"We are too," she motioned to her family. "We're heading to Roosevelt Lodge tomorrow."

Cathy pocketed her phone. "We hope you enjoy it. We'll be there in three days."

"Oh—" Alice opened her mouth and closed it.

The woman whispered to her husband as they walked away.

Heather watched them go, puzzled by Alice's hesitancy. "What was that about? Usually, you're happy to take photos with your fans."

Alice looked around. She seemed to relax when no one else was nearby. As they strolled toward their rooms, she filled them in. "I didn't want to worry you, especially because of Mary's illness, but I have a stalker. It's been on my mind for so long that it felt good not to talk about it." She swallowed. "I don't want him to find out I'm here. One social media post and, well, you know how it is..."

"Oh, Alice." Heather stared at her. "Why didn't you say something sooner?"

"I figured we'd be totally off the grid here. Cell service spotty, rental car, different hotels each night." Alice shrugged. "I know you all never post anything, but others might and I can't take that chance."

Cathy raised a clenched fist and shook it. "Who is he? I'll give him a knuckle sandwich. Is he an old flame or something? He'll regret it." She slammed her fist into her palm.

"You betcha, we'll take him on," said Heather, her fist raised too. Jennifer joined them.

"He calls himself Nelson." With tears in her eyes, Alice hugged each of them in the middle of the quiet lobby. "You're the best friends anyone could ask for."

"But you don't know him?" Jennifer asked. "Don't most stalkers know their victims?"

Alice nodded, took a long shaky exhale, and dabbed at her eyes. "I looked it up when I realized what was happening. Over eighty percent know their victims. I seem to be one of the few that don't."

"Alice—" began Jennifer.

"No." Alice interrupted. "This is what I didn't want to happen. I want to forget him, even just for a short while."

"We could have postponed this trip," Heather finally said.

"No way. I will not let that wacko ruin my life. This was too important. And he's had a hold on my family for too long. I wanted to be here for Mary and for you all. And for me."

"All right," said Jennifer. "So we need to be prepared. Is there anything we should know? Has he threatened violence?"

Alice paused. "Not in so many words."

Heather turned as she entered the elevator. "What does that mean? What happened?"

"At first the attention was flattering. I thought he was just a super fan. Then he began calling and hanging up. I blocked his number, no problem. But that set him off and his threats became aggressive online. It's like he was jealous of seeing photos of me at events with other people. Then the bad reviews started. After a while, at every public event, someone would come up to me and say, something along the lines of 'your friend Nelson sent me.'"

Cathy's jaw dropped. "Why have you never told us this before?"

"I thought he'd lose interest."

Heather pushed the button for their floor and waited for the doors to close before she asked, "Why not just report him?"

"I have. I began documenting every action. Every call. Every text. He has no prior convictions for stalking and he's only bothering me, not threatening me. I've been trying to ignore him."

"And? How's that going?" asked Jennifer.

"I was doing okay. And then he started to harass Arabella. She made the mistake of chiming in on Facebook to defend me. And, well, you know her temper. So, now my daughter is a target too."

Cathy shook her clenched fist again. "Oh, no."

"So I closed my social media accounts. It's tough because I want to communicate with my fans, but...." Alice sighed. "He still posts veiled threats and false information about me online but at least I don't have to see it."

"You said you lost your phone," Jennifer said, "but you changed your number, didn't you? Did it work?"

"For a while." Alice shook her head. "He began texting me

again a month ago. On my new number. I blocked it again, of course."

"How did he get it?" asked Heather.

"I don't know." Alice signed. "Someone must have leaked it. Or somehow he tapped into my phone."

"That's why you're so brief on the phone now," Heather wondered out loud.

Alice nodded. "I'm sorry. I didn't want to drag you into my mess. But it gets worse. Gifts began to appear at home."

Cathy gasped. "He has your home address?"

"Yes," Alice said. "And then my car was acting up and the mechanic found a GPS tracker. That was the same week that Mary died."

Heather was speechless. She led the way out of the elevator and turned left toward their rooms.

"And since then?" asked Jennifer.

"I have enough evidence for a judge to issue a restraining order on him and had my lawyer send him a letter."

"Did it get better?" asked Cathy.

"I thought so but..." Alice rubbed her eyes. "He filed a restraining order out on me last week."

Jennifer screeched. "What?"

"Shhh. You'll wake the other guests. Yes, he had copies of emails that I sent him. Showing repeated harassment and threats."

"You didn't—No, of course not," Heather said firmly.

"Another judge is looking at the evidence. I'm waiting to hear. Ironic isn't it? He may be successful in filing a restraining order against me, the victim?" Alice clapped her hands. "Now, that's enough talk. We're here, in Yellowstone National Park, one of the most spectacular places in the world."

"Done." Heather looked at the others, reading the concern on their faces. But she hugged Alice and said, "Anything for you. We'll keep an eye out, make sure no one takes any photos. A hat and sunglasses should help."

Heather was sharing a room with Jennifer and they said goodnight to Alice and Cathy outside their room.

"I wish we could help Alice," she said as she closed the door.

"Me too. There's not much we can do. And I think she's right. We need to make the most of every moment. Mary's death has taught us that." Her friend fiddled with an earring as she peered out their room window before closing the curtain. "I'll never get used to seeing elk wandering around outside. But, do you think we should have reported those men? What if we learn that an elk, bison, bear, or wolf is killed and we could have stopped it?"

"I don't know. But did you see one of them eyeing Alice? Perhaps they were just showing off to the movie star?"

"I suppose. Wouldn't be the first time. I'll never forgive myself if an animal is hurt though."

"No, me neither. If we hear something else, we'll report it. Agreed?"

Jennifer agreed and with that, Heather fell into a deep sleep. After a quick breakfast the next morning, they piled into their rental Subaru Outback and drove along the Obsidian River, stopping at various sites including the Obsidian Cliff on their way to their next night at the Old Faithful Inn.

Before the Norris junction, they visited the Museum of the National Park Ranger and then followed the valley along the Gibbon River. They stopped multiple times to watch elk and bison feeding in the distance and, at one, a coyote trotted by. Heather pulled out the spotting scope and binoculars they'd rented. As an amateur birder, she made sure they had good equipment.

"No bears or wolves, though. I want to see a grizzly bear next," said Cathy.

"Me too," said Alice. "As long as we are far, far away."

"I'd love to see a bighorn sheep." Jennifer checked her book. "We might see one near Mount Everts, east of here."

"I'd like to see a Sandhill crane," shared Heather. "That was Mary's favorite bird."

Heather didn't have to wait long before she stepped in to protect Alice. As she was taking a photo of Alice in front of Firehole Falls where ancient lava flows formed the canyon walls, a family walked by. The mother gave them a look of recognition and lifted her phone. Heather pulled Alice away. "Come on, let's grab our stuff. I want to go for a dip. It's supposed to be fifteen degrees warmer than the surrounding water."

Near Old Faithful, they had another scare when a man recognized Alice but Cathy persuaded him it wasn't her.

Later that night, they took photos of themselves in the Old Faithful Inn standing in front of the massive seven-story stone fireplace dominating the open lobby. After dinner, Heather read Mary's next note where she described in more detail where to spread her ashes.

Jennifer's eyes filled with tears. "Writing us those instructions must have been hard."

Alice sniffled as she nodded. "I'm glad Mary shared that she was named for the Mary of Yellowstone. Spreading her ashes here makes even more sense."

The letter included a continuation of Harriet Monroe's poem. Jennifer read it this time.

"Laughing geysers that dance in the sun, and
spread their robes like lace over the rocks;
Raging geysers that rush out of hell with a great
noise, and blurt out vast dragon-gulps of steam,

and, finishing, sink back wearily into darkness."

Cathy wiped her eyes and sighed. "Even on my best days, I could never write such beautiful descriptions. Monroe brings the images to life. Each different geyser has so much personality."

After a night at Old Faithful Inn, they woke early to climb the trail to Observation Point to see the many geysers of the Upper Geyser Basin area.

On their way back to the car, Heather noticed a Bear Aware concession with bear spray rentals and she picked up four canisters. *Just in case*, she thought. They were hiking and she wanted to be prepared.

They drove over the continental divide at Craig Pass and then headed toward West Thumb Junction, along Lake Yellowstone. After searching for water birds with a spotting scope, they returned to their car and drove north along the Yellowstone River.

Heather announced, "Next stop, Mary Mountain Trailhead."

With her guidebook on her lap, Jennifer read while they drove. "The book says the trail will lead us to a great view of Hayden Valley. It's too far to make it all the way to Mary's Lake, but we should see bison on the way."

They parked the car and Heather checked her day pack. Water, snacks, cell phone—although that wouldn't help much since service had continued to be spotty at best—first aid kit, extra clothes, sunglasses, and sunscreen.

"You have the special permit, right, Heather. To spread the ashes?" asked Jennifer.

Heather patted her pack. "Yup, got it."

At the trailhead, they took a quick photo beside the trail sign and Heather handed them each a canister of bear spray. "We should be prepared," she said, and they spent five minutes going over how to use it.

After hiking for over an hour, Jennifer was the first one to notice wolf tracks in a spot with dried mud. They also waited for fifteen minutes for a bison to move from the trail.

Jennifer whispered. "Don't get too close. At least twenty-five yards away. And watch out if his tail goes straight up."

"Why, what does that mean?" Alice asked.

"He may charge."

"Okay…" Cathy exhaled deeply. "Good to know."

Heather took a long swig of her water as she watched the animal lumber away, glad to see its tail switching gracefully. They continued along and she lost track of the time until the wide expanse of grassland appeared before them.

Alice stopped suddenly ahead of her. "Wow."

Jennifer shielded her eyes as she scanned the expansive valley. "This is…stunning. I can see why Mary wanted us to spread her ashes here."

Heather removed the small wooden box from her pack. Inside was a plastic bag, tied tight. "Good thing I brought a jack knife," she muttered as she struggled to open the thick material. "This is as stubborn as Mary herself." And they all laughed, breaking the tension of the moment.

Cathy read the Mary Oliver poem 'When Death Comes,' as their friend Mary had requested. They stood in a circle and, one after the other, took turns spreading Mary's ashes.

Heather watched the fine material disperse in the wind and mix with the soil. It reminded her of the line of the Monroe poem, '... and finishing, sink back wearily into darkness.' No one else would ever know they'd laid their friend to rest there. But at least they did. They'd never forget.

"It feels right for Mary to be in this place she loved so well," she said as the last of the ash floated to the ground.

Cathy sniffed. "What a privilege. To do this for her. And to do it with you all."

Heather wiped her eyes. "I think I'm going to run out of tears."

During their return trip, they saw a pair of Sandhill cranes in a wet open meadow. "Hurrah for Mary." Heather quickly pulled the binoculars from her pack. "Mary had told me that they have the most amazing courtship dance."

"It's like Mary is here with us," said Jennifer, "just as she said."

They told more of their favorite stories of Mary as they hiked back to the trailhead.

Dusty and tired, that night they stayed in one of the cabins of the Canyon Lodge. They hadn't forgotten about Alice but Heather saw no one who recognized her. After a hot shower and dinner, Heather read Mary's next letter. The poem continued.

> "'Glad geysers, nymphs of the sun, that rise,
> slim and nude, out of the hot dark earth,
> and stand poised in beauty a moment,
> veiling their brows and breasts in mist;
> Winged geysers, spirits of fire,
> that rise tall and straight like a sequoia,
> and plume the sky with foam:'"

Jennifer sighed. "I like the image of winged geysers and spirits of fire. That's how I see Mary. Our Sandhill crane."

"Hmm. Me too," Heather said. "I assume the last envelope includes the end of the poem."

"What are these?" Cathy pulled out four pieces of paper from the envelope. "Huh. Four tickets to the Roosevelt Stagecoach for tomorrow afternoon. She thought of everything. It says here that 'guests will travel an old stagecoach road through the sage-covered meadow of Pleasant Valley,' in a replica Tally-Ho stage-coach."

"Tally-Ho?" Cathy laughed. "I like them just for their name alone."

Heather slept like a log that night. Putting Mary to rest in a place she loved was more cathartic than she'd realized.

The next morning, Alice was driving as Heather stared out the window. "This is Dunraven Pass, the highest elevation on one of the main roads."

They reached the Roosevelt Corral with thirty minutes to spare. They were joined by eight others and the guide took a group photo in front of the shiny yellow stage coach with black trim.

Heather loved the swaying back-and-forth motion of the stagecoach and hearing the clip-clop of the horses. They surveyed the hills dotted with trees looking for signs of animals and the earthy spice smell of the sage filled the air as they moved through the meadows.

Alice stretched her back as they stepped down from the carriage. "That was just long enough."

"I loved it," said Cathy. "Riding in a carriage makes me want to write a historical romance. Can you imagine the scene—"

Jennifer laughed and held up a hand to stop her. "You write it, I'll read it."

As they sat on the front porch of the Roosevelt Lodge in

wooden rocking chairs, Heather opened the last envelope and read Mary's messy script one last time.

> *"'O wild choral fountains, forever singing and seething, forever boiling in deep places and leaping forth for bright moments into the air,*
> *How do you like it up here?*
> *Why must you go back to the spirits of darkness?*
> *What do you tell them down there about*
> *your little glorious life in the sun?'"*

Heather scanned the valley as the words hung in the air then looked at the page again. "Mary underlined the last sentence." Heather read it again.

Alice examined the piece of paper and flipped it over. "That's it?"

"She was a person of few words." Jennifer hummed. "I think she's telling us that she had a glorious life in the sun. And now it's up to us to make the most of our own glorious lives."

Heather stopped her chair from rocking. "I think that's perfect. A good reminder for us all."

That night, their last night together, they slept in the Roosevelt Lodge Cabins.

"Sleep well," said Heather, "We have a seven a.m. tour to the Lamar Valley to see wildlife on a 'Wake Up Wildlife' tour. We should see plenty of elk, moose, and bison."

Cathy clapped her hands. "And maybe bears and gray wolves too? Can't wait."

THE TOUR IN THE YELLOW MINIBUS WAS ALL IT WAS SUPPOSED TO BE.

They saw lots of wildlife, including birds, so Heather was happy.

"The muffins they gave us were tasty," said Cathy, "But not as good as yours, of course," she said to Heather.

"Ugh, now I'm hungry again," Alice complained as she rubbed her stomach. "Heather, you do make the best muffins."

Heather felt herself flush with their support. "You all are the best." She may not be a movie star or a novelist or a fashionista librarian but she ran her own business and was good at filling bellies. "That was a great tour but we still haven't seen any bears or wolves."

"We might not, you know," reminded Jennifer pointing to a page in her guidebook. "My book says that gray wolves are known to hang out in the Lamar Valley but often follow the elk to higher elevations in the summer."

Cathy smiled. "It doesn't matter. This trip has been worth every moment."

They all agreed, but just in case, they stopped at several scenic outlooks and planned one more hike as they drove back toward the northern entrance of the park.

"The ranger I asked said we had a good chance of seeing black bears on this section of road today," said Alice.

"Stay one hundred yards away from bears and wolves," reminded Jennifer.

Heather shivered. "A football field distance is too close for my taste."

Jennifer read more from her book. "Did you know that more people are injured from bison in Yellowstone than by any other animal?"

"Yes, as you keep reminding us," laughed Alice.

"Next stop the Hellroaring Creek Trailhead," Cathy announced. "What do you say? I read about it last night. We cross the Yellowstone River on a suspension bridge as the water roars under our feet."

Jennifer added, "The guide says that trail goes through a Douglas fir forest. And that we might see black bears."

"My kind of trail. Let's do it," urged Alice.

Heather checked her day pack. She slipped the bear spray into the holster at her waist and handed out the three other canisters. The trail headed down toward the river.

"Remember, save some energy," Alice cautioned. "We'll need to go up this trail on the way back."

"What song should we sing?" asked Jennifer.

"Let's start with 'The bear went over the mountain.' That seems appropriate," suggested Alice. Heather loved to sing at the top of her lungs and joined in.

Their trip had been a success in many ways. They'd had a meaningful trip celebrating their friend Mary and spreading her ashes. They'd forged new bonds amongst them. It was a different dynamic without Mary but even in death, she was bringing them together.

"Umphf." Heather stopped as she bumped into Cathy who'd stopped in the middle of the trail.

Alice gasped.

Heather peered around her, expecting to see a large animal in the trail. Her heart started to pound as she watched Cathy and then Alice pull out their bear spray. She heard the sound of velcro from Jennifer behind her as she also opened her spray holster.

She reached for her own, but with her shaking hands, she fumbled the canister. She grasped it a second time and succeeded.

"What is it?" Heather whispered. Her throat felt dry and she could barely talk.

Cathy was breathing heavily. "I heard a stick breaking up ahead. Like something was walking. Something big."

Alice looked around. Her eyes were wide. "What should we do?"

"Back away slowly. Don't run," said Jennifer. "We'll be fine."

"I wish I'd paid more attention to what to do," admitted Alice.

Jennifer said calmly. "Take the spray out of the holster," she looked around, and each one of them held their spray. "Okay, good. Then remove the safety clip, back away slowly together, avoid eye contact, speak softly, and say 'Go away bear.'"

Heather's brain started working again. "Remember what the directions said. Use two hands, one on the canister, one on the trigger."

"I remember now," said Alice. "It's effective about a car length away."

"Aim downward, just below the bear's face," added Cathy.

"And press for two seconds," Heather finished.

Jennifer then added, "To be effective the bear spray has to hit the eyes and nose of the bear."

Heather's heart raced faster. "Maybe it's nothing."

They heard footsteps.

More footsteps, faster now, and louder, closer. More running, branches breaking. More running.

"Steady," said Jennifer. "Let's go back the way we came." They began to back up slowly as if one person.

Then Heather heard loud swearing. And a man shot out of the woods straight at them, holding his side and screaming.

"What the—" said Cathy.

The man ran straight past them, without even glancing

their way. They stopped and stared, watching him cross back over the river toward the trailhead, the way they'd come.

"What was that all about?" Heather pressed a hand to her heart. "It certainly got my adrenaline going."

Heather slid the bear spray into the holster and bent over to catch her breath. "I think I've had enough excitement for one day. We should head back."

Jennifer nodded vigorously. "I don't know what scared him, but that sounds like a good idea."

They were halfway back to the trailhead when they heard talking behind them and three gray and green figures appeared. The unmistakable figures of three Yellowstone Rangers were heading their way. And they were moving fast.

The first one asked, "Did you see a man running for his life?"

Alice's eyes were wide. "Green T-shirt? Camouflage pants? Baseball cap? Long brown curly hair? Mustache? Blood dripping down his leg?"

"That's the guy," the second one said as he scanned each of them. "Is everyone all right here?"

"Rick?" Cathy exclaimed and hugged the first man. "Is that you? I've never been so glad to see anyone in my life. Look everyone, the bartender is also a ranger."

Heather whispered to Alice. "Ranger Rick? Seriously?"

Jennifer looked at the other two men. "Hey, you look familiar too." She slapped her forehead. "The two guys in the Map Room Bar. The poachers..."

Rick introduced the two men. "Special Agents Sam and Robert. They work for the ISB. The National Park Service Investigative Services Branch," he explained. "They assist in criminal investigations."

Sam scratched his chin. "Poachers? You thought we were poachers?"

"What are you doing here?" interrupted Cathy. "How did you find us?"

Rick lifted his distinctive Stetson-style ranger hat and repositioned it on his head. "Mary asked us to watch out for you while you were here." He loosened a rock with the tip of his boot. "Sorry about her death. What a terrible loss."

"Thank you," said Jennifer, her eyes on Robert. He was carrying a camera and she must have connected the dots the same time Heather did. "Ahhhh. When you mentioned shooting them between the eyes, you meant with the camera."

Sam nodded. "If we can document the bad behavior of our visitors then we can better protect the wildlife. Photographs help identify perpetrators and, with evidence, we fine them—or more—if necessary."

Rick added, "We had a tip that a man had threatened a well-known actor. Miss Darling, we knew that must mean you. The folks at Roosevelt gave us your plan for the day. Must have arrived at the trail just ahead of you."

"So what did he do?" asked Heather.

"He got too close to a bison. Bothered a baby elk too." Robert patted the giant lens around his neck. "I got it all on camera."

"Alice, did you know him?" asked Heather.

Alice inhaled a deep breath. "My stalker." She turned to the men. "His name is Nelson. I have a restraining order on him. In New York."

"You recognized him?" asked Cathy.

When Alice nodded, Robert said, "We'll look into it. If there's a pattern of stalking it could go badly for him. Interstate stalking laws have a harsher penalty."

"I think he put a GPS tracker in my car at home," admitted Alice.

"Well then, we'll walk you back to your car and make sure he didn't tamper with it," said Rick. "When he tries to leave the park, we'll stop him."

"I can't believe it," muttered Alice. "I can't believe he followed me all the way out here."

There was no sign of Nelson at the trailhead. After a quick check of the car, the four women piled into the Subaru and waved to the men. Cathy clasped a card with Ranger Rick's phone number in her hand.

As Heather started the car and began to drive away, Alice cleared her throat. "Now that we're on our own. I have a confession... I left a trail of where I'd be. For Nelson. I couldn't leave as many clues as I'd have liked. But apparently, it was enough."

Heather didn't take her eyes off the road ahead. "You were leading him right to you?"

"Yes. Using social media with others posting photos of me and where I was."

Heather squeezed the steering wheel. "Wow."

"I'm sorry I didn't tell you but I didn't want you all to get in trouble. And frankly, I'm a better liar than any of you."

"About that—Should we tell her?" asked Jennifer, from the second row. She'd stuck her head between Heather and Alice in the front seat.

"Tell me what?"

Cathy's head also appeared from the back seat. "We also have something to admit..."

"What?" asked Alice again, her head swinging back and forth as she looked at each of them.

Heather glanced at her. "We knew that you were leaving breadcrumbs for your stalker." She added, "More than crumbs. Full slices of bread more like."

Alice's eyes were wide and she made a round 'O' with her mouth. "How did you figure it out?"

Cathy laughed. "We know you. And we're on social media too, you know. And we have our phones. And it may be spotty, but there is some Wi-Fi here."

"You could have been seriously hurt. Or worse," Heather said.

"You're lucky," Jennifer said, then asked, "What would you have done if he hadn't gotten gored? If he attacked you instead?"

Alice scoffed. "It's not luck. Why do you think I choose to do this with you all? I could have led him anywhere. Any time. I knew that things would be worse for him if he crossed state lines so it made sense to try. I knew the clues would be impossible for him to ignore. You're all highly capable women and friends who would do anything for me, as I would do for you. We had our brains and that's enough. The security of the bear spray was a bonus."

"Quite the plot twist," Cathy said. "Are you sure you aren't the writer?"

"I get it," said Jennifer. "Now that there is a reason to look, they also might find evidence on his computer about his false accusations about you."

"I'm hoping," nodded Alice.

"Well played." Heather patted Alice's arm. "We have another admission. Mary warned us that you were dealing with something. We figured you would tell us when you were ready. So, when you did, and we realized what you were doing..."

Jennifer finished her sentence. "We might have added a crumb or two of our own."

Heather laughed. "Or three. One of the photos we posted had our exact location."

"When and where," Cathy added. "We wanted to make damn sure that he never hurt you again. And we trusted that you knew what you were doing."

Alice's eyes filled with tears. "What would I do without you all?"

"I can imagine the headline in the local paper tomorrow." Cathy gestured with her hand. "Man hiking off-trail gored by Bison. Runs for his life."

Jennifer snorted. "That reminds me, what's that infamous question that women are being asked, 'Would you rather be stuck in the woods with a man or a bear?' After this experience, how would you answer that?"

"Definitely, a bear," said Alice. "Even before this trip."

"Bear, no question," agreed Heather. "As long as I had pepper spray with me."

Cathy grinned. "I'd say bear, too, unless the man's name was Ranger Rick."

They all laughed and Heather shook her head. "Let's stop ahead. I'll pull out the spotting scope one last time. We still haven't seen a wolf and dusk is one of the best times."

"Jennifer's book did say that the gray wolf is a pack animal. They often work as a group to take down their prey. Lucky me you're my group." Alice smiled at each of them. "Mary was right. What a 'glorious life in the sun.'"

SALLY MILLIKEN WRITES CONTEMPORARY AND HISTORICAL MYSTERIES and crime. Her stories have been published online in *Punk Noir* and *Stone's Throw*, as well as in the anthologies "Malice, Matrimony and Murder" and "Hook, Line, and Sinker: the 7th Guppy Anthology." The flash fiction story 'Adam-13' was the winner of the 2023 Golden Donut Award. She recently won first prize in the Bethlehem Writers Story Contest. She is working on her first novel, a historical mystery set in 1882 Massachusetts. Follow her on Instagram @sallyhistorymystery. Find out more at *www.sallymillikenauthor.com*

7
THE DEAD BEAR AFFAIR
KENZIE LAPPIN

Daggett roared along on the snowmobile, ignoring the snow flying into her face. So she was going a little fast. What was life if you couldn't live a little?

Mary Daggett—Daggett to her friends, Ranger Daggett if you made her mad, and Mary only to her old tottering grandmother—loved the off-season at Yellowstone. Up here on the central plateau, she was far away from any semblance of humanity. No tourists, no cars, and, at this time of year, almost no chance of running into anyone unexpected.

Presumably there were people who joined the Park Rangers because they just *loved* people, but Daggett was content enough with the woods.

As she ramped over a log, she startled a flock of nearby birds, who went fluttering angrily into the air. Guiltily, she reduced speed and started going more carefully. She glided forward for a moment longer, then came to a total stop.

The scientists didn't like it when she scared the animals away. They *really* didn't like it.

She shut off the snowmobile, swung her legs over the side,

and abandoned her helmet in the saddlebag. With her braids now swinging loose, she replaced the helmet with her winter ranger flat-hat. She liked to pretend it gave her authority.

In November, almost all roads into Yellowstone National Park were closed. The only way you could get anywhere was over-snow travel. Not too long ago, a snow-coach had puked up five over-excited bison scientists and their gear into the wilderness, and rapidly run away.

Presumably this was because the lead scientist, Joanna Folger, was highly annoying.

Daggett had made Science Outpost 20 part of her regular patrol, mostly because she worried the scientists were totally going to die out here.

She walked the rest of the way rather than face the dire wrath of Dr. Folger. She didn't mind. The quiet of the woods here was gorgeous, the sky clear, not threatening more snow for now, and the air crisp in her lungs.

She was never quite sure where she was going to find Folger or her little grad student assistants. They followed the path of the bison as they wandered for winter pastures, searching for new grazing paths. Today she took her best guess and went where she last remembered a new trail camera.

It was a good guess, too. Folger was crouched down in the snow only a couple hundred feet away from the camera.

Daggett crunched quietly up to her in the snow.

Folger didn't notice, excitedly picking at something in her gloved hands, occasionally referring to a waterproofed notebook on the ground by her feet.

"I told you last time I was here to carry bear spray if you're going to be alone in the woods," Daggett said, right into Folger's ear.

Folger screeched in surprise, startling more birds. She fell on her ass into the snow and glared up at Daggett. "Must you do that every time, Ranger Daggett?"

Daggett shrugged. "Get better at situational awareness."

Folger rolled her eyes. "Is there a reason you're out here?"

"Came to check on you," Daggett said. "There's no cell or internet out here. If your interns finally got cabin fever and broke the radio into a million pieces, you couldn't even call for help. Just making sure you're not dead yet."

"Thanks," Folger said. "So glad to know if we die someone will find our corpses."

Daggett grinned. She crouched down. "What are you working on?"

Folger lit up. She was far better with animals and with nature than she was with people, which was probably why Daggett liked her, for all her flaws.

She showed Daggett what she had in her hands—it was a sample container.

"Shit," Daggett said neutrally, uncertain whether to be sympathetic or if this was a good sign.

"That's right, it's shit!" Folger said excitedly.

"Hate to tell you this, Joanna, but that's a little too small to be bison droppings," Daggett told her. The specimen container was a tiny sample of something gross, maybe rabbit poop or some other little critter.

"Oh, ha-*ha*," she said. "It's from a cowbird! They travel behind the bison, collecting seeds, insects, all that good stuff. To find evidence of cowbirds here is a good sign. Means we're right about the current path of the bison."

"You know," Daggett said, "I could take you to a bunch of spots with bison. There's tons of them trying to warm up in lower elevations. I saw a big herd near Old Faithful the other day, even."

"I don't care where they *go*," Folger said. "We're studying how they get there!"

"It's the journey, not the destination, that sort of thing?" Daggett asked.

"Exactly."

Daggett kind of got what she meant. Hard not to, when you spent all your time outdoors like she did, watching nature unfold around you.

"Well," Daggett said. "I brought your scientists a new box of Ramen. Last time I was here, they were out, and they looked like they were considering mutiny."

"An angel among men," declared Folger. "Come on. Let's go back to base camp anyway. You didn't bring that awful snowmobile, did you?"

"Considering I didn't walk six hours to get here, yes I did," Daggett said. "Don't fret. It's far enough away *you* didn't hear me."

"I don't pay that much attention to anything but nature," admitted Folger.

That was fair enough.

Folger packed her gear into her backpack, and they set off for the short trek to Science Outpost 20. It was a prefab building, more like a shack, which had been airlifted into the middle of Yellowstone some years ago to be the center of some different group of scientists' observation. It was barely a cabin, with a generator and heat so they didn't die, limited water systems, and apparently was so exciting to the scientists they couldn't contain themselves.

Daggett walked first to tramp down the snow for Folger, but there was already a slight path as the scientists had trekked back and forth and back and forth for a couple weeks.

Halfway back to the observation outpost, Daggett stopped.

"What?" asked Folger impatiently.

"Another case of following something that leads to something else," Daggett said, squinting up into the trees, half snow-blind. She pointed. "Turkey vulture."

"This isn't a Western," Folger said. "That doesn't indicate gloom and doom. They have to eat—it's probably hunting rabbits."

"Maybe if there was just one. There are three."

Daggett tromped off the path, towards the vultures. The one they'd seen was cawing busily in a tree, but she had heard the other two calling, and was able to find them and their prey easily enough.

"Oh, poor thing," Folger said sympathetically.

Daggett grimaced, but dug around in her pockets for her emergency whistle. They were far enough from the outpost that Folger's people probably wouldn't come running to investigate.

The sharp sound startled the vultures, awkwardly hopping across the snow before fluttering grumpily away.

They had been scavenging a dead grizzly bear. It was hard to tell how old the body was, preserved as it was in the snow and obviously only recently found by the birds. She could still smell musty animal-stink, and maybe a hint of gunpowder.

She hauled herself over the bank and went down the small hill.

"You shouldn't touch a dead animal," Folger said nervously.

"It was shot," Daggett said, ignoring her, gently nudging the bear with her foot to make sure it wasn't going to twitch. No, it was solidly dead, and she crouched down to get a better look.

"Someone shot it and then just left it?" Folger asked, confused. "They didn't want, you know, the pelt or the meat or anything?"

Daggett had a suspicion. She checked the paws—sure enough, all the claws on every foot had been cut off. "Poachers," she said darkly.

"Poachers?" Folger repeated, just as contemptuously. She might have hated them more than Daggett did. "Grizzly bears are endangered."

"They like to take trophies, but it's a pain in the ass to haul a whole illegal animal without getting caught. So, claws."

"Poor thing," Folger said again.

"You got a camera in your field pack?" Daggett asked. She had one, but it was in the saddlebags of the snowmobile. She brushed her hands off on her pants and clambered back up the rise.

"Sure, but shouldn't you call it in before documenting?" Folger swung her backpack around to the front and pulled out a nice nature camera in a case.

"It's the middle of November. We're five hours from the nearest open road. We'd be lucky to get someone out here for a *human* murder."

"Do me a favor and tell me if you catch the guy," Folger said. "I'd like to kick him in the balls."

Hunting was illegal in Yellowstone. There were occasional official round-ups for diseased or problem animals, but it was certainly something the Park Services knew about ahead of time. Of course, that didn't really stop people, not if they were determined enough. In the tourist season these things were hard enough to solve. In the off months, where there were never any witnesses and even getting into the park was hard, things would be way, way more complicated.

Folger grumbled under her breath the whole way back to

the outpost. If poachers were afoot, she vowed, her whole study might be interrupted, and, worse, they might even touch her precious research subjects. She seemed to be having so much fun complaining Daggett didn't have the heart to tell her nobody really killed bison except the local ranchers, and that was only when they strayed to the edges of the park, far away from them.

Daggett's backpack full of ramen was met with much excitement in the outpost. It always felt nice to have people happy to see you, even if it only lasted as long as it took to heat a pot of water over a hotplate.

While the others were lost in throes of artificial flavoring packet-induced ecstasy, Folger called over one of her grad students. Marshall slept with a bison-shaped stuffed animal on his little cot, and he wasn't even the weirdest one here. He had big glasses and seemed very excited when Folger handed him the sample of cowbird poop.

She told him about the dead bear, though, and his face turned grave.

"I don't suppose you have any footage from your trail cams at that time?" Daggett asked.

"Point it out on the map," Marshall said, and knocked aside a series of scientific journals—and one copy of *Lord of the Rings*—to reveal a field map with all the trail cams marked.

"We weren't near any," Folger said, even as Daggett pointed out an area on the map well away from any of their monitored areas. The cameras were designed to catch bison on their way to and from their foraging grounds, but they were motion-activated and she had hoped they would catch their poachers red-handed.

"Damn," Daggett said. "Can I use your radio?"

She did, but the poor little thing had to be coaxed into life before it would contact the closest Ranger station. This was part of the reason Daggett was so worried about the scientists out here.

The news was just as she expected. No, they could not send a team out for one single dead bear, and no, the nearest Fish and Wildlife agent was busy, and besides, a pair of tourists had gotten themselves lost up near Mammoth and everyone was far more worried about them than an animal dying in the middle of a forest.

"I'm supposed to document everything and they'll review the case when it starts to thaw," Daggett told Folger apologetically.

Folger made that face that was surely the bane of whoever had sent her out to freeze her ass off in the middle of nowhere. She had a stubborn jut to her chin. "They'll never see justice?" she asked, outraged.

"It is how it is," Daggett said. "I'll try my best."

Folger glared. "Animals can't speak up. So humans just have to speak louder in their name to make up for it."

Daggett thought, as she sped as quietly as she could back across the snow, that explained a lot about Folger.

DAGGETT MADE AS MANY CALLS AS SHE COULD THAT NIGHT, BUT THERE really wasn't much she could do. None of her local contacts had heard anyone bragging about killing a bear, no one had spotted anyone coming in or out of restricted areas, and even the local snowmobile rental guy hadn't had any new customers lately.

Her satellite phone started making sounds like it wanted to kill itself, or probably it was running out of battery, so she set it aside to charge and stared up at the ceiling. She was a Park

Ranger—she was supposed to protect the park, wasn't she? And all its little creatures, animal and tourist.

She needed to get to the bottom of this. There would be *no* poaching in her park. By the time someone else was able to investigate, it would be too late, and all the leads would be quite literally cold (or soggy, in this case).

It was too bad the trail cameras hadn't caught anything.

The poachers must have gone quite a damn way to hunt there—they wouldn't have come from Mammoth or the open road, because that was way too far a trek even for trophy hunting. So they had to be camped out somewhere nearby. Daggett knew her park. The scientists were on a pretty major game path, which was probably why the hunters had chosen that area.

It was just bad luck they hadn't been in an area picked up by the cameras when they shot the bear.

Well, not *there*, anyway. She brightened. They hadn't been caught on tape during the crime. How about before?

Daggett had told Folger that, for now, she didn't want her or any of her kids out in the woods without a group. She was glad to know they'd followed her advice, even if that meant she *was* greeted the next morning by a pack of tiny college students screaming and aiming shovels at her.

"That's what you get for sneaking up on people," Folger said, satisfied, once the sheepish science minions had led Daggett back to the cabin.

"Marshall has a wimpy swing anyway," Daggett sniffed. "Can we go inside? I want to take a look—"

"First, you'd better take a look at this," Folger said grimly. "You'll never guess what we found this morning."

A hundred yards off an animal trail, Folger led Daggett to a dead wolf. A gray wolf—another creature who'd just barely eked off the endangered species list.

This was a rather more gruesome crime scene. Daggett hoped none of the kids had found it.

Someone had cut off the wolf's claws too, but also the head, apparently happy for a more portable trophy. It had been shot a couple times with a heavy-duty hunting rifle.

"We heard wolves howling last night, more agitated than usual, but not the shot," Folger said. "Found this when Roan wandered off to pee during field observation. We took pictures of it already."

"Must have snuck up on it when it was separated from the pack," Daggett said. She was perturbed. She'd thought that the poachers wouldn't dare push their luck by returning to Outpost 20. If she had thought they would come back, she would have come armed with her rarely-used rifle.

"And they avoided our field cameras again."

"Damn," Daggett said.

Folger squinted nervously. "You really don't think they'll go after my bison?"

"*No,* I don't think—"

A gunshot was amazingly loud. In a forest, surrounded by mostly snow and scrubby little trees, it bounced off everywhere and rang around Daggett's ears. A tree several feet to their right exploded in shards of bark and wood.

Folger shrieked, even as they both ducked down instinctively. Weirdly, Daggett mostly thought, *Hey! Destroying a tree is punishable with up to a year in prison!*

Then she remembered someone was shooting at her and she grabbed Folger by the arm.

There were no further shots. But she was risking nothing. She pulled Folger behind her and they booked it at full speed back to the outpost. Daggett was way faster, but Folger was familiar with the land after a couple weeks here and managed to avoid tripping up too badly. They zig-zagged and generally hauled ass and made it back without seeing anyone else, and without being shot at again.

Daggett made sure all the interns were inside and safe, and that the door was locked. Then she sat down hard on a chair. The interns huddled in the tiny back room, presumably to avoid Folger's wrath.

"Someone shot at us!" Folger said disbelievingly, shrilly. "They tried to kill us!"

"They weren't trying to kill us," Daggett said, using a glare to try to disguise the way her heart was beating far too rapidly.

"Excuse me, I think a bullet is a very definite indication of an intention to murder."

"Unless they're the worst shot in the world, they weren't trying to hit us. They were trying to scare us off."

Folger tipped her chin up again. "We almost died."

"I wouldn't have had you run if I thought there was a real chance they'd shoot at us," Daggett said. "In that case, we would hunker down and figure something else out. We were in the open for a moment—they didn't shoot. Trying to warn us away from the site."

"You think the poachers know we're on to them?"

"I think my uniform could spook anyone," Daggett said. If the ranger hat didn't give it away, the green jacket bundled over several other layers must have done the trick. "They must have come back to make sure no one was poking around." She had caught her breath by now. "I'm going to call for backup."

Or at least she was going to try. When she went for the radio, it only made sad staticky sounds. Daggett slapped the radio box—her tried and true method for repair—but it was nothing doing.

"What's wrong with this thing now?" Folger said impatiently, and also gave the radio a good whack. It was good to know that was universal. It squealed and refused to work, no matter how they tuned it.

Finally Daggett gave up with a frustrated huff of air. "There must be a storm front moving in. Cloud cover is probably blocking radio transmissions." And she had, of course, forgotten the sat phone back in her little cabin.

"Well, now what?" Folger asked.

Daggett chewed her lip. They couldn't stay out here forever, but going out might not be a good idea either, especially if the shooter moved from warning shots to serious business. "I have a radio on my snowmobile..."

"Great idea, get shot," Folger said. "If our radio doesn't work, I doubt yours will either. So, even better, your sacrifice will be for nothing."

Daggett rolled her eyes.

"Hey, why were you here in the first place?" Folger asked suddenly. "You said you wanted to see something?"

"Yeah, well, it was what you said. You follow the bison, because if you know where someone's been, you can learn all sorts of things about them." Reacting to Folger's raised eyebrow, Daggett added, "I want to see the trail cams."

"We already checked, and they didn't catch either shooting."

"Nope. But maybe they caught the poachers at different times, times when they didn't know they had to be careful—something about the journey, you said?"

"Hmm. For an outdoor kind of person, you're not that dumb. Let's take a look."

THE TRAIL CAMS WERE MOTION-ACTIVATED, SO IT WASN'T LIKE THEY had to dig through months of footage, unfiltered. Unfortunately, though, even in winter, there were all sorts of critters

THE DEAD BEAR AFFAIR

crawling across Yellowstone, from birds to Folger's bison to coyotes and even a wolverine.

So there was a lot to look at.

Daggett enlisted the interns to sift through the footage too. They were happy to help, but she had a suspicion that was only because they wanted to see any bison that had passed through frame. Either way, help was help, and, finally, they hit pay dirt.

The trail cameras had caught the poachers in frame about five times in total. It was lucky, in a way, that they were so isolated out here. If they had been here in summer, or closer to a popular destination, it would have been impossible to say for sure than any humans captured on tape had anything to do with the poaching. As it was, when they caught flashes of two men, wearing warm-weather gear and carrying definitely illegal hunting rifles, it was obvious why they were there.

The glimpses were only fragmentary. The cameras were at the right height—a bison was taller than a human, and they hoped to catch them as well as their calves—but humans just didn't move along the same trails as bison did.

They caught an elbow, the back of a head, and finally a glimpse of two distinct faces. Daggett screenshotted that immediately, intending to send that to the nearest Ranger station as soon as she had the chance. Which, hopefully, would be soon.

"So, what does this tell us?" asked Folger. "Beyond that I know who to punch in the face next time I see them."

The map of the trail cameras was still out from the previous day. Daggett traced a finger along the path of the cameras that had caught the poachers, as well as where they'd found the two animal bodies.

"They're making a trail southwest." Folger followed the path with her eyes.

"Must be trying to escape the park," Daggett said.

"We have to catch them before they do!" Folger said. "We can't let them get away. A couple blurry pictures aren't going to be enough, especially when they don't actually show anything happening. We don't know their names, or what state they're from, or *anything*—"

"Okay, *okay,*" Daggett said. "We need to radio for backup. No one might care about a dead bear, but a poaching ring and shooting at a Park Ranger is going to stir up some trouble. I'll have to take a look at my own radio, and if not, we're not too far away from some of the tourist centers. They'll be abandoned right now, of course, but there should be a radio we can use."

"You shouldn't go out alone."

"I'll be okay," Daggett said, only slightly uncertainly.

Folger glared. For some reason, Daggett actually found herself intimidated.

"I'll go with you," Folger said.

"I can't just—"

Folger glared harder.

Daggett made a point of telling the rest of the scientists to stay where they were. One of the students was a little older than the others, having gone into the illustrious field of bison-study only after leaving her previous field, working construction. There was exactly one gun at Science Outpost 20, and they had brought it solely to scare away coyotes. The older student agreed to keep it with her and keep the kids locked inside.

And then Daggett and Folger departed.

It just wasn't worth the fight. And Daggett was scared of her.

They were careful on their way back to where Daggett had parked the snowmobile, but there were no signs of poachers or sudden bursts of gunfire. And no further sign of more dead animals, either. Daggett wished she could be relieved about that, but instead she was worried. What had the poachers gotten away with before she had stumbled upon them?

The snowmobile was still where Daggett had left it, not even dusted with snow. Whatever storm was brewing, it hadn't gotten here yet. They waded through the snow over to it.

Daggett put a leg up over her snowmobile and clicked the handset of her radio without much hope. And indeed, she was greeted with the same out-of-range static as had been on Folger's radio.

"Nothing," she said, frustrated.

"Did you really think something would go our way today?"

"Not really."

Daggett started the snowmobile. Folger suddenly looked wary.

"Don't tell me you're fine with possibly encountering poachers, but a ride on a snowmobile scares you?" Daggett asked, grinning, speaking a little louder to be heard over the sound of the engine.

"They go *fast*, Mary!"

Daggett threw back her head and laughed. "You wanted to come. Get on."

Daggett gave Folger her helmet. She hadn't thought to bring a spare, but she did have an extra pair of heavy-duty goggles which she snapped on over her head to protect from snow and glare.

And then she set off, roaring at maybe slightly unnecessary high speeds. Folger clung to the back, and kept her screams at least mostly quiet.

She brought them into the woods. She had thought to drive towards the basin, where there was a visitor's center and she could access a radio. In fact, it was a regular tourist's destination—they were heading right for the famous Old Faithful geyser. It was an hour or so's ride, but she had plenty of fuel; it didn't worry her.

What did worry her was that, while it was the closest sign of civilization... it was also the direction they thought the poachers were heading.

Maybe they were going to the West Thumb instead or maybe they had gone to try to meet back up with a road through some other route. Maybe she and Folger were walking into trouble. She wished she hadn't brought Dr. Folger if that was the case.

So she went fast, but, as she got closer, she got more and more cautious.

It paid off—she saw something. They were still some ways away from the stretch of land where Old Faithful and its assorted lodges, tourist centers, and parking lots were all hunched together. They could just see over the tips of the trees.

Daggett stopped the snowmobile and squinted out in the sudden silence. Without the omnipresent roaring of the engine, her ears rang and the world seemed too still.

"What?" Folger asked, taking off the helmet.

"Smoke," Daggett said contemplatively.

"Like a forest fire?!?"

"Like a chimney. Someone's in The Old Faithful Inn."

"I thought it was closed," Folger asked.

"It is," Daggett said. "I think we just found our quarry."

"Let's go get them!"

"Slow down, tiger. We're going around. We'll head up to the Thumb. It's not that far out of the way."

Folger flicked her on the ear, the easiest piece of exposed skin in reach. "By the time we get there, they'll *definitely* be gone!"

"Well, what do you want me to do?" Daggett asked, bewildered. The ear flick had been so unexpected yet hilarious she had to hold back a snort.

"I still have my camera," Folger said. "We can get better pictures of their faces, maybe catch them hauling illegal animal parts... *Something* we can bring in as absolute proof of wrongdoing."

"Hey, Yellowstone Batman, we're not vigilantes," Daggett said. "And I'm not putting a civilian in danger."

As a Park Ranger, Daggett technically had the authority to arrest people, but in practice, she had only done so once or twice with drunk guests, and there was the small detail of the poachers being armed and her very much not.

"I'm putting *myself* in danger," said Folger, surprisingly brave. Or maybe not surprisingly. Whatever. "You can't really stop me."

Daggett wavered.

"If you don't go, I'm going to go on my own and definitely get myself killed," Folger said, a little too smugly for the situation.

Daggett huffed. "So you'd rather get killed dramatically together, is that what you're saying?"

"All for a good cause, Ranger. All for a good cause."

THEY BROUGHT THE SNOWMOBILE A LITTLE CLOSER, THEN PARKED IT IN the cover of the trees before getting off to walk more stealthily the rest of the way.

It was a good idea—although Folger's footsteps couldn't exactly be called quiet—because as they got closer, they definitively saw signs of life.

There were two snowmobiles, shiny and high-end, parked outside the inn, along with a four-wheel drive vehicle with the biggest and nicest tires Daggett had ever seen. Someone had laboriously shoveled a narrow canal in the snow leading up to The Old Faithful Inn's front doors.

"They're squatting," Daggett said. It wasn't the worst idea; everything around here was normally buckled up tight for the winter. No one would be around and no one would notice two malcontents coming and going as they pleased.

She and Folger were still in the cover of the brush.

The doors opened, and the two poachers came out. They seemed like they were in a hurry. They really had been spooked by seeing Daggett hanging around, and they were leaving town.

Even as she watched, they hauled a couple backpacks into the car, then went back inside at a hurried clip.

Folger fumbled for her camera. "We haven't actually seen them do anything relating to hunting yet," she said glumly, trying to get a picture of them as they disappeared back into the hotel. "At this rate, they'll only be arrested for breaking and entering and those poor animals will never get justice."

"We need to look at their operations inside," Daggett said. She took the camera from Folger and put the strap around her own neck. "They're both inside now, so at least we know where they are. They'd see us, though, so it's too risky to go into the hotel by their entrance—"

"Come on, you know this place," Folger said. "You're practically a walking tourist pamphlet for everything in this park! I bet you know another way in."

Daggett grinned. Well, she *did*.

They went around the back, to the employee entrance. They worked together for a few minutes to clear a bare path in the snow, just enough that the door could squeak open and Daggett could theoretically slide in.

Just as she moved to do so, Folger snagged her arm. "What do we do when we get inside?"

"*We?* Nothing. *I* will go in and see what I can see. So far we haven't witnessed anything actionable. If I do, I can testify to that, even if we don't get any pictures." She sensed the coming argument. "And I will *try* to get pictures. But in the meanwhile, they're both in there, so you should be safe out *here*. Okay? Sit and stay."

Folger gave her an expression that was suspiciously like a pout.

"At least let me go inside," she said. "It's cold."

"And you'll stay away from the bad guys," Daggett said, suspicious.

"And I'll stay away from the bad guys," Folger conceded.

"And you'll stay where I leave you," Daggett added.

"Come *on.*"

Daggett raised an eyebrow.

"Oh, fine, I'll stay right there while you do the exciting stuff. I hope you're happy."

"Ecstatic."

They squeezed themselves through the door and into a narrow employee hallway with no working lights. Daggett left Folger there, still complaining to herself in a whisper, and made her way into the hotel proper.

She came out in a corner where she could essentially hide behind the bellhop desk as she got slowly closer.

The Old Faithful Inn was more than a hundred and twenty years old. It was a gorgeous old place. All wood and natural lines, with four stories of balconies inside, all sorts of original fixtures, and nice electric lighting during usual operating times. As it was, things were lit by—firelight?—and apparently a portable floodlight.

Most of the hotel furniture was covered in dust-cloths or

into storage, but a table had obviously been dusted off and was upright with some chip and snack wrappers scattered atop.

Someone, by accident or whimsy, had left the countdown clock uncovered. TIME TILL PREDICTED ERUPTION (+/-10 MINUTES):, with the little hands ticking away until the next time the geyser was set to go off.

Daggett crept inside into near silence. The only sound, in fact, was the roaring of the fire. The poachers had set the fireplace to blazing—the huge one in the middle of the room. There were sleeping bags spread out around the warmth. They must have gotten cold sleeping in the rooms; the radiators wouldn't work yet and the place was old and drafty.

Hold on. *Three* sleeping bags?

Uh-oh. They had made an assumption—just because they had only *seen* two, didn't mean there wasn't another. There were only two snowmobiles, but two people could easily share one. Daggett and Folger had already proved that. The poachers might have traveled here three at a time in the Jeep and then split off on the snow vehicles as needed.

She turned around immediately to go back to where she'd left Folger.

It was too late.

There was a noise off to her left, right in her blind spot. She whirled to look, and came face-to-face with one of the poachers, who'd been trying to sneak up on her.

Caught out, he went for broke and lunged, trying to grab her.

Daggett was *not* very cool with that and she punched him right in the nose.

He didn't seem to be expecting it, and wheeled backwards, almost falling. Unfortunately, it seemed he hadn't been alone, just jumped the gun, because a second later the second poacher came up from behind and tried to snatch her arm.

Daggett wriggled away and drove the heel of her fist into his throat.

While the two men were stumbling around, gasping, she vaulted the counter and beat feet. She broke for the front door the men had cleared out, keeping an eye for the mysterious third one. And she almost made it out, too.

But then her attention was caught by something, and she felt herself slowing out of pure curiosity.

A line of tipped-over gasoline containers, smelling so strongly of gas that it was obvious all their contents were currently on the floor.

Daggett was furious. They were planning on torching the evidence!

As a Park Ranger, she had a natural hatred towards fire. And poachers. And creeps who tried to grab her. And—well, she didn't need to go on. If she hadn't gotten here, if she and Folger hadn't come to investigate, they would have burned this whole place down.

Yeah. No more running. She was *catching* these men, and she was going to put them in jail.

The revelation came just on time, too, because there was the third guy. He was dressed, like the others, in camouflage chic. It wasn't even good camo for the area—they had probably bought the most expensive or prestigious gear and been done with it.

This one looked kind of surprised to see her, but he was more ready than his buddies and brought a heavy handgun up to defend himself. He aimed, but clearly wasn't willing to actually shoot directly *at* a defenseless woman. Would have been nice if they'd had the scruples before.

He was standing too close. Daggett was good with guns as a matter of necessity, a childhood spent hunting deer for meat or scaring off coyotes. She grabbed the gun.

It was a terrible idea, really—gun safety 101 suggested that perhaps a tussle over one was not the best plan—but it didn't go off, and when she grabbed his wrist hard, he let go.

And the gun was hers.

"Freeze!" she said. "Park *Ranger!*"

As it went, it wasn't the most intimidating of warnings, but coupled with the gun and doubtless the anger in her eyes, it seemed to do the trick. She pointed the gun at the one in front of her, who froze.

He gave her kind of a sketchy look. "Um, we're just here to, um, see the geyser..."

"With an illegal handgun?" Daggett asked.

He paled. "Um..."

"Throw your guns down," she said. "All three of you. And come here where I can see you."

They came with great hesitation.

But she saw their hunting rifles go down on the floor—yep, the same caliber which had shot at her and Folger—and she relaxed, a little.

They came closer, close enough for her to say, with the sternness that was the fear of tourists, hikers, and other Rangers alike, "Do you know just how many federal crimes you've committed?"

She could see up close they were all essentially boys, probably only in their twenties. They got a closer look at her, too, though, and she didn't think that was probably a good thing.

"Hey, it's just one lady!" one of them said. "She doesn't look that strong!"

Just as Daggett had decided it might be time to release a warning shot into the ceiling to show how much she was totally *not* just one lady, one of the men knocked purposely into the table and flipped it, sending trash flying everywhere.

It was a sufficient distraction as Daggett was forced to

duck, and all three took advantage of it, splitting off and juking in different directions like a football team.

Daggett swore under her breath, but didn't even try to shoot.

Two of the men ran for the front door. The third, apparently playing the odds, turned and ran deeper into the inn.

There was no hesitation.

Daggett abandoned the first two and went after the lone wolf. He was going back to where she'd left Folger.

Folger had not stayed put, of course. She had wandered further out, towards the main room. She must have been trying to watch—and in doing so, put herself in danger.

Or maybe not. When Daggett got there, breathing hard and gun at the ready, the poacher who had gone after Folger was already lying on the floor, rocking back and forth and whimpering and crying.

"She's evil," the man groaned when Daggett peered down at him and nudged him with a curious toe.

Folger was waving a hand over her own eyes, trying to clear the air. She had an empty can of bear spray in her hands; Daggett was abruptly proud.

"I wouldn't recommend using this stuff indoors," she said, coughing. Actually judging by the way the poacher was cradling certain parts of his anatomy, Daggett figured that probably wasn't all she'd done to take him out. Folger was not above kicking a man while he was down. "I got him—go get the other ones!"

Daggett followed her advice and hared back to where she'd seen the other two escape. She reached the front door just in time to hear the snowmobiles start up, one after another, and the guys hurriedly trying to get them moving.

They were only a few feet away. Moving almost without her own volition, Daggett sprinted towards them. They were clearly startled, and more than a little scared of the madwoman bull-rushing them apparently without fear or reservation.

She couldn't bring herself to even try to shoot them. She had always only planned to use the gun to get them to comply. She was not actually willing to shoot a couple now-unarmed kids.

One of them got the snowmobile going and slid forward a few feet, but by that time, Daggett had already reached the second. She tackled him off the sled.

They *oomphed* down together into the snow, so cold it took Daggett's breath away.

The man scrabbled, surprised, and tried to escape her grip, kicking and attempting to army-crawl forward so he could get to his feet.

"Just—!" she said. "Just stay down!"

Too close a range to get out the gun, even just to use it to threaten. She hauled off and kicked him down into the powdery snow. Crouching next to him, she looked for his buddy.

What she wouldn't give for a little Ranger backup right now. It was possible she hadn't been making the best choices, as of late. Maybe she was just having too much fun.

The one on the snowmobile had recovered from his shock. He skidded up beside them, sending dust and exhaust fumes kicking up into both Daggett and his friend's faces. When Daggett rolled to the side to cough, the one on the snowmobile hauled his friend up onto the back of his sled.

The two of them took off together, racing for freedom.

They left the second snowmobile behind.

In for a penny...?

Without letting herself think about it too hard, Daggett leaped onto the second one, which was still running. She jammed the throttle and shot forward, riding hard after the poachers.

The snowmobile roared along, fast and a little dangerous, just the way she liked it.

She chased them, closing in.

Almost close enough to touch. She'd run down a couple joyriders in the park before; all she needed to do was circle around front and halt their way forward. Faced with a very stubborn and very authoritative Park Ranger directly in their path, they'd stop.

Right now, they still thought they could get away.

Daggett was catching up, at which point she would force them to walk all the way back to the Inn. And, depending on how much lip they gave her, maybe she'd let Folger have them. But maybe that was cruel and unusual punishment.

There was a big clearing outside of Old Faithful Inn, the one leading to the eponymous Old Faithful geyser, bracketed by boardwalks and other marks of tourism.

On the sides, there were copses of trees, a good place for the two poachers to get lost in during Daggett's pursuit for them. If they played it right, maybe slid around a corner while she was still searching for them and shut off the engine and prayed, she could go totally past them without ever knowing.

But maybe it looked more attractive to a novice snowmobiler, the big stretch of open space and snow that was Old Faithful.

Not a good idea. The water in that geyser got up to 200 degrees. Not to mention at any point there was a chance at punching through the geothermal crust and falling right into any number of nasty toxic gasses or boiling water.

Daggett was forced to turn off, doing a quick sideways slide, kicking snow, before she could fully stop the snowmobile.

The poachers had no such common sense; they kept going, apparently heartened by the fact she wasn't following.

It was too far to yell a warning to them; she winced and fought the urge to cover her eyes. They were heading straight for Old Faithful. By now the geyser was spitting steam and starting to bubble over; it was about to erupt.

They got closer and closer.

Suddenly, a shadow crossed the poachers' path.

Daggett couldn't believe it. It was a *bison*.

They liked to hang out by hot springs and geysers during the winter months, because the boiling water and steam heated things up for them. There was a little family of them lingering in the warmth, one coming a little further out, right towards the snowmobilers. It wasn't even charging or particularly interested in them, just standing disinterestedly, chewing something.

Daggett had never been stupid enough to see one up close before, but she imagined Folger would probably be peeing her pants if she was here right now. She saw the bison—a second later, the poachers did too.

It lumbered into the path of the snowmobile.

The driver yanked them to the right, desperately, trying to stop before barreling straight into a thousand pounds of pure muscle and fur.

They *did* stop, but the snowmobile skipped and skidded, tipping over. Both men fell off and rolled so they wouldn't be crushed by the vehicle.

Old Faithful erupted right on time.

The bison, silhouetted by the spray and bounce of the water, looked majestically into the sun. The light glittered off the snow and the prismatic sprays of superheated steam. And, off to the side, the two poachers, who were sitting up and cursing now, but seemed to have mostly given up on life.

The bison wandered away, bored, leaving deep prints behind which filled softly with water.

It would make for a great postcard. *Welcome to Yellowstone!*

THE OLD FAITHFUL SNOW LODGE WOULD BE OPENING UP FOR THE winter soon—right across from where Daggett had had her little adventure. The roads would open back up for snowcoaches, and tourists would begin to trickle in. The lights were coming back on.

It was kind of a shame. Daggett had liked the solitude.

Well, kind of, anyway.

Outpost 20 was awash with activity. Daggett found herself hanging around, watching the scientists buzz back and forth with total geeky excitement.

Folger wouldn't shut up. She'd gotten ahold of a newspaper, and was reading all about the arrest of the three Yellowstone poachers. She was ecstatic.

"They totally caught them red-handed," Folger said. "When faced with everything, they confessed it all. They found all the animal trophies we reported, plus evidence of a few more, and a whole dead eagle. Disgusting people."

"Enough for federal prison for a long time," Daggett said, pretty satisfied. She'd read the article too. The poachers had been a bunch of rich college boys seeking out a thrill on winter break. They planned to keep some of the trophies and sell the rest to their buddies. They had wanted a more exciting experience than regular hunting. She supposed they'd gotten it.

"And that's not the best part," Folger said, gleefully flipping the paper around so Daggett could see the headline on the front page.

BISON GETS REVENGE! YELLOWSTONE BUFFALO STOPS POACHERS!

"A bit of an exaggeration," said Daggett, who rather thought most of the death-defying heroics had kind of been *hers*. She had gotten in a little bit of hot water over her methodology, but in the end, they'd caught and arrested the poachers. Who wouldn't be happy about that? She'd probably get a ceremony or something. "I don't see how that's the best part, seeing as how they seem like they've totally forgotten about *us*."

"Are you kidding? Do you know how long my research is going to be funded? *Forever.*"

Daggett couldn't help but smile. It was good to know some people had their priorities.

KENZIE LAPPIN IS A WRITER WITH SHORT STORIES IN PUBLICATIONS such as Dreadstone Press, Brigids Gate Press, Apex Magazine, WordFire Press, Air And Nothingness Press, and more. Check her out on X at @KenzieLappin.

8

YELLOW STONE
R.T. LAWTON

Beaumont and Yarnell had flown into Billings, Montana, to pick up a rented black panel van. The next stop on their list was a big box hardware store to acquire a couple of short handled sledge hammers, some cold chisels, work gloves, head lamps, a few large moving pads to deaden sound, and anything else they might need to peel an old-style safe. Naturally, they paid cash for everything so as not to leave much of a trail behind themselves.

Late that afternoon, they drove south to Cooke City, population about one hundred, on the southern Montana border and spent the night in an old motel. Bed time came early. The next part of the plan was to get to the park before the sun came up. Since the Northeast entrance was only four miles down the highway, they hoped to get there before any of the park employees were manning the entrance booth. It wasn't that they were too cheap to pay the entry fee, it was just that in their line of work, it was best if no one saw them to even remember they had been there.

The sky was still dark when Beaumont slowed their rental

van as they approached the Northeast Entrance to Yellowstone Park. His headlights lit up the outside of the booth.

"Doesn't look like they've opened for business yet," said Yarnell in a low voice.

"If nobody's here," replied Beaumont, "then you don't need to be whispering."

"Sorry," whispered Yarnell. "Force of habit when it's dark out and we're thinking about burglarizing a place."

Beaumont ignored him and drove past the empty booth.

Continuing along the unlit roadway, they passed through large areas of grasslands on either side where the headlights picked out shaggy-haired animals with gleaming horns on their head.

"Look," cried Yarnell, "It's buffalo."

"Bison," contradicted Beaumont. "Buffalo are like water buffalo and Cape Buffalo, which don't have a hump between their shoulders. Bison do have a hump above their shoulders and are found in Europe and North America."

"The westerns always call them buffalo," Yarnell argued.

"That's because it's a common misconception left over from early explorers who didn't know any better."

"Sounds like you've been reading a lot of books lately."

"Just doing some research on the area before we got here. One can never have too much information."

Yarnell let that one go in order to avoid any more argument. He sat back and stared out the passenger window. That is until Beaumont slammed on the brakes just as two very large somethings, hairy and brown, with glowing eyes and white canine teeth came out of the roadside ditch, sauntered across the asphalt, and disappeared into a stand of pine trees and bushes at the edge of the grasslands.

"What the hell was that?" exclaimed Beaumont.

"That was a couple of bears," Yarnell calmly replied. "You

know they do have bears in Jellystone Park. I've seen them on television."

"Yellowstone," replied Beaumont. "Jellystone was a cartoon. Those two bears you saw on tv aren't real, they're cartoon characters."

"They're as real as Ranger Smith is," said Yarnell. "Just wait. If we get unlucky on this job, you'll see for yourself."

Now it was Beaumont's turn to be silent. Which lasted until Beaumont pulled into the parking lot for the Albright Education Center in the Mammoth Springs District just as the sun broke over the horizon.

Yarnell straightened up in the seat and looked at the stone buildings. "What's this? Looks like old cavalry barracks. They've even got stables for horses."

"That's what the buildings were," said Beaumont. "The army protected the park before the Park Service was born." Then he pointed through the windshield. "See that building over there, that's Ranger Headquarters. That's where our safe is supposed to be, sitting in the Chief Ranger's back office."

"If that's where Marty said it would be then that's where we will find it."

"You sound pretty certain."

"Marty used to work for a cleaning service, until he got caught going through the client's desk for valuables late one night. Seems his supervisor and one of the park rangers dropped in unannounced to check his work. Unfortunately for Marty, he was halfway through counting out the currency from the district's cash box at the time."

"What happened then?"

"Marty grabbed the box and took off running, but them Rangers are pretty fast on their feet. The ranger ran Marty down and collared him."

"They probably have to be fast from working around all them bears," said Beaumont.

"And buffaloes," said Yarnell. "You see the horns on them things?"

"Bison," said Beaumont.

"Jellystone," muttered Yarnell.

"It's like this," retorted Beaumont, "Native American tribes in the area described a place along the river bank where the stones were yellow and that's how the park got its name. It wasn't named after jelly."

Yarnell decided life might be more pleasant if he switched the subject of their conversation over to the valuable object they were here to lift.

"So how much does *Old Yeller* weigh?" he inquired.

Beaumont immediately launched into a lengthy explanation of how gold was weighed in troy ounces with ten troy ounces to a troy pound and whereas an avoirdupois ounce weighed 28.349. grams, a troy ounce weighed 31.1035 grams.

With all those numbers in his head, Yarnell was having trouble keeping up. All he really wanted to know was whether the oversized gold nugget could be carried out by one man or if it was going to take two.

At that point, the sound of knuckles rapping on the driver's side window interrupted the math lecture.

"Excuse me, sir," said an official voice, "You have stopped your van in the middle of the roadway and are blocking traffic."

Beaumont glanced in his rearview mirror. He didn't see any vehicles behind him, but considered it best not to argue the point at this time.

"May I see your park pass, please?" continued the voice.

Both Beaumont and Yarnell turned to the driver's side window.

A hand outside the glass made a gesture that meant lower your window.

Beaumont reluctantly did so.

A narrow face topped with a Smokey the Bear hat bent down to look at them.

"Sir, you do have a park pass, don't you?"

"Uh, well, no, not yet," replied Beaumont. "We were in a hurry to get to the park, so we arrived early and there was no one in the entrance booth."

"That's perfectly understandable," said the slim ranger. "Fortunately, you are able to purchase passes at any of the stores and ranger stations. Our headquarters over there will be glad to serve you." His long arm and index finger pointed the way.

"We'll go there right now," said Beaumont. Then, he raised the driver's side window and shifted the transmission into DRIVE.

"Did you see his name tag?" asked Yarnell as they pulled away.

"Nope, I was too busy looking at the narrow face and flat-brimmed hat of the law that was filling our window frame."

"That was Ranger Smith," said Yarnell, "just like in Jellystone. Even kinda looks like him."

"Smith is a common name, plenty of them out there, so don't start in on that again. Besides, he just gave us the perfect excuse to go inside and look around before we do the job."

Beaumont turned the van into a lot near the headquarters building and parked close to the front entrance. He reached in his pocket and handed thirty-five dollars to Yarnell.

"When we go inside, you buy the park pass and talk to the guy for a while to keep him busy. I'll look around for alarms and cameras. See if I can locate that safe."

As they walked up the front stairs and entered the building,

Beaumont made mental notes about the security cameras focused on the front door and the hard-wired alarm system on the windows and the front door. To Beaumont's eyes, the equipment appeared to be old and out of date, but it probably gave the client a sense of security. Just what Beaumont wanted to see.

Eventually, he saw the second thing he was looking for. By standing in a certain place, he could look down a short hallway, through an open office door, past the waiting room and see the old-timey safe sitting along the back wall in the Chief Ranger's office.

On his way out of the building, Beaumont picked up a multi-colored brochure telling the history of *Old Yeller*, one of the largest gold nuggets ever found in Montana, and how it was displayed in the Albright Education Center on a daily basis for the public to see, this being the last day the stone was available before returning to the Montana Museum of Mining. What the brochure didn't mention was that at night the giant nugget rested in the Chief Ranger's old-timey safe. Beaumont and Yarnell had already acquired insider information on that point.

"That was worth the price of a park pass," he said to Yarnell as the two of them returned to the van, "just to be able to see the layout of the place in broad daylight. Your ranger did us a favor."

"And that's probably why he's watching us right now," replied Yarnell.

Beaumont swiveled his head around. Yep, Ranger Smith was looking in their direction from another parking lot.

"Quick," said Beaumont, "hold up the pass to show him we're legit now. We don't need him following us all over the park."

"That *is* how Ranger Smith catches Yogi Bear and his little sidekick Boo-Boo, by following them around when they go stealing picnic baskets."

"We've got to ditch him then."

Yarnell started rubbing his stomach. "I'm getting a bad feeling about this job."

"C'mon," said Beaumont, "we'll get you something to eat. That always makes you feel better. Then, we'll play tourist until we lose him."

Beaumont continually glanced in his rearview mirror as he drove to the nearest bar and grill to get some takeout burgers, fries, and drinks. Yep, Ranger Smith was back there at some distance, following them in his forest green pickup. Beaumont didn't bother to mention the situation to Yarnell, who was busy munching on his second bacon cheeseburger already. No sense keeping his partner riled up.

By consulting a map of the park, Beaumont figured they could visit several interesting sites while making a large loop on park roads which would then lead them back to Mammoth Hot Springs and the Chief Ranger's office. To kill time until the sun went down, they stopped at several springs and geysers, including Old Faithful. By the time they got that far, Beaumont could look over his shoulder and no longer see any forest green pickup following them. He relaxed and started to enjoy playing tourist.

Before they got back to Mammoth, they had to make one more stop for Yarnell to get a couple more bags of delicious smelling bacon cheeseburgers.

By positioning their black rental van between a couple of empty forest green pickups in a convenient parking lot, Beaumont and Yarnell could observe both the educational center and the rangers' headquarters building. When the lights went out in the educational building, they watched four rangers transport the gold nugget over to the Chief Ranger's office. After a short while, the lights started going off in the ranger building. The last man out locked the doors and set the alarm as he went. Several employee vehicles gradually found their way out of the main lot and drove off in different directions. Soon, everything was dark and quiet.

Two hours they waited, noting the regularity of the on-the-hour roving patrol which consisted of one ranger in a pickup. He never stopped to shake the door handles or check the windows of the building.

After the midnight patrol had made its most recent drive-by, Beaumont took a small flashlight out of his pocket and spread the hand-drawn map they'd gotten from Marty out across the console between them. Using a ballpoint as a pointer, he went over their entry plan one last time.

"We'll leave the van here," he said, "take all our gear across the parking lot to the window into the supply room at the side of the building, where you'll jump the alarm wires, and we'll go in. After that, we'll go into the waiting room and through the Chief Ranger's office door."

Yarnell merely nodded his head.

They eased out of the van's front doors, went to the rear door and started unloading their equipment to carry with them. All doors were softly shut as they moved around the van. Then, they trotted across the parking lot to the designated window at the side of the building. Yarnell used a glass cutter to make a hole large enough for him to work through, then peeled the insulation off of a couple of wires so he could attach a jumper cable with an alligator clip on each end. With a silent prayer to Saint Dismas, Yarnell raised the window and went in. Everything remained quiet.

Beaumont handed their equipment in through the open window to Yarnell, and then crawled in himself, with help from his partner. They opened the supply room door and entered the waiting room. Yarnell paused at the Chief Ranger's office door. Light was coming in around the glass in the upper part of the door.

Yarnell put his face up to a crack between the glass and the wood frame bordering the glass. He backed away quickly, bumping into Beaumont behind him.

"There's some people moving around in the office," he hissed softly.

"That's impossible," said Beaumont.

Yarnell quickly clamped one hand across Beaumont's mouth to deaden the volume. He moved his lips close to Beaumont's ear so he wouldn't have to speak very loud.

"There's at least two in the Chief Ranger's office, and I saw one more guy just pop up out of the floor."

"What do you mean pop up out of the floor?"

"It's as if they dug a tunnel and it comes up in the Chief Ranger's office."

"What? Let me see."

Beaumont crawled up to the office door and peered through the crack.

"Damn, somebody's trying to steal our gold nugget. Where'd they come from?"

"You mean other than out of the floor?"

Beaumont put his face up to the glass again and took another look.

"They don't look to be in the kind of shape to dig a tunnel very far, so it's got to be someplace close by."

Yarnell pulled Marty's map out of his pocket and checked out the rear of the headquarters building.

"There's what may be a two-stall garage across the alley," said Yarnell. "From what I remember on one of our drive-bys, it would probably fit a couple of dump trucks, but from all appearances it hadn't been used for several years, except for maybe storing obsolete office furniture and stuff."

"Well, I'll bet that's where these guys started their tunnel. They probably took the dirt away in a dump truck in the dark of night and no one ever got wind of what was going on. You'd better go back out the supply room window and peek around the corner, see what's going on. Make it fast."

Yarnell tip-toed back to the supply room, made his way out of the open window and peered around the corner. A dump truck and a construction pickup, both empty of any drivers were parked near the two-stall garage. The garage itself seemed to be unpopulated, but a corner of whatever the guys had used to cover all the garage windows had come untaped and gave off a sliver of light. Yarnell raced back to the supply room and made his report.

"So that's how it is then," muttered Beaumont. "As far as I'm concerned, if we don't get the gold, nobody does. We'll have to hurry though because last time I looked through the crack in the door, they were dragging a cutting torch out of the hole. It won't take them long to cut through the metal sheets in that old safe."

"Some burglars take no pride in their work techniques," replied Yarnell.

Beaumont nodded while he contemplated the pros and cons of the evening.

"Here's what we're gonna do," he finally said. "You go move our van over here for a quick get-away. Then hot wire that dump truck and the construction pickup that you saw. Drive both trucks up against the two garage doors until the doors can't be opened."

"What will you be doing?"

"I'll be rigging that old alarm to go off ten minutes after we've left the scene."

Doing some thinking of his own, Yarnell trotted to the van and drove it back with its headlights out. With the assistance of a large screwdriver, he then started both trucks and left them idling where they were parked. He glanced at his watch. They had about fifteen minutes before the on-the-hour patrol made its next drive-by. He'd have to hurry.

On their way out of the park, Beaumont and Yarnell were approaching the booth for the Northeast Entrance. Once again, their headlights showed the booth to be dark and empty.

"Looks just like it did when we came through from Cooke City," said Beaumont.

"Except we were looking at the other side," replied Yarnell.

"I feel bad we didn't get the gold," continued Beaumont. "You sure you got those two trucks up against the garage doors tight enough so them other burglars won't be able to open the doors and escape?"

"I did better than that."

Beaumont had kept on talking and didn't immediately recognize what Yarnell had said.

"What do you mean?"

"There was a side door in the garage and I didn't want to take the chance of them getting out that way."

"There's something you're not telling me."

"Before I went for the van, I heard a rustling noise in some nearby bushes Sounded like a large animal. Then, after I drove the dump truck up to the garage door and killed the engine, I heard some heavy sniffing sounds like a couple of bears searching for food coming from the same bushes."

"What did you do?" Beaumont asked in an accusatory tone.

"I opened the second garage door. Then, I took a couple of

the leftover bacon cheeseburgers out of the sack, tore off some pieces, and laid a trail from the bushes, through the open door, to the tunnel edge and threw the rest of the burgers into the tunnel. After that, I called out to Yogi and Boo-Boo."

"You talked to cartoon bears?"

"Yep, and they came out of the bushes, ate the pieces of hamburger, went into the garage, and crawled down into the tunnel to get the last of the burgers. That's when I closed the second garage door and leaned the front end of the construction pickup against it. When them three burglars run into those two hungry bears, they'll be glad to get arrested."

R.T. LAWTON IS A RETIRED FEDERAL LAW ENFORCEMENT AGENT, PAST member of the Mystery Writers of America board of directors, a 2022 Edgar Award winner for Best Short Story, and has over 160 short stories in various anthologies and other publications, including 52 sold to *Alfred Hitchcock Mystery Magazine*. He currently has nine short story collections in paperback and e-format for purchase on Amazon.

He has presented surveillance workshops at Left Coast Crime Conference, Bouchercon, and Pikes Peak Writers' Conference.

9
WHAT ROAMS AT NIGHT
ALYSSA BOWEN

I am probably a little bit crazy.

There's no other way I would be driving into Yellowstone National Park and preparing to spend the next few weeks virtually alone, with little-to-no cell service, and keeping watch over the Northeast Entrance. This is a dead end right now. The park is closed where the roads washed out in multiple places along Lamar Valley. Besides construction vehicles, the entrance is open for bicycle and foot traffic only, but they're hoping they can get it open to vehicles soon.

Because of the damage from the floods, I'll be the only person at this entrance for a while. They're overwhelmed in the other areas dealing with a more restrictive entrance policy and the unhappy tourists. They want someone to be here to keep an eye out for roaming guests and help anyone with questions about what they're supposed to do from here, to give them a map and outline the rules since the flood.

This is my first official posting as a park ranger, and there's supposed to be someone seasoned here to meet me. I steer my pickup through the entrance and up towards the residence area.

It's hard to see from the road with the pine trees blocking most of the views of the cabins. The only sign of life I see is a lone bison looming off to the side and chomping on something without a care in the world. I park the truck at a dormitory, and there's not much in sight. Trees, lots of them, obstruct much of any kind of view.

The cool, sharp mountain air is so different from the suffocating humidity of eastern Oklahoma. The lack of any human sound. No honking cars or screaming neighbor kids or ex-husbands telling you to keep that job at the bank because it's good money, and it doesn't matter that your boss is a creep.

It frees me, that pushy thought of why I've run away to where I can be alone for a while, and I practically bounce up the steps to the first cabin with a bit of a smile on my face. I no longer have to answer to my ex-husband, to talk to him, to ever see him again. I can do whatever I want.

There are no assholes here.

"Hey, what do you think you're doing?" I miss the top step and trip, barely catching myself on my palm instead of my face.

"This is employee housing. No visitors. And this entrance isn't open. You need to head back towards Silver Gate if you're looking for facilities," the voice calls, not stopping to ask if I'm okay. I find my feet and stand up.

"I'm supposed to be here," I grit out, trying to keep my voice calm. I will not snap on day one.

He's got on NPS standard-issue green pants with a white t-shirt and a Doc Holliday mustache and soul patch that makes me want to roll my eyes. Another hipster who moved out here when it became popular during the pandemic. It's not a new fad for me. Living in the Mountain West is a dream I've held for as long as I can remember.

"No one is supposed to be here."

"*You* are here," I let the tiniest bit of sarcasm seep in.

"I'm park law enforcement. I'm meeting someone here today to show them around."

"Me. I'm the person you're meeting to show around."

"No, it's a guy."

"How do you know it's a guy?"

He practically growls before saying, "Well, this would be the first time I've met a girl named Martin."

"You must have missed the comma. The name is Elizabeth Martin."

His eyes narrow. "Elizabeth."

"You can call me Beth."

"Beth."

"Are you going to keep repeating my name, or are you going to tell me yours?"

"Coleman Fisher."

"Nice to meet you, Ranger Fisher. You are a ranger, right? You only look like about half of one right now."

He looks down at his shirt. "I fished on my break. I was changing back into uniform and heard a car drive up. You're early."

"Timeliness offends you. Got it."

"I'm going to walk back to my truck and get the keys. I'll be back."

I wait for him like a teenager, arms crossed over my stomach and scowl on my face, but then I see another bison making its way through the trees, and the tension seeps from my body like steam from a geyser. That is why I'm here. Because this place and the animals that roam it are magical. Because when I see a bison stomping through the woods or hear a wolf calling to its pack or hold the cool, slick body of a cutthroat trout in my hands, I feel alive in a way I don't anywhere else. I need this escape, and I need it to go well, so I will put on my cheerful face and make the best of this grumpy ranger showing me around.

He comes back, but this time, he's added the ranger standard tan button up shirt and a bullet proof vest with tactical belt. He hooks a thumb towards the smaller cabin on the northwest side of the compound. "They have you in that cabin over there."

"Oh ok."

"First time here?" he asks, and I fall into step beside him as he walks across the gravel parking lot.

"My first time to work. I usually just come to camp."

He makes a sound akin to a grunt whose meaning seems somewhere between approval and disinterest. I take it as a good sign.

The cabin is farther into the tree line. It isn't anything fancy on the outside, just wooden siding painted brown to give log cabin vibes. It's long and rectangular with a porch covering the front and a couple of chairs set in one corner.

The screen door creaks when he opens it—as any good screen door should—and he flips the keys up into his hand to unlock the door. It takes him a minute of working the key, and I'm a bit worried the grumpy park ranger is about to get grumpier, but I finally hear the clunk of the deadbolt turning. He holds a hand up for me to enter first, and when I bump into the door on my way inside, I notice how heavy it is. Bear proof? Hopefully.

The inside is simple too. A green futon, an armchair whose wooden frame matches the wood of the floor, and a coffee table with an array of Yellowstone literature spread across it. Bear safety, maps, hiking trails, camping guidelines. All things I'm familiar with but probably need to read over again if I'm going to be helping people.

"Bathroom is here," he says and opens the door to the left. "Main bedroom is upstairs, but you could fold the futon out if you wanna stay down here."

Stairs are a bit of a stretch. They're steep enough that they could probably be called a ladder but sturdy enough that they could sell them as stairs if they were on Zillow. He moves past the stairs and states the obvious one more time, "Kitchen."

I can't help but poke the bear a little bit. He's so serious, and it should not be this serious of a situation. "Man, you must have a side job selling real estate."

He snorts in what I think is amusement and says, "I figured you could find your way around a cabin, so I was saving my breath for the important part."

"Which is?"

"Water usage." He sets a hand on the sink. "There's no running water to the cabins right now. They hope to have it fixed soon, but the line was busted in the flooding. There's a water tank outside that you can use to fill buckets for cooking or washing dishes. I'd recommend getting some gallon bottles to fill up and keep inside for drinking next time you go to town. I'll show you."

I follow him out the same door we came through and around to the back of the cabin. There's a fire pit there with a lone chair next to it. The water tank is black and sitting on a table up against the house. The table is long enough it could be a prep area if I wanted to cook over the fire instead of inside.

"Like camping, you'll need to dump any water down the vault toilet, so you don't attract bears."

"Oh."

"Oh?"

"I—I was prepared for the shower thing and the water thing and the alone thing, but I wasn't thinking about having to leave the cabin at night, alone, if I needed to use the bathroom."

"Scared of the dark?"

"I'm scared of what roams around here, whether I can see it or not," I snap.

"You could use a chamber pot and then dump it in the vault in the morning."

I am stunned into silence for a moment. It's not a bad idea, but this was not what I envisioned talking about on this first day at my dream job. And it's definitely not something I would have chosen to talk about with a relatively attractive man I'd never met before. "Okay, let's stop talking about my restroom usage. What else do I need to know?"

"Do you know how to use bear spray?"

"Aim it at their feet, and when they're incapacitated, escape."

"Right. Cell service isn't good here. We should have a satellite phone for you in the next few days, but the wireless internet is working decently for now."

"Who do I call in an emergency? Who would be closest?"

"Nine-one-one if it's an emergency. I can give you a pamphlet that has our office number if it's not urgent."

"Right."

"Are you going to be okay out here?"

"Yes, definitely, one hundred percent," I lie and wonder if it was a good idea to listen to that last true crime podcast on the drive. "I'm very cautious. And I was mainly wondering if I'd have company anywhere close."

His eyebrows are raised, and it irritates me that he doesn't believe me even if he is correct that I'm nervous. "I can give you my number, just in case. I'm not exactly close, but I'd at least be able to find help for you quickly. We're hoping to have someone over here soon. It's been chaotic trying to get everything organized after the floods."

"I'm sure."

We walk in silence over to my car, but when he gets there, he asks, "Can I help you unload anything?"

"Wow, Doc Holliday has manners too."

"Recanting my offer," he grunts, but I swear this time he's trying not to smile. "Here's my card if you need something."

I climb into my truck and watch him walk away.

THE FIRST WEEK GOES SMOOTHLY. I SETTLE INTO THE CABIN, AND IT feels homey, even with no running water or cell phone service besides Wi-Fi. There's more traffic than I expected going into and out of the park on bikes, but it's not overwhelming, and there are days I go hours without having someone come through. The people I see the most are the construction workers driving through on their way to work on the road. I haven't driven down that way, but from the videos the park has posted, I know they have their work cut out for them.

I go into Silver Gate for dinner once and for ice cream in Cooke City another night. There's something about huckleberry ice cream in a waffle cone in the mountains that can't be beat.

It's Sunday night before my Monday day off. I'm going to get up early and walk down into the park. I set out my hiking boots and settle under the covers of my bed with the newest book from my favorite author. The Cooke City Coffee Shop also sells books, and they ordered this one for me. I am asleep before I read two pages.

I know it's a dream. I'm running, but I'm not sure if it's away from someone or if I'm the one in pursuit. I hear someone screaming, and I'm not sure if they're scared of me or trying to help. I come to, but I'm still in that hazy post-dream state. Was I chasing someone in the dream? I want to fall back into it and dream my way out of the fear. What were they saying in the dream? Were they screaming for help?

The scream pierces the dark, even though it's not extremely close, and my eyes fly open. That's not my dream. Is it? I lay still. It's my imagination. I shift to my left until I feel the wall of the cabin against my shoulder and try to burrow in to go back to sleep. The next time it comes, there's no denying it.

"Help!" The scream is louder this time, and another one follows quickly. It's a woman, I think, and this time she adds something else. Did she say, 'he's trying to get me?' I still haven't moved when she screams again. She's getting closer. She's definitely saying someone's trying to get her. Over and over, maybe five times she calls out, and I lay perfectly still, my heart's pounding making it hard to hear what she's saying. When it falls silent for the longest amount of time since I woke, I go for my phone.

I reach for it, but my hand brushes the lamp. Since it's one of those tap lights, it comes on and lights up the room. I scramble to turn it back off, knocking my phone and book to the ground in the process.

"Damn it," I whisper and hop off the bed, panicked, like somehow that noise or that light will draw attention from whoever is chasing this woman to me. It's dark outside in a way that only exists when you're hundreds of miles from a city. My light would stand out. I'm debating what I should do when she screams again. It feels close, but it's hard to tell inside the cabin, and the distance of sound is always hazy in the mountains anyways. There are no words this time, just one long scream that makes the hair on my arms stand and my face numb.

This is not happening. It can't be. I've read enough crime novels and thrillers that it should make me exempt of actually being in one. And for someone who has watched almost every detective show known to man, I have no idea what I should do. I look at my phone. It's two-fourteen, and I have no service, not even SOS to call nine-one-one. With the road closures, it would take hours for any kind of law enforcement to get here. The only emergency help close by would be the volunteer fire department.

There's an octagonal window over my bed, so I climb up to look out. It's dark, but maybe if someone has a flashlight, I could see them? It takes a minute for my eyes to adjust, but I can make out the other buildings. I scan the woods, but I see nothing. Should I go downstairs? Try to get a better angle? No, nothing that might bring attention to this cabin. If I tripped or knocked something over in the dark that was loud, someone might notice. What if the woman screaming comes to my door? Do I let her in? What if it's a trick, and they're after me? What if she lures whoever is chasing her here?

I'm about to sit down when I see them. Headlights, coming from the direction of the park. That can't be right. The park is closed to vehicles right now, and even if it wasn't, there's no reason for them to be in there at this hour. There're no open campgrounds, no stores. The car stops for a moment then drives out the exit, but they circle and drive back the way they came. The lights disappear, and I scan the woods again looking for anything that might signal what is going on. I check my phone. It's been ten minutes since I heard the last scream, maybe fifteen minutes total since I woke up.

The car is back, but this time when it slows, it turns into the drive of the residence. *Please don't see my car, please don't notice there's someone here*, I beg and cover my mouth to keep from audibly crying as the tears spill over my eyes.

The car circles slowly and aims its lights towards the west, where it sounded like the screams came from. It stops, for what feels like hours but is likely less than a minute, then reverses slowly onto the street and slinks back the way it came.

I don't know how long I stand there before finally collapsing on the bed. I drag my bear spray and my phone with me into the corner of the bed which is pushed up against the wall opposite the stairs. I'm not leaving this room until it's light outside. I wish I was brave enough to sprint to my car and take off, but I'm not, and this little corner is about the safest place I could be. If anyone comes in, they'll have to come up, and I can incapacitate them with the almost lethal pepper spray.

I try to get a call out, but it won't ring. I contemplate calling my mom on Facetime to have her call the police, but I know that it'll only cause her to panic and start driving to Montana which won't help. I'm not sure the police coming at this moment would do anything but make me feel safe. It's too dark to do anything outside. With the number of dangerous animals that live here, we'd be more apt to get someone in a search party hurt than we would to actually help someone while it's dark.

I stay in the corner of the bed, periodically getting up to look outside, for hours. Eventually, my heart rate slows to a normal pace, but I'm never relaxed and never able to fall back to sleep. When the light starts to seep into the windows, I get dressed. I wait though, until it's past the early morning dimness and shadows, until I can actually see all the way to the park's entrance and through the trees in the other direction before I descend the stairs. I grab an energy drink from the fridge, throw my fanny pack over my shoulder, and after looking out all the windows for any signs of life, I turn the deadbolt and step outside. Head on a swivel, I lock the door and make a mad dash for my car.

Even though I obtain phone service somewhere along the way, I don't stop to call. I drive until I reach Mammoth and run inside, a whirl of messy hair and puffy eyes and terror. There are a few people scattered around, but it's certainly not busy. I march up to the guy at the desk and say, "My name is Elizabeth Martin, and I'm stationed at the northeast entrance. Last night, there was some kind of accident in the woods."

His eyes dart over to me and back to the computer, his fingers not slowing. "What kind of accident?"

"I'm not exactly sure," I say. "I was sleeping, and when I woke up, someone was screaming in the woods."

"Screaming?"

He sounds bored, and I'm about to snap at him when a hand wraps around my arm and a voice says, "I'll talk to her, Brett."

I flinch and go to pull away, but I recognize the voice. "Coleman."

"Let's go to my office, Beth."

I'm not entirely opposed to his hand on my arm because it's gentle, and I've felt so alone and terrified since I woke up to the screaming that his touch feels like comfort. He moves it to my back and directs me through the door in the corner into an office. "What's going on?"

"Last night, I woke up about two in the morning, and there was a woman screaming in the woods outside the cabin."

His lips twitch, his mustache along with them, and curl up in concern. He motions to the chair pulled out into the middle of the room, so I sit, but he leans against his desk, crossing his arms over his chest. "Go on, tell me everything."

"At first, I thought I was dreaming, but then it happened again. She was screaming, and was saying something like, 'Help! He's trying to get me!' Or 'Help! They're trying to get me.' She kept getting closer to the cabin, and I tried to look out the window, but I didn't see anything. It was so dark, and there were no lights or anything, but it happened five or six times, and then finally, there was one really long scream, like she was terrified." I shiver and realize I'm shaking. Reliving it is a nightmare.

"I tried to call out, but I didn't have any service, and I don't have a satellite phone yet. I was too scared to try to run to my car, so I waited until daylight to come here. But then, there were headlights."

"Like headlamps?"

"No, like a car. It came from the west and drove out the entrance then back inside. Then it came again and pulled up the driveway. It stopped at that west corner which is where the screams sounded like they were coming from and sat there with its headlights on like they were looking for someone. Then it went back the way it came. I didn't hear it again."

"That's—" He searches for the word, so I help him out.

"Terrifying, weird, intense. Coleman, there should be no cars coming from that direction at night. What were they doing?"

He shakes his head, obviously contemplating everything I said. "And you're sure the screams were a woman? Couldn't have been a mountain lion?"

"I'm a woman out there alone. I get people questioning my judgement and what I heard. I might question myself, but—the car. I was wide awake then, and no matter how you slice it, there should not have been a car there. It can't be a coincidence. I don't know if it was someone looking to help or hurt her, but I don't have any explanation because no one should be in there after dark."

"Did you let anyone in yesterday that seemed suspicious?"

"No, yesterday was slow. I let in a family in the morning on their bikes and a few older men who are staying in Silver Gate and have been walking in to fish. There were a couple of ladies who were going on a hike. They all came out. I didn't let in any couples except the one with the kids."

"What about construction trucks? Could it have been one of those last night?"

"No," I shake my head adamantly. "It was car of some kind, four doors, dark in color. Black or charcoal or something."

"Who's working the gate today?"

"It was supposed to be my day off. I don't know if someone got there to cover for me or not. As soon as it was light out, I got in my car and drove away."

Coleman runs a hand down his face and goes around the other side of the desk. "Ok, do you mind writing all that down? I'll talk to my boss about going back with you and checking things out."

"You believe me?"

"You didn't think I would?"

I shrug. "I'm still deciding if you're more Doc Holliday or Johnny Ringo."

He rolls his eyes at that, but he hands me a piece of paper and a pen, and my shaking hand brushes his as I take them. "I'll fill out the top portion, but if you can fill in the bottom portion with your version of events and contact info, we'll go from there. I'll be back."

He comes back in when I'm finishing writing everything out and takes it with another Arnold Schwarzenegger comment, closing the door behind him. When he returns, another guy walks in behind him. The new guy is older, bald, and by the way he moves past us both into the room and immediately starts talking, in charge.

"So you think there was someone attacked in the woods?"

"I have no idea. But someone was, at the very least, in fear for their life."

"But you think that she thought she was being chased by someone?"

"I wouldn't begin to assume what she was thinking, but she was scared. This is Yellowstone National Park. She could've been chased by a bear or a wolf or a human, but based on the car that showed up, my thought was human."

"And regardless of what actually happened, the park is closed to traffic at that entrance," Coleman adds. "Whoever was in there was in there illegally, and that's a matter for us, sir."

The boss looks back and forth between us and then shrugs, scratching the top of his head. "Okay."

Coleman follows him out the door and pulls it behind him, but it doesn't quite shut. "I really think we should check this out."

"She's cute, she's scared, you have a protector complex, I get it. But we're spread thin as it is."

"It has nothing to do with any of that. She's a park employee, and she's over there alone and far from help."

"Which she signed up for."

"That doesn't mean we don't have a duty to her and whoever she heard in the woods to check it out. If it's nothing, great. But if someone's hurt or up to something over there, we better take care of it."

My face is bright red when he comes back in, and he notices. "You hear all that?"

"Yep."

"It's been a mess the last month. He's under a lot of stress."

"Hey, at least he thinks I'm cute," I joke, and he scoffs out a half-laugh.

"I need to wrap up a few things here before I head that way. Do you want to wait for me, or do you want to go on back?"

It's a long drive, and I probably ought to make it while I'm still hopped up on caffeine. It's daylight now, and with my heart beating at a normal pace, I think I'm fine being there on my own. "I think I'll get some food and drive back if you think you'll be there before dark."

He checks his watch. "I think I can be there in time to look around some tonight then we can get up early and do a wider search."

"I'm going to help?"

"Unless you don't want to. Wider search area with two people."

"No, I want to help. During daylight hours," I clarify.

"If I'm not there, and you're nervous, go into town and wait for me at the Royal Wulff," he says, referencing the hotel and restaurant in Silver Gate. "You'll have phone service there, so I can call you, or you can call me."

"You need my number?"

He holds up the folder. "You put it here. Did you save mine the other day?"

I nod, and we stand there looking at each other. I wonder if he thinks I'm cute, and I feel my cheeks start to burn again. "Welp, I guess I'll see you later, Coleman."

"Be careful, Beth."

I'M HESITANT TO GO TO MY CABIN BY MYSELF, BUT AT SIX O'CLOCK, IT'S still plenty daylight. I grip my bear spray tight in my hand and edge up to the door, my back to the cabin. Nothing looks out of place on the outside or the inside, and I collapse on the couch to wait.

It's dusk when I hear a car approach, and I hop up to look. It's an official vehicle, but I still wait until I see him climb out before I open the door. He waves a hello and stretches, and I barely avoid staring as the black t-shirt he's now wearing pulls tight across his back. "That's a heck of a drive to make twice in a day."

"Yeah, it sucked."

"We won't go far since it's getting low light, but you want to give me the run down of where you thought things were happening?"

He puts on his tactical belt and throws what looks to be a badge around his neck. I grab my bear spray because you can never be too careful, even with someone who is carrying at least one firearm and his own bear spray. "I never saw the person, but from inside, it sounded like the screams were coming from this direction."

I point west, and we begin walking that way across the parking lot. "The car pulled up here and pointed its headlights that way."

We look at the ground, and I am vindicated at least by the tire tracks in the dirt. I don't blame him for glancing over at my truck whose tires have way too much tread to have made these, but I'm glad to have this one confirmation that I'm not crazy.

"Let's walk this northwest perimeter. Stay about six feet from me, and look for anything suspicious. Footprints, trash, that kind of thing."

We make a loop around the north and west sides of the housing complex in mostly silence. I stop a few times to inspect something closer, and so does he, but it's always something that doesn't matter, something a four-legged animal did. When we get back to the cabin, it's almost dark. "You care if I borrow some of your water for a shower? I brought a refill for you."

"Go for it," I tell him. "You hungry?"

"Starving actually."

"You like pasta?"

"Does it have meat?"

I laugh, reminded of my dad who doesn't feel any meal is complete without a good helping of protein. "No vegetarians around these parts."

I've got the chicken cooking and the pasta water started when he knocks on the door to be let in. "It's Fisher."

I don't look at him when I let him in, hurrying to get back to the stove. "You want something to drink? I've got water and diet Dr. Pepper."

"Honestly, diet Dr. Pepper sounds great."

"Cans are in the fridge, ice is in the ice chest by the back door. Cups are in the—" My words stall out when I take in his face. "You shaved."

He shrugs. "I got tired of you calling me Doc Holliday."

"I only called you that twice."

"I've only ever met you twice, so who knows how many times it could've added up to?"

I can't help but laugh at that as he grabs a cup from the cabinet next to me. "Besides, I've always thought myself a little more Augustus McCrae than Doc Holliday."

"Then you should've left the soul patch off," I say, still laughing at this grumpy yet funny park ranger who seems to be a better sport than I first thought. "To be fair, with your dark hair, I probably would've called you Tom Selleck."

"How about you call me Fisher like everyone else does?"

"Fisher who was fishing the first time we met." He settles

me with a stare that tells me this isn't the first time someone has made the jump between his hobby and his name.

"How about we compromise, and I'll call you Coleman?"

He grunts in what I think is agreement.

After dinner, he goes outside with me and offers to help with the dishes, but I make him stand guard while I take care of them. After we dump the bucket of water down the vault toilet and both use the facilities, he says, "I have a key to the other building, so I'm going to grab my stuff and head to bed. Thought we'd get up early and get to it."

"Wait, you're staying over there?"

"Where did you think I was staying?"

"If you're over there and something happens, I'll be over here and have no way to contact you."

"You want me to stay in your cabin?"

"You're not gonna, like, try anything are you?"

"I think I can refrain," he says, sarcastically, and I'm not sure if it really stings or not because neither of us seem serious.

"Hey, your boss thinks I'm cute," I remind him and head back inside, "and just your luck—the futon is pretty comfy!"

He drops his bag next to the ice chest, and I fold my hands together. "It feels more awkward now that we're actually in here."

"Yep."

"I'm exhausted, so if you're okay with it, I'm going to go on up and try to sleep."

"Goodnight, Beth," he says when I've put my foot on the first step.

"Goodnight, Coleman."

This time when I wake, there's a hand over my mouth. I gasp and prepare to scream, but then Coleman is whispering in my ear. "There's something outside."

He moves his hand, but he stays crouched next to me. "What? Did you hear them?" I hiss.

"I'm not sure what woke me up, but I heard someone or something walking by that other cabin. When I got up to look, I didn't see anything, but I saw movement in the trees. I want to go out there, but I need you to the lock the door behind me."

"No, absolutely not. You're not going out there."

"Why am I here if not to investigate and figure out what is going on?"

"I thought you were here to protect me and investigate tomorrow. In the daylight."

I'm sitting up now, holding my comforter across my chest.

"I need to go. It could be whoever was chasing that poor woman last night."

"What are you going to do if you find them?"

"Arrest them."

"I don't like this."

"Neither do I, but come on. I need to go now before they get away. You lock up behind me and keep an eye out best you can."

I notice when I go to follow that he has his vest on again and his gun on his belt. I hope he needs neither, but I'm glad he's being cautious. The vest will protect from a bullet and maybe a little from a bear.

Our eyes meet at the door, and if this was a movie this would be the moment we kiss, that moment before the hero goes after the bad guy. But he just nods, and I just pat him on the shoulder as he turns to go.

I lock up behind him and watch as far as I can see in the dark. It's cloudy, so it seems even darker than the night before. I catch a hint of movement as he comes around the front of one of the other buildings, but then he disappears again. I scan the trees, hoping to see something, anything that might tell me what is out there, hiding in the woods, but I mostly see darkness and the hazy shadows of where pine trees hover.

Movement to the right. Is that Coleman? It was gone into the darkness as soon as I noticed it. I stare until my eyes start to burn and finally let myself blink. I don't feel as scared for myself tonight. I'm more worried about what happened to that girl in the woods, what could happen to Coleman out there alone. I wish I'd gone with him.

It's barely a few minutes later when I see his form walking back towards my cabin. He's not hunched in his previous sneaking body language, his gun looks holstered, he doesn't look like he's worried about anything. I open the door right when he reaches the porch, and he hangs his head as he passes through.

"It was a moose calf."

My shoulders drop, but he still looks tense. "Why aren't you relieved?"

He shrugs out of his vest and unwinds the holster from his body, laying them both on top of his bag and his gun on the end table by the futon. "I woke you up, scared you—hell, I scared myself—all over a damn moose."

He collapses onto the futon and rubs his face. I can't help it. I start to laugh. The absurdity of it all, the chance that the night after I'd heard something traumatic going on in the woods, a moose would wander through. "At least it wasn't an angry moose."

He grumbles something, and I sit down on the other side of the futon from him. "Hey, don't feel bad, for real. Something human was roaming the woods yesterday, so tonight when you heard something, it's natural you thought it might be human again."

"I'm glad I didn't walk up on Momma Moose. That would've been all I wrote." I nod in agreement. Moose are as dangerous, if not more so, than grizzly bears because they are massive and can be aggressive, especially cows with a calf.

"Silver linings."

He kicks his shoes off and sets his feet up on the coffee table, slouching down to get comfy. I put my feet up too, and we both take a deep breath at the same time. We glance at each other, and this time, he busts out laughing along with me. Finally, we are quiet, and then, we are asleep.

THERE'S A CRICK IN MY NECK WHEN I WAKE, AND I GROAN AS I TRY TO stretch it out. The sun is creeping through the windows, and though I don't see Coleman on the couch next to me, I smell coffee percolating in the kitchen, so he can't be too far. Instead of waiting to run into him in an awkward, morning after we slept next to each other on a futon moment, I sneak up to the loft to change clothes. I go ahead and put on my uniform pants and a tan, NPS sweater to go to work after we search. It'll be chilly first thing.

Coleman is leaning against the kitchen counter, cup of coffee in one hand and phone in the other. "You get on the Wi-Fi?"

"Yeah, it's slow, but I was able to check my email."

"Thanks for making coffee."

"You bet. You ready to go for a walk in the woods?"

"Let me drink a little bit of this first."

I carry my coffee to the bathroom which I've been using to get ready in the morning, even if there's no water. I am fairly simple in my preparation. A good, thick moisturizer to combat the dry, mountain air. Sunscreen to protect against the sun at ten-thousand-feet elevation. A braid to keep my hair out of my face. I only wear my hat when I'm officially on the clock.

"So what's the plan?"

"We'll grid search as best we can with two people. Look for anything out of the ordinary, anything we can use to identify what happened here the other night."

"And if we don't find anything?"

"Then we don't. There's not much more we can do. I'll ask around the construction site and around town a bit, but we don't have a crime on our hands if we don't have a person."

We set out about twenty feet from each other, walking north. There's less room that direction since it essentially dead ends with a hill so steep you'd have to scramble up it. We turn west and then back south, back and forth. After about an hour of slow, deliberate walking, we run into a ravine that falls to the north.

"Golly, I wouldn't want to run up on this in the dark." I mutter.

"I wouldn't want to be running in any of this at night," he adds. The ravine isn't too deep, but it's steep enough that if you ran off the side, you'd likely drop and then tumble down. Rocks and downed trees are thick enough there'd be no way to avoid them if you fell in. We can see down into it, and there isn't any sign of life. Or death.

We skirt around, continuing our search and jump a bedded mule deer buck who takes off, bouncing as they do until he's out of sight. We've both stopped to watch him. "I love to watch them hop."

"Yeah, me too," he agrees. I'm about to take a step forward, but he calls me over. "I don't know how much farther we can really go. We've already been out here for over two hours. Let's go back to the cabin and drive down the road a bit. Maybe we'll see something that'll give us a clue to the car."

He must see the protest on my face because he adds, "I don't want to give up either, but it's a needle in a haystack to find anything out here without better clues."

He's right, I know he is. I have no idea where the sound actually came from. The mountains and the cabin could've warped that. But the way the car aimed, I really thought this was the right direction.

"I'm a grown man, and in full disclosure, I was scared in these woods last night too."

I turn in a circle to take it in. Trees everywhere, both standing and fallen, rocks and boulders popping up unexpectedly. You can't see the road anymore from where we're standing, can't see the cabins. We can faintly hear the Soda Butte, but it's barely loud enough to lead you to it. If you were out here at night, there's any number of hazards that could maim or kill you in minutes, and that's not even counting the animals.

We cover new ground on the way back to the cabin but don't find anything. "Before I head out, let's drive down to the first trailhead. There's a picnic area, maybe they stopped there."

We see it at the same time when we're pulling into the parking area and both speak up. "Do you see that—"

"Is that a sleeping bag?"

He parks, and we leap out of the truck, both hoofing it past the picnic tables and up the hill to where an aqua blue sleeping bag is bunched up on the ground, shredded by what was likely a bear. The leaves next to it are flattened like a tent was set up, but there's nothing else to tell us what happened here. If she'd run from here to my cabin, it would've been at least three quarters of a mile.

Coleman picks up the sleeping back and looks through it. A protein bar wrapper falls out. "There's a name on the tag. Like someone took it to camp and wrote their name on it, so it wouldn't get stolen."

"Can you read it?"

"Sarah Calvin."

We put it in the backseat of the truck and drive towards cell service. It takes getting to Cooke City and stopping at the top of town to get enough service for him to get a call out. When he gets off, he says, "Sarah Calvin lives in Red Lodge. She's twenty years old and has obtained backcountry permits from the park in previous years."

"So you have her contact information?"

"Yes."

"So we can try to find her?"

"I will, but we can't leave the gate open, or we might run into another situation like this."

I know he's right, but I hate having to stay home. "How will you let me know what you find out?"

"You should be able to get a message since you'll be on Wi-Fi."

"That's not the same."

"I'll find a way to get in touch."

THE DAY IS LONGER THAN ANY I CAN REMEMBER, EVEN THOUGH QUITE a few people come through the gate. I try to smile, to be upbeat for the guests, but I'm distracted, wondering what's happening, what Coleman found out. It's getting near closing time when I see a white truck approach, and I shove up the window to talk to him. "Did you find her?"

"Hello to you too."

"Cut it out. I've been dying to hear from you all day."

He holds up a grocery store bag from the passenger seat. "Can I have the keys? I'll cook dinner tonight."

"You're going to cook me dinner?"

"Yes, but I need to get inside."

"I want answers."

"I'll tell you when you get up there."

I want to throw the keys at him, but I hand them instead and harumph back into my chair to watch the last twenty minutes tick by.

The grill is already going by the time I make it up the hill, and he's putting what looks to be burger patties on. "Well?"

"You want to change clothes first? Relax a little?"

"No, I want you to tell me what happened!"

He chuckles and shuts the grill lid, hanging the spatula on the hook. He opens an ice chest that he must have brought with him and offers me a beer which I take but don't open yet. "I found Sarah at Prindy's Place Diner where she works."

He plops into the porch chair and kicks the other one in my direction, so I sit too. "Go on."

"She and her boyfriend and their friends like to camp, but last week she watched this scary movie where a woman is stalked in the woods by a bear and a man, and it freaked her out. They decided they'd sneak into the park when the gate attendant wasn't there and camp when no one was around, and she went along with it even though she was nervous."

"Oh gosh," I say, seeing the writing on the wall.

"They'd all been drinking, and she wandered out to use the bathroom and got turned around. She doesn't remember a whole lot, but she started running, thinking she was heading back to camp, but she was actually heading in the opposite direction. The boyfriend started chasing her to try and catch her before she got hurt. Probably scared her more, and a friend of hers got in the car and drove down the road to try to find her that way. She tripped, and the boyfriend caught up with her. They left the next morning just after daylight, probably right before you left."

"What about the sleeping bag?"

"They left it, so a bear must have gotten to it after they left."

It's a while before I say anything else. "I feel dumb."

"Why?"

"Because it was some drunk kid, and I thought she was being chased by a serial killer or something."

"She thought she was being chased by a serial killer, so you were kind of right."

I hold the bottle up to the chair and knock the bottlecap off before taking a long swig. "Kind of right."

"Lotta scary things roam these parts at night. For as scared as she was, she's lucky she didn't run into any of them."

"You're right."

"But I'm completely right, not like you, who's just kind of right."

I roll my eyes and take another drink of my beer.

"Whatever you say, Doc Holliday."

ALYSSA BOWEN BEGAN WRITING STORIES AS A CHILD UNDER THE OAK trees of southeastern Oklahoma but has long felt called to the West. She still writes stories but now from the northwestern part of the state where she lives with her husband, two dogs, and cat. She is an avid outdoorswoman and loves to spend time in the mountains with a fly rod, spotting scope, or book in her hands. Along with writing and exploring the outdoors, she loves being Mrs. Coach to her husband's university baseball team. She believes Yellowstone National Park is one of the most magical (and dangerous) places on earth and does her best to return every year. Her story, "What Roams at Night" is loosely based on an experience she and her husband had during a recent visit.

Alyssa has a bachelor's degree in English from the University of Arkansas and a master's degree in American studies from Northwestern Oklahoma State University. Her creative thesis, *A Girl Called Harvey*, was inspired by women in the West. You can find her on Instagram at @awelltraveledhomebody

10

Honeymoon Trip

Julie Fasciana

Yellowstone, 1933

Josephine Jacobson stood on the West Yellowstone train platform, gazing down from the railing. She felt the same rush of excitement she had on her previous visit. Even though that trip, ten years earlier, had been a working vacation where she'd been employed as a maid in one of the lodges, her time in Yellowstone National Park had been joyful.

Today, she was returning to the park with her husband, George, on a long-postponed honeymoon, yet she felt no joy. Only sorrow. And fear.

In her memories, it was always summer in Yellowstone, the backdrop to the mountains the vivid blue-green of the dense forest. In late September, the aspens and cottonwoods were on their way to their winter bareness. The leaves that remained whispered their farewells in yellow, dark orange, and brown hues.

She closed her eyes and breathed deeply. The scents of pine mixed with sulfur mixed with juniper welcomed her, letting her know that, even on this dark day, she was home. Yellowstone would bear witness to what she must do.

Yellowstone would understand.

George joined Josephine on the train platform's lookout point. "What a pity that Baby isn't here to see this. She would've loved it."

Josephine didn't bother to remind him that Mae wasn't a baby. He well knew how old she was. Damn well.

Besides, it wouldn't do to get into an argument now. "You're right. Mae would love it here. But this is our honeymoon."

George shrugged. "It's not like we're kids starting out. You're what? Fifty-seven? And, we're not even newlyweds. We've been hitched for six years now."

"Mae is having fun with her big sister."

George grunted. "Big sister who's old enough to be her mother. I don't know who you two think you're—"

Josephine turned to face him. She assumed it was her glare that stopped him from finishing the sentence. She said, "Mae loves postcards. I sent her one from Rapid City. I'll pick one up in the lodge after we settle into our cabin."

George chuckled. "Baby does love to get mail. I'll send her a card too."

Josephine hoped her returning smile reached her eyes.

Following wooden signs, George led them to the lodge. When Josephine had worked at the park, she'd climbed this trail hundreds of times. She could've been the one leading the way. Which is why she'd chosen this trail to perform the task she was about to carry out.

When the boulder she was looking for came into view, Josephine called to George that she needed to rest.

"For God's sake, Mother. I'm the one carrying this trunk of bricks."

"Keep going. I'll catch up to you." As she knew he would, George forged ahead without a backward glance.

Making sure no one was around, Josephine removed a glass bottle wrapped in a handkerchief from her carpet bag. Then she retrieved a photograph of George. On the back, she'd written, "This is him. Burn. JJ." She formed the photograph into a tube and stuffed it into the bottle, plugging it shut with the handkerchief. She tucked the bottle behind the rock, half-burying it with handfuls of dirt, scrubby grass and dried leaves.

In a final phone call before Josephine left for the trip, her friend Cora had suggested the hidden photo as a way to ensure that, if she or her sister, Annabelle, encountered George at the lodge, they would recognize him and make sure he didn't see their faces.

Satisfied that only someone who knew the bottle was there could find it, she hurried back to George.

Josephine and George were the only occupants of the lodge restaurant that evening. It would soon close for the season. George took a sip from his cup. He took great pride in being a teetotaler. His night cap was always coffee, never whiskey.

Ironically, Josephine wished that he was one of the drunkards the women in her family were attracted to. If he had been, everything she and the girls had to do tonight would be easier, perhaps even unnecessary.

Josephine's thoughts wandered to 1905, when almost a spinster at age twenty-nine, she'd felt lucky to meet and marry handsome Axel. He'd turned out to be a drunkard who couldn't keep a job. In spite of his violent temper, or perhaps because of it, Josephine gave him a daughter she'd named Lillian, followed by four sons. When Axel headed off to Alaska to make his fortune as a gold miner, long after the rush had ended, Josephine was relieved to see him go. She was not sorry when a letter arrived from the mining company informing her that he'd "lost his way" on his return to his barrack and was found frozen in a snowbank. The letter didn't say where Axel had been returning from but Josephine knew it was the saloon. She didn't bother responding to the letter's request for instructions on what to do with her husband's remains. If she had, it would have been along the lines of, "Leave him in the snow. At least a bear will get a meal out of him."

As her own mother had done after the early death of a drunkard husband, Josephine took a job as a maid, or housekeeper, as the refined lady of the house preferred to call her. The position paid Josephine enough to rent a tiny house on the property where her children lived and where she returned each night to tend to them and sleep for a few hours.

After working for the lady for six years, Josephine made a decision. She was taking a vacation, albeit, a working one. With the older boys self-sufficient enough to care for the younger ones and Lillian old enough to serve in her place as housekeeper, Josephine applied for a summer job as a maid in Yellowstone National Park. The work would be back-breaking for a woman her age, but how else was she going to scratch her traveling itch and see the country?

Her sons were not happy about the idea, and Lillian didn't want to work as a housekeeper. But to Josephine's surprise, her employer supported the trip. "What a grand idea! Have a marvelous time, my dear."

JOSEPHINE'S REVERIE ENDED WHEN THE YOUNG WAITRESS CAME TO their table with the coffee pot. "Have a refill, George," Josephine said. "I'm going to look at the postcards."

At the front desk, Josephine ignored the postcard stand.

Instead, she told the clerk at reception she wanted to leave a note. He supplied her with a sheet of paper, envelope and pen. Josephine wrote, "Arrived. Cabin 5. Burn this. JJ." Then she sealed the envelope, addressing it to "Cora or Annabelle."

The clerk scanned the envelope. "One of them will be working tomorrow morning. We'll make sure they get the message."

In fact, Josephine knew but didn't tell the clerk, one of the girls would pick up the note that night.

SOON AFTER ARRIVING AT THE PARK FOR HER SUMMER AS A MAID IN 1923, Josephine became friends with two robust sisters, Cora and Annabelle, who'd grown up on a ranch and married ranching brothers. Both were tall and strong. "Strong as men," Cora liked to say, pumping her bicep. Cora, two years older than Annabelle, was bossy but jolly with it. Annabelle, kind and quiet, was her sister's right hand. When their ranch fell victim to drastic price declines, the sisters had taken jobs as maids at the park.

In late August that year, Josephine, Cora and Annabelle had unexpectedly been given the same Sunday off. At six o'clock that morning, Cora burst into the bunkhouse. "Wake up, sleepyheads. We're going to do some sightseeing like normal tourists. We're not letting Josie leave the park without seeing Old Faithful."

"Breakfast first," Annabelle said, her voice rough from sleep.

"Of course!" Cora pulled three egg sandwiches out of her knapsack. "And I got more for lunch, too. But hurry up. We gotta be at the lodge by seven to catch a ride with Jasper."

Jasper's job at the central lodge where they all worked was

to deliver provisions to the outlying lodges. He waved to the women as they hurried up the hill from the bunkhouse. "Good morning, ladies! Fine day to be off work."

Jasper's wagon let them off near a wooden sign indicating that Old Faithful was four miles away.

"Four miles?" Annabelle said.

"We do twice that much every shift," Cora said.

The women hiked, occasionally pointing out a sight in the deep valley below. A mama grizzly lumbered alongside a stream while her cubs struggled to keep up. The women watched in awe as an enormous paw reached into the stream and pulled up a fish which she ate whole.

Annabelle was the first to spot a herd of grazing bison.

"They look like toys from up here," Josephine said.

"And it's darn good thing we're that far away from them," Cora said. "Those brutes could kill us if we got in their way."

As they came around a bend, the rotten egg smell of sulfur overtook the atmosphere.

"That stench means we're getting close," Cora said.

Another wooden sign at a turn-off pointed one direction for Old Faithful and another for Sulphur Caldron.

"What's Sulphur Caldron?" Josephine asked.

"You don't want to know. I seen it once." Cora shuddered. "The presence of the devil was there, I tell you. I felt lucky to get out alive."

Finally they arrived at Old Faithful. A group of people standing as close to the geyser as the park rangers allowed began counting down the seconds until the eruption.

"Sixty, fifty-nine, fifty-eight..."

Josephine said, "I thought the geyser goes off at varying intervals. How do they know when to start counting?"

"People who study the geyser recognize the signs of a big eruption versus a normal one," Cora said. "Bigger ones take longer to form. But no matter the size, Old Faithful's eruption is a sight you'll remember for the rest of your life."

And indeed it was. Josephine found herself clapping at the majestic plume of water. "Is this a big or normal eruption?"

"This is normal. The big ones get as high as them old trees." Cora pointed to a stand of pines in the distance. "But a normal is still...well, you saw it. More'n a hundred feet, I'd guess."

"I felt a few drops of hot water," Josephine said.

"Me, too," Cora said. "Some people have gotten burned pretty bad. That's why I had us stand back so far."

That night as the three friends sat at the campfire they'd built outside the bunkhouse, Josephine said, "I've only known you girls a couple of months but I'm already wondering what I'm going to do without you."

"Don't you have no friends back home in St. Paul?" Annabelle said.

Josephine shook her head. "After I finish working at the house and taking care of those boys, I don't have energy for anything." She chuckled. "If I had an extra hour, I'd take a nap."

Cora laughed loudly. "A nap? What's that?"

But Annabelle's face was serious. "Friends are important, Josie. If I didn't have Cora, I don't know what I'd do. Go crazy, more'n likely."

None of the women was as shocked as Josephine herself when she began to cry. Sob. Loudly. As if her heart was breaking. Because, in fact, it was.

Josephine gazed into the fire. She didn't dare look into the girls' eyes. She was about to tell them something she'd never told anyone. Her mother, God rest her soul, knew, of course. But no one else.

"I had two younger sisters," Josephine said. "When we

were thirteen, eleven, and eight, my mother put us in an orphanage. She'd married a drunkard, too, and, when he died, she had to work as a maid." She glanced at the girls who were listening intently. "You could say I followed in her footsteps." She chuckled at her joke but this time neither sister laughed in return.

"You said you *had* two sisters," Annabelle said. "What happened to them?"

Josephine took a moment to answer. When she did, her voice was choked with tears. "We got sick a lot in that orphanage. There were always germs brewing. My little sisters weren't as strong as I was. They both got pneumonia, six months apart. I sat with them while they choked to death."

Josephine's face was in her hands as she let out all the tears, all the sobs, all the screams, that she'd never released for the little girls she'd loved so much. She'd been strong for them, strong for her mother who survived only two years after the loss of her younger daughters. No one had ever been strong for Josephine.

Until today. As Josephine regained her composure, she was surrounded by Cora on one side, Annabelle on the other. They were holding her, patting her back, telling her they loved her.

"What were their names?" Annabelle asked.

"The older one was Patricia. I called her Patsy. Nina was the little one."

"Pretty names."

"They were pretty girls and so sweet. I never told anyone about them before."

"I'm glad you told us," Cora said.

"And you got two sisters again," Annabelle said. "Me and Cora."

"That you do," Cora said.

Two weeks before her working vacation was to end, Josephine received a telegram. Her employer's cable said that Josephine's services would no longer be required. Her children could stay in the small house until her seasonal position at the park ended, but, upon her return, they must find new lodgings.

A brief letter from Lillian explained everything. She was expecting a baby. The father was the refined lady's not-so-refined husband.

Cora and Annabelle saw Josephine off at the train station. The women hugged and promised to keep in touch. "Just write to Cora or Annabelle at Double P Ranch, Idaho Falls. We'll get the letter."

"I'll do that," Josephine said, giving each of them another quick hug as the train approached the platform. She hadn't told the girls about Lillian's situation, but they noticed she hadn't been herself since the telegram arrived. They asked what was wrong, of course, but when she told them everything was fine, they let her be. She loved them for that.

On the first day of what promised to be a dismal journey back to St. Paul, a tall man of approximately Josephine's own age, boarded the train at Bozeman, Montana. His name was George Jacobson. He traveled the country as a steam engine repairman, and was on his way to his next assignment in Chicago.

George was a quiet man who enjoyed reading. He handed over his copy of *Innocents Abroad* when he finished it. Josephine, in turn, erased the answers in the collection of puzzles she'd cut out of the newspaper so he could work them.

He kept a cribbage board in his tool case and tried to teach her the game. They both knew he could find a better match in the club car. But teetotaler George disdained the company of men who drank.

Josephine and George sat together even as passengers departed and empty seats became available. Occasionally, when napping, George's head would drop onto her shoulder but she didn't wake him. She liked the sweaty, hard-working smell of him. Upon waking, he would apologize profusely, blushing like a boy.

When the train pulled into St. Paul's Union Station, George carried Josephine's suitcase to the main concourse. With a tip of his hat, he made his way back to the train for the remainder of his journey to Chicago. Josephine never expected to see him again.

Lillian had a baby girl she named Mae. Josephine convinced Lillian not to give up her dream of going to nursing school. She took her granddaughter in, telling anyone who asked that she was the baby's mother.

Eventually, Josephine found work in a yellow brick mansion on Portland Avenue in Minneapolis. The house had once been majestic but was now in a sorry state. In exchange for room and board for the youngest boys and baby Mae, Josephine worked for next to nothing. But at least she hadn't been forced to put her children in an orphanage.

Her fancy title was gone as well. She was back to being a maid.

As the years in Minneapolis passed, Mae stayed with Josephine, whom she called Mama. Lillian married and had another child, a son. Her eyes watered every time she saw Mae but she and Josephine agreed it was best if the little girl continued to believe Lillian was her sister.

Josephine's wages gradually increased as her need for room and board decreased. Now only Mae lived with her on Portland Avenue. The younger boys had been parceled off to live with the new families formed by Lillian's marriage and that of her oldest son. Second son, Jonathan, had received a full scholarship to Carleton College.

When Mae was four years old, Josephine scraped together enough money to buy her a red wool coat with a white fur collar for Christmas. Josephine never had the luxury to be clothes-proud, either for herself or her children. She knew it was partly her pride in managing to purchase such a lovely coat for Mae that caused her to take the little girl to as many Christmas events as she could. She was parading her. Mae didn't mind. She loved the attention. The small girl with dark curls and large brown eyes drew smiles everywhere she went.

Josephine had saved the best event for last as a surprise for Mae. On Christmas Eve, she used her afternoon off for a trip to Dayton's Department Store to see the famous windows.

As Josephine had expected, Mae was delighted. "Oh, Mama, look! Ballerinas!"

"Yes, that's a scene from the Nutcracker Suite. Do you remember us listening to the music on the radio last Christmas?"

Mae shook her head.

"We'll listen again tonight."

Josephine felt a tap on her shoulder. She turned to see George Jacobson, a bit grayer, but otherwise the same as when she'd last seen him.

"Mr. Jacobson! What a surprise!"

"So, you remember me. Please call me George."

The way he looked at her warmed Josephine's cheeks.

HONEYMOON TRIP

Bending down on one knee, he gazed into Mae's eyes. "Who is this lovely young lady?"

"This is Mae, my daughter."

George's face betrayed momentary puzzlement but he recovered quickly. "Aren't you a pretty one!" He opened his coat and retrieved a brown paper bag from his vest pocket. "I must have known I was going to meet you today. I bought these candy canes for someone but I wasn't sure who. Now I know." He held the bag out to her.

"May I take one, Mama?"

"Yes," Josephine said. "Say thank you."

"Thank you," Mae said.

"Take them all darlin'. I bought them for you."

Mae's eyes grew wide. "But I never saw you before."

George chuckled at the earnest little girl. "Christmas is a time for magic."

He stood up. "I'm staying at the Marquette. They do a nice lunch there. May I buy you ladies a meal?"

Josephine had planned to take Mae on the streetcar to Lillian's house for Christmas Eve supper but Lillian wouldn't mind if they didn't come. Now with two young boys to play Mrs. Santa for, her hands were full.

In the New Year, George was to start a job in Nashville. When she and Mae said good-bye to him over cocoa at the Marquette coffee shop on New Year's Eve, Josephine once again believed that would be the last time she'd see him. Instead, the fifty-two-year-old woman and the fifty-six-year-old man began courting through letters and weekly phone calls. George always asked after Mae.

One day, George wrote that he would be on the Empire Builder on March 15, pulling into the Milwaukee Road station in downtown Minneapolis at eight p.m. He hoped Josephine and Mae would be there to meet him.

When Josephine, Mae, and George were snuggled in a booth that night in the depot coffee shop, George produced a box from his vest pocket. It contained a gold ring with a small diamond. "Will you marry me, Josephine?"

"I will." Smiling, George slipped the ring on her finger.

He reached into his pocket again, this time extracting a second box which he opened and held out to Mae. She stared at it. "I saw this pretty little ring and thought of you. That's a pearl, honey. Your birth stone."

Happy tears stung Josephine's eyes. She couldn't imagine what a bachelor with a steady job saw in her. But she deserved some good fortune after the years of hardship. And so did little Mae.

IN 1932 GEORGE took an assignment for the CENTRAL RAILROAD of New Jersey. On a sweltering Jersey City evening in July, George and Josephine sat on the fire escape of their apartment.

"I'm finally ready, Mother," he announced banging his Coca-Cola bottle on the steel landing.

"Ready for what?"

"To stop traveling. It's a fine life for a bachelor but not for a family man." He pulled a letter out of his shirt pocket. "A friend of mine wrote me that there's a tidy little house in Grand Rapids, Minnesota, that has been foreclosed on. I can get it for a song. And the paper mill there could use a man with my skills. I'm taking you and Mae back home to Minnesota, Mother."

"What's Grand Rapids like?" Josephine said. "Shouldn't Mae and I see it first?"

"No need. It's a pretty town. On the Mississippi. Lots of

lakes nearby. I'm heading there tomorrow to find out about the job. I'll send for you and Mae."

Disappointment rose in Josephine's chest. Her wanderlust was still with her. George's traveling life had been a joy for her. They'd lived in six states in five years. While George worked, she'd enjoyed exploring their adopted hometowns with Mae.

Mae, sweating through her short, cotton nightdress, came onto the fire escape. "I'm so hot, Mama. Can I sleep out here tonight?"

"No, darling, it's not safe. But I've got some ice cream. I'll bring you a scoop. What about you, George?"

"Sure, I'll take some, Mother."

When Josephine returned to the fire escape, she found George and Mae sitting side-by-side on the stairs, their bodies pressed together. George had wrapped one of Mae's curls around his finger. "You're going to have your own bedroom with your own pretty bed. No more of this cot in the kitchen nonsense."

"Really, Papa George? Do you promise?"

George kissed the top of Mae's head. "I promise."

IN GRAND RAPIDS, WITH MAE NOW A THIRD GRADER, JOSEPHINE didn't have much to do during the day. She'd never expected to have a life of leisure and, now that she did, she wasn't sure she liked it. But she reminded herself of how lucky she was and found ways to occupy her time. She kept the small house spotless. She made sure Mae did her lessons. She walked the seven blocks to the business district for provisions every day. The line outside the soup kitchen was yet another reminder of her good fortune. She was glad that George enjoyed his own daily walks to the paper mill. A shiny new car parked outside the house would've rubbed salt in the wounds of the many who couldn't find work in the hard times.

She was also glad to have a phone. She called Lillian in St. Paul once a week, her one extravagance. Long-distance was expensive. "Can't she ever call you?" George grumbled.

One Saturday afternoon, as Josephine walked home carrying groceries for Sunday dinner, a rain shower came out of nowhere. Neighbors Albert Johnson and his wife, Louise, who lived in the big house at the top of hill, pulled up beside her in their powder blue Packard. "Josephine!" Louise called. "Hop in!"

Gratefully, Josephine did so. Minutes later she was at her back door, surprised to find it locked. She didn't carry a house key because she never locked the door, but she kept a spare underneath the cement flowerpot, now overflowing with purple azaleas. She attempted to lift the pot but she couldn't do it. She'd had no trouble lifting it a month ago when she'd planted the flowers.

Then she noticed that her hands were shaking.

She took a breath to steady herself, then lifted the pot and slid out the key. Leaving her groceries and pocketbook to get soaked in the rain, she climbed the stairs. Her hands still shook as she inserted the key. The sound of giggling came from Mae's bedroom. Josephine held her breath as she moved toward the sound. The giggling was becoming frenzied, hysterical even. Then she heard a shriek. "Papa George! Stop! That hurts!"

Josephine pushed open the bedroom door. Mae, dressed in the short Shirley Temple dress George had purchased for her at Maitland's Department Store, lay face down across George's lap. The skirt of her dress was up, exposing her naked bottom.

Josephine stepped into the room. "What's going on in here?"

"We're just having fun, Mother. Aren't we, Mae?"

HONEYMOON TRIP

Mae climbed off George's lap, her eyes trained on the floor. Her cheeks were wet and gleamed a bright angry red.

Josephine saw George's foot move, as if he were kicking something under the bed. She pretended not to notice. She was not at all certain what to do in this moment but antagonizing George didn't seem like good idea.

"George, dear, would you mind going outside and picking up the groceries and my pocketbook? I dropped them when I tripped looking for the spare key."

"Do it yourself, Mother. You're already wet."

"I asked you to do it. Please."

George stood up and headed for the door, scowling at Josephine as he left the room.

"Are you okay, darling?" Josephine whispered to Mae, who nodded. She kissed the girl's cheek. "Grab a set of clean clothes and head to the bathroom. I'll be there in a minute to help you take a bath."

"I'm nine, Mama. I don't need your help to take a bath. Besides, I always take my Saturday bath before bed."

"Please, darling. Just do as I say."

Mae opened bureau drawers and retrieved a clean set of clothes. When the girl was out of the room, Josephine bent down to peer under the bed. There, as she'd suspected, were Mae's lacy underpants.

They were stained with blood.

THE FOLLOWING MONDAY WHEN GEORGE WAS AT WORK, JOSEPHINE went to the Carnegie library. Even though the librarian was not a busy-body, Josephine didn't seek her help. The card catalog identified a holding called *Yellowstone National Park: A Geographical Treatise*.

Josephine located the book and sat with it at a table. Published in 1918, the book was written by a geologist who'd led early expeditions into the park. The treatise provided an alphabetical listing of every geological formation the teams had encountered, including the entry she was looking for: Sulphur Caldron.

The boiling pot of muddy sulfuric acid was sixty-by-one-hundred feet in diameter and approximately sixty feet deep with a temperature of 190 degrees. "The sulfur smell here was stronger than other pools the team encountered," the geologist wrote, "forcing many men to cover their faces with their handkerchiefs." He added that the caldron was "fraught with dangers brought about by the extraordinarily high acidity level, higher than any other thermal pool in Yellowstone. Simply put, the acid could destroy human flesh in short order."

That night after Mae and George were asleep, Josephine wrote a letter, ending it with, "Burn after reading. JJ." The next day she went to the post office to mail it. The address was "Cora or Annabelle, Double P Ranch, Idaho Falls, Idaho."

Josephine continued to share a bed with George, but now she slept with one eye open, making sure he didn't go into Mae's room. She made up for her sleep deprivation with naps when he was at work.

One day the trilling of the telephone awakened her. "Josie, this is Cora. Annabelle and I want to help you. We have a plan. I'm going to tell you what needs to be done on your end. You ready?"

Heart pounding, Josephine listened as Cora dictated a series of tasks. The final instruction was, "Don't contact us again until you arrange the trip."

Josephine's days were busy with preparations. She ordered a huge trunk from Montgomery Ward, which arrived when George was at work. She dragged it to the shed. She told

George the family needed a vacation and asked him to take off a week in late September.

"But Mae has school."

"She needs a break, too," Josephine said.

On the last Thursday of September, Josephine called Lillian to ask if Mae could stay with her for a few days. "If I put her on the three o'clock bus, will you meet her?"

"Today, you mean?"

"Yes. Today." Josephine hadn't intended the urgency that came through in her voice—she didn't want to alarm Lillian—but it had the desired effect.

"Of course, Mother."

"Thank you, honey," Josephine said. Then she set to work preparing George's favorite meal of pot roast with potatoes, carrots and onions.

When George arrived home from work that evening, Josephine presented him with the train tickets and confirmation of their stay in a cabin near West Yellowstone Lodge.

"There's no ticket for Baby," he said.

"She's taking her vacation in St. Paul with Lillian."

George's eyes narrowed. "You made all these arrangements without even asking me?"

"I wanted it to be a surprise for our anniversary."

"We were married in March."

"I mean the tenth anniversary of when we met on the train coming home from Yellowstone."

George stared at his plate, his appetite seemingly gone.

Josephine had cried rarely in her life and she had never pretend-cried. Now fake tears gushed out along with snuffling and gasping. For Mae's sake, she could be Mary Pickford.

George moved to her side of the table. He patted her shoulder. "There, there, Mother. Don't cry. We'll go."

Wiping tears from her eyes, she smiled up at her husband. "Thank you, dear."

Convincing George to go to Yellowstone had been the final task. The next day she would send the girls a telegram.

Cabin 5 was chilly that night but Josephine told George not to build a fire. "We'll be in bed soon," she gave as the reason.

At nine o'clock, George's typical bedtime, he opened the trunk. "Where are my things?"

"I unpacked. Everything's in the bureau drawers."

"For God's sake, Mother, we're only here for two days."

When George came in from the outhouse, he was wearing just his undershorts. He grinned at her as climbed into bed. "Since this is our honeymoon, I figured we'd do what newlyweds do."

Josephine forced herself to smile. "I want to do that, too, but…" She shivered but the lack of a fire was not the reason.

George grinned. "Get over here, Mother. I'll warm you up."

"A little later."

When she returned from her own visit to the outhouse, she was dressed in wool pajamas.

"You changed in the privy? How many times have I seen you in your altogether?" He looked at her feet. "You've still got your boots on."

"I'm cold."

"Why didn't you let me…Never mind!" George threw the detective magazine he'd been reading on the floor and turned off the lantern. "Don't wake me up when you get into bed."

Josephine had no plans to get into bed next to him that night or any other.

When George began to snore, she checked the clock: 10:30.

The girls would arrive in ninety minutes. She tiptoed to the door and unlocked it. Then, as Cora had instructed, she turned on the lantern and placed it outside the door.

At midnight, the cabin door opened. Cora, a rifle strapped across her chest, came silently into the room. Annabelle was behind her, carrying ropes and a tarp.

Cora nodded to Annabelle who moved to the bed and began wrapping the tarp around George's head. He stirred, then shouted, "What in tarnation...?" He struggled mightily against Annabelle. It took all the man-strength she possessed to hold him down. Cora moved next to them, placed the rifle against George's head and fired it. George slumped down. The tarp began performing its job of preventing blood from spilling onto the bed.

The girls made quick work of removing George's undershorts, sliding him off the bed and tying the ropes around his body. When they finished, they had made two large loops, one at his chest, the other around his legs.

"What are the loops for?" Josephine whispered.

"We don't need to whisper. George can't hear nothin'," Cora said. "Those are the handles that we'll use to drag him to Sulphur Caldron."

"I'll just grab my coat and—"

"You can't come with us," Cora said. "If anything goes wrong, you can't have no connection to us."

"If anything goes wrong, I'm taking responsibility."

Cora locked eyes with her. "Okay, then. Help us get him into the trunk."

Annabelle dragged George to the center of the room while Cora moved the trunk next to his body.

Cora and Annabelle each took a handle. "Get ready to support his back, Josie," Cora said. "On three."

"One, two, three," Cora counted. Seconds later, George's

body was mostly in the trunk. Cora adjusted him, folding up his legs at the knees and crossing his arms over his body. His head still hung out of the trunk. "Don't look, Josie," she said.

Josephine turned away, wincing at the cracking sound. She couldn't stop herself from taking a peek. George's head dangled at an impossible angle. Cora had broken his neck.

"Now, girls, take all those clothes out of the bureau and cover him up."

Cora and Annabelle lifted the trunk onto their truck's flatbed and secured it with a rope. Then the women took off in the rickety truck with Annabelle driving. They were headed for Grand Loop Road.

Josephine closed her eyes trying to shut out the horror, an impossible task. She opened her eyes when she heard soft crying. Cora!

"What is it, sister?" Annabelle said.

"He was a human being and I killed him. What if our Lord don't forgive me?"

"He'll forgive you. Men like him is sick. Killing them ain't no worse than putting down a horse with a broken leg."

"You make a good point, sister. Bless you," Cora said, followed immediately by, "There's the spot. Stop."

Minutes later, George's naked, rope-trussed body lay on the ground. Annabelle and Josephine put the clothing back in the trunk. If anyone should open it, they would see the belongings of a normal couple on a normal trip.

Cora lifted the trunk back onto the flatbed. Then she took out a lantern and handed it to Josephine. "Lead the way."

Sparkling stars illuminated the path as the women trudged down the trail on the cold, clear night. In the distance, coyotes called. Owls responded. The howling wind shook the trees, sending their remaining leaves fluttering to the ground.

At one point, Annabelle cried out. She'd stumbled and nearly fallen.

Josephine saw that George's body had become stuck on some rocks. She knelt down and moved the rocks out of the way.

Cora, breathless from exertion, said, "It's only a quarter mile but it feels like twenty-five dragging this fool." When they reached Sulphur Caldron, she removed a knife from her belt and cut the ropes. They rolled George to the edge of the pit, pushing him until his body slid in and a swirl of bubbles consumed him.

The area surrounding the caldron was a hellscape of steaming mud, dead trees and fog. The rotten egg smell roiled Josephine's stomach; she choked back vomit. She remembered Cora saying she'd felt "the presence of the devil" here. Josephine felt it, too. This was the right place for George.

She heard herself say, "Double, double, toil and trouble..." The line from *Macbeth* seemed like an appropriate farewell.

"The acid will destroy his body," Cora said. "Next spring, if his skeleton floats up, everyone will think he was some drunk who lost his way."

Just like Axel, Josephine thought. *Except that George was a teetotaler.*

Cora wrapped her arms around the others. "You two okay?"

Josephine, her voice cracking, said, "Thank you, girls. I'll never be able to repay you."

"Repay us?" Annabelle said. "We wanted to help you. You're our sister."

"That you are," Cora said.

On the train ride home, Josephine thought about her future. The little house was paid for but she would need an income. With luck she could find work as a housekeeper. Maybe the kind Johnsons on the hill could use her help.

What to tell Mae though? In spite of everything, the girl loved Papa George. Josephine decided on a version of the truth. He went down a bad path and didn't return. No one knew what became of him.

And, if Josephine was lucky, no one ever would.

Julie Fasciana's passion for crime fiction began early. As a child she skipped Nancy Drew and went straight to her library's Doubleday Crime Club selections. She continues to read and write fiction daily when she's not working as a technical writer or taking walks with her dog in her beautiful St. Paul neighborhood.

"Honeymoon Trip" is her third published crime short story. She is the author of "Missing," which is included in the anthology, *It was a Dark and Story Night, Dontcha Know* and "Makeover," a selection in *Cooked to Death Volume 4: Cold Cut Files*.

Julie dedicates this story to Anne Mureé with love and gratitude.

11

TERRACES
KATIE THOMAS

She entered the musty-smelling building with trepidation. *What am I doing here?* Vivian watched the random assortment of incoming seasonal employees, spilling into the orientation room in Mammoth Hot Springs Hotel. In all her life, Viv had never stopped at Mammoth, despite having grown up in nearby Livingston. She had always visited Old Faithful, the Firehole River, the falls at Yellowstone Grand Canyon. But somehow, here she was, attending her first day of training for a summer job as a housekeeper in Yellowstone National Park.

It was the day after Memorial Day in 1973, and summer season hadn't really begun. Snow was still visible in the surrounding mountains, and temperatures dropped down to the twenties at night. But new staff were encouraged to start as early as possible, to prepare for the busy summer ahead. Everyone was wearing the standard-issue maroon polo shirt and khaki pants. Viv's long black hair was tied back in a braid. She wasn't crazy about the outfit, but she was crazy about the man she'd followed to Yellowstone. Trevor had worked in the park the previous summer as a groundskeeper, had loved it, and had convinced Viv to join him this year.

In fact, several of their friends decided to join as well. Viv and Trevor had a close network of friends, whom they'd met during their freshman year at Lewis and Clark College in Portland, Oregon. The group had bonded over the past year as they roamed the Oregon coastline backpacking, camping, kayaking, whale-watching, and hot-springing. Most of the 20-year-olds had never been to Montana or Wyoming before, and they were excited to see the geysers and mountains as well as the bison, elk, and bears.

This last desire despite the fact that a young man had been killed and partially eaten by a grizzly bear near Old Faithful the previous summer. They'd all heard the story about the two hitchhikers who had gone into the park, set up an illegal camp on a hillside above Old Faithful, and proceeded to treat their campsite like a garbage can. They made a mess, left food scattered around the camp, and went down to the lodge's bar. When they came back around 2 a.m., they surprised a 250-pound sow grizzly. The bear charged one of the men, dragged him away, and ate both his legs and an arm.

Viv was contemplating this story when the head of housekeeping, a round, kindly-looking grandma-type with a large cloud of white hair and their same uniform, called the room to order.

"Hello, everybody, and welcome to Mammoth Hot Springs!" she announced. "My name is Flo Banta, I've been working for the park concessionaire service for 20 years, and I've served in every department. I'm your go-to for everything you need to know."

Flo went on to break down the steps of each day's work, her impressive bouffant staying firmly in place as she gestured and animated her lecture. She reminded Viv of Mrs. Claus – so jolly, apple-cheeked, and approachable.

At the lunch break, Trevor met Viv and their friends in the Employee Dining Room—the EDR. The building was park-service beige, like everything else designated for staff, and smelled of perpetual steam table. The food was cheap, and barely edible. But they loaded up their trays, sat down, and took turns talking about the various jobs they were about to start. Trevor was back in the maintenance department, Sasha was a hotel porter, Duncan was a busboy in the dining room, Alex was a waiter, and Nancy and Carrie were housekeepers with Viv.

"I just want to get out there and start backpacking," Duncan said. "The job seems fine. And it's only in the evenings, so I'll be able to be gone during the days."

Duncan reminded Viv of the images she'd seen of Jesus, except that his long hair and beard were red. He was short, stocky, strong, and had worked as a tracker in the Cascade Mountains the previous summer. Funny and charming, everyone adored Duncan. In particular, Viv suspected Nancy of being secretly in love with him.

Trevor agreed: "I have to work some weekdays, but not all. I'll go with you as much as I can."

Taking off his trucker hat, Trevor shook out his curly black hair and smiled at Viv with his brown eyes and friendly eyebrows. Viv melted a little bit; her love for him was no secret. Trevor had moved to Oregon from Phoenix, and they'd met in Geology 101. They'd been inseparable ever since. She loved that they were almost the same height and build, making their bodies fit perfectly together.

"Me too," added Alex, a tall Oregonian who had grown up with Duncan in Corvallis. "I'm hoping to make some decent tips this summer, because I need new stuff. None of this gear is cheap." Alex was the exact opposite of his best friend: blonde, introverted, and cerebral. Though he loved the outdoors, his face was usually stuck in a book. He was a good balance for the rest of them.

Nancy, a stout, strong-willed woman from eastern Washington who preferred the company of the boys and generally roughing it, cleared her throat. "I'm also here for the mountains," she reminded them. "I'll be out there every damn chance I get." Nancy had worked as a river guide and a wildland firefighter, always volunteering for the most backbreaking trench-digging work, and was happiest when covered in dirt and sweat.

"Same here," Carrie said. "This place is so amazing. I can't believe that elk just wander through town." Carrie was petite and southern. She'd grown up among the dripping heat and feral pigs of Louisiana, and was experiencing a bit of culture shock. It had taken some convincing from the others to get Carrie to agree to a summer in the park, but Viv could see she was excited and captivated by their surroundings.

Always the last one to comment, Sasha said dryly, "Yeah. Maybe the elk'll lead us on our hikes and show us the way." Sasha came from the unhappiest of homes and had a constant attitude, making her a bit out of place in their crowd. But after a while they all grew to love her, and it was mutual. She entertained them with her sarcasm and wit without even trying, her bedroom eyes and dark bob lending her a sultry, contrary manner.

"You guys are nuts," Viv told them. Having grown up in Livingston, she'd heard more horror stories about grizzly attacks than the others, and her parents had a friend who'd been attacked and survived. "I wouldn't sleep out there with the grizzly bears cruising everywhere. I'll hike with you, as long as there are trees to climb – but no overnights for me."

Viv and her friends quickly found plenty of ways to enjoy playing in the park. There were day hikes, fishing excursions, backpacking trips, and swimming in the Gardner River. They got to know their fellow employees and learned from Flo that the ubiquitous gopher-looking creatures were referred to as whistle pigs on account of the shrill little noises they made.

Everyone grew accustomed to the constant odor of sulfur in the air as they explored the Terraces, the unusual geothermal feature that attracted visitors to Mammoth. Chalky white layers of looming travertine deposits, some with rounded edges shaped by slopes and water volume, blended into browns and rusty oranges, giving the Terraces a soft, almost edible look. The formations particularly interested Trevor, who was majoring in geology. He often walked the Terrace boardwalks alone for hours, studying and taking notes about the combinations of carbon dioxide, limestone, and 170-degree water.

In the evenings, they all played cards, board games, or frisbee (while watching in disbelief as tourists tried to pet the elk), and often drove into the town of Gardiner for burgers at the Corral. But their favorite activity by far was soaking in the legendary Boiling River.

To avoid the crowds, and to get a thrill, Viv and Trevor especially liked to sneak out of their dorms late at night, hike down the steep and cactus-ridden hillsides, and dip into the swirling indigo water in the pitch dark. When they had the pools to themselves, they fooled around until one or both of them became paranoid about the bacteria in the water, and eventually went back up to the dorms. It was their place – such a magical miracle of nature, a hot tub in the middle of the wilderness – and even the threat of grizzlies didn't stop Viv from going as often as possible.

"Nancy?" Viv called one day, as she knocked on her friend's

door. Nancy's room was down the hall from Viv's, which Viv shared with Carrie, in Spruce dorm. Nancy roomed with Sasha, while Trevor, Duncan, and Alex shared a large room in Aspen, the men's dorm. Couples were only allowed to share employee housing if they were married. Being twenty years old, Viv was used to her relationship being subject to policies like these. *Besides, it's just for the summer,* she reasoned, as she knocked again.

Nancy came to the door. She'd been drying her hair, which was long, thick, and the color of maple syrup. "Sorry, I couldn't hear you over the hairdryer," she said. "Ready to go?" They were going to hike Bunsen Peak, a precipitous two-mile climb about five miles south of Mammoth. It wasn't challenging enough for Nancy, but she chose it for Viv's sake because, unlike her friend, Viv wasn't looking to push herself. She appreciated the beauty of the park, but preferred hikes on the less strenuous side. Nancy not only feared nothing but seemed to need to prove her resilience. But despite her tough-girl persona, Nancy was extremely gentle and loving deep down, a vulnerability which had drawn Viv to her when they first met.

"Morning, ladies!" Coming down the hall were Flo and her assistant, Victor Thompson, the general manager of housekeeping, who oversaw the daily operations. "Where are you two off to today?"

"We're going to Bunsen Peak," Viv answered. "Have you guys hiked it?"

"I have, yep," said Victor. "It's really nice. A bit steep, but great views." Standing there in his long-sleeved white button-down and tie, Victor struck Viv as a bit overdressed for the job – he was from San Diego and always looked as if he were about to enter a board meeting. But he treated the staff well.

Flo laughed jovially. "Not this old gal – can you imagine trying to tote this body up a hill?" She shook her frosty head.

"The last time my late husband, God rest his soul, tried to get me to hike, I says, 'Bill,' I says, 'I'll be waiting right here with doughnuts and coffee for you when you come back.' Course, that was back when I worked in the staff kitchen. Between baking desserts and cutting meat, it's no wonder I put on this extra layer. I wouldn't have been able to keep up. No ma'am, no hikes for me."

Everyone chuckled politely, and then they went their separate ways, Flo and Victor heading toward the housekeeping office, Viv and Nancy to Viv's blue 1969 Chevy pickup. Viv thought she saw Flo spit on the ground as they walked away, but immediately dismissed the thought – a woman like Flo wouldn't spit.

"I hope we see a griz," Nancy huffed, as they started up the trail.

"Dammit, Nancy, bite your tongue," snapped Viv. "You know how I feel about that."

Nancy laughed. "And you know we're like 100 times more likely to be struck by lightning. You should be more worried about rattlesnakes."

Whatever. Viv followed her friend up the switchbacks. She'd feel better if this hike were happening in Oregon, where she happened to know that the last recorded grizzly died in the 1930s. But slowly Viv relaxed as they passed other hikers, chatted, and took in the scenery. They had to pick their way around the abundant prickly-pear cactus, but were rewarded with brilliant wildflowers in all colors, and the occasional red-tailed hawk.

After reaching the top, the women stopped to drink some water and admire the views. Aspen and fir trees lined creeks in the valleys below, mixed with stands of lodgepole pines and spruce, forming a collage of greens. They could see a herd of antelope grazing in the tall grasses way down along the river, near a small gathering of bison. It was about 3:30 in the afternoon, and the sun was burning hot. They drained their water bottles and made their way back down. They were back at the dorms by 5 p.m.

"Well, I'm ready for a disgusting EDR dinner, how about you?" Viv joked. "I can taste the stale bread now."

Nancy replied, "Actually, I'm heading back out. I'm not tired, and there's still a lot of daylight left."

Viv felt a bit uneasy. "Are you taking the guys with you? I don't really like you going out by yourself."

"Naw, I'll be okay," Nancy told her. "I can run faster than a grizzly, and besides, I stink. They won't want to eat me."

"Hilarious, Nancy." Viv rolled her eyes and tried to evoke Sasha's sarcasm. "Well, be safe, and please come back before dark. You know I worry."

"You don't have to worry. I'll be fine."

But Nancy wasn't fine.

Viv and the rest of the group had their usual early EDR dinner, then Duncan and Alex headed to the dining room to start their evening shifts while the others went into Gardiner to pick up some beer. They came back to the dorms for what was becoming a regular poker game for whoever wasn't on the clock.

Around 7:30, Viv thought, *Nancy should be back by now.* But she told herself she was being paranoid. The game went on, a group of their co-workers from Spain joined in, someone brought in a guitar and began strumming and singing. By 10, when the sun had disappeared behind Electric Peak, Viv couldn't contain her anxiety.

"Trevor, where the hell could Nancy be? She should have been back hours ago." Viv was struggling to keep her voice level. Her gut told her that something terrible had happened.

"Don't worry, babe – I bet she's just hanging out in

someone else's room," Trevor answered, looking up from his *Roadside Geology* book. "You know Nancy, someone probably challenged her to arm-wrestle, and then she had to beat everyone on the floor." He laughed, and Viv almost joined him. That was just the sort of thing Nancy would do.

The others didn't seem particularly worried about her; they all seemed to think Trevor was right. One of their new Spanish friends, Miguel, said Nancy was the toughest woman he'd ever met. And Sasha reminded them that Nancy had wanted to check out the trails around Sheepeater Cliff; she'd probably just gotten excited and hiked farther than planned.

"I'm sure she'll be back any second," Sasha told Viv, sensing her friend's fear. "I'll give her a good lecture about not doing this in the future, when she comes to bed."

With nothing else to do but finally go to bed themselves, Viv and Carrie eased everyone out and Viv walked Trevor back to his room. She wasn't in the mood to go inside with him tonight.

The next morning, Viv and Carrie woke to someone banging on their door. "Wake up, everyone," someone shouted from the hallway. "Emergency meeting outside." It was 5:45 a.m. Their housekeeping shift didn't begin until 7. *What could the emergency be?* Viv thought, and then immediately knew. *Nancy.*

Gathered in the courtyard outside, Flo and Victor were taking a quick staff roll call, making sure everyone from housekeeping was there. The other departments were slowly trickling in, employees rubbing their eyes and still waking up as they stumbled toward the courtyard in pajamas and sweats. Chuck Barrett, the Area Manager, was addressing the crowd. Viv located Trevor and ran to him, trying and failing to maintain a neutral expression. Trevor could see her dread.

"For those of you just arriving," Chuck was saying, "we

have some very unfortunate news. One of our housekeeping staff, Nancy Greene, was found dead early this morning." Viv's throat released a strangled cry among the gasps of the group.

"Nancy's injuries are consistent with a bear mauling," Chuck continued, "and we suspect the same grizzly that killed a man at Old Faithful last summer." He continued speaking, but Viv couldn't hear his words. She suddenly felt like she was going to throw up, thinking about what she'd read about bear attacks and her friend dying in such an unspeakable way.

Trevor whispered, "Let's sit down, Vivian. You need to breathe." He eased her onto the lawn and motioned for Duncan and Alex to join them. Sasha and Carrie were already behind them, clutching each other and crying. Viv couldn't cry yet; she refused to believe this was really happening. Her stomach was in her throat and she felt paralyzed. Trevor's arm around her told her she was really here and this was actually happening, but she couldn't move. Viv was vaguely aware of Flo and Victor, coming to check in with them specifically – Victor knew these were Nancy's closest companions. Viv heard Sasha explaining to Flo that she hadn't been in the room when Nancy and Viv returned from hiking Bunsen, but that she knew Nancy had gone back out, alone. Flo made a sound almost like a laugh, but it must have been more of a grunt – obviously no one knew how to react to the horrible news.

The rest of the day was a blur. They were given the option of taking the day off, but Viv knew she needed to keep moving to stay sane. She alternated between shock, revulsion, rage, and heartbreak. Scrubbing toilets, she thought about whichever unfortunate staff had to inform Nancy's parents. Washing windows, she thought about what state Nancy's body must be in, and where it might be now (where did they take dead bodies from Yellowstone? To Gardiner? Livingston? Billings?). Sweeping porches, she thought about the bear, and what it must look, sound, and smell like. It had to be rabid, or injured, or something bad. Bears didn't usually kill humans unless something was wrong with them – unless, of course, it was a protective sow with cubs. And Chuck had said there was no sign of cubs.

That night, she and Trevor skipped dinner in the EDR. Like zombies, they finished their respective work for the day, showered, and met in Viv's room to figure out how to survive the long night ahead.

"How are we supposed to sleep tonight?" Carrie asked, lying on her bunk with her eyes fixed on the ceiling. "Or do anything normal again, ever?"

"Let's get some booze," Trevor said in a flat tone. "I need to not think anymore."

"Yeah." Viv felt like she was in a trance. "I'm never fucking going outside again, by the way, so one of you'll have to go get Sasha. Duncan and Alex won't get off work till late."

"Viv, come on. Don't be dramatic. I think we can safely cross the village in the daylight. Let's go together." Trevor took her hand, and slowly they walked with Carrie over to Aspen, to where Sasha was coming back from dinner.

"Whose turn is it to buy?" Vivian asked, not looking at them. "Let's find oblivion."

Soon it was mid-July. Nancy's parents had let them know that funeral services wouldn't be until September, back in Oregon. Viv and her friends were trying to enjoy the rest of their summer, trying to put Nancy's death out of their minds and carry on. There hadn't been any more reported bear incidents, which helped somewhat. But Viv was more hesitant than ever to venture away from their little pocket of civilization.

"Hey, Viv, let's go. They're waiting for us." It was Trevor, meeting Viv to drive over to Tom Miner Basin and collect

Duncan and Alex, who had gone out backpacking two days earlier. Viv wanted to tag along so she could see the area, another place she had never explored. A hot summer breeze swept through Mammoth even though it was only 9:00 a.m., and Viv was looking forward to a dip in the Yellowstone River on the way.

The narrow hills flanking the river were dry and brown. The July sun had turned this landscape into a desert, where sagebrush and rattlers flourished. But the Yellowstone River was full and wide, with people boating the rapids and fishing along the banks. Trevor drove past several fishing access points before stopping at La Duke, near Devil's Slide. After a quick skinny-dip, the pair continued down Highway 89 until they reached the turnoff at Teepee Creek.

"I can't believe those guys climbed Ramshorn," Viv said, staring out the window at the approaching mountains, hearing only the wind and occasional bird calls.

"Well, they tried – we don't know if they made it to the top," answered Trevor, looking over at her. "I'm sure they're capable of it, but you never know. Either way, I'm proud of them for trying."

"Yeah, me too," Viv agreed. "But I still worry."

"You don't need to, babe – there's Duncan right there."

Viv looked up ahead and indeed saw a figure running toward them, a figure whose red head and beard gave him away. But shouldn't there be a tall, blonde-headed figure with him? And why was he running?

Pulling up to the campsite, Viv could see panic on Duncan's ashen face.

"Oh my God, you guys, oh my God!" Duncan shouted, tears streaming down his cheeks as he flung the driver's-side door open and pulled Trevor out. "Alex is dead! Oh my fucking God, Alex is dead."

"WHAT?" Trevor and Viv both screamed.

Alex was sobbing, holding on to Trevor's arm as Trevor grabbed him by both shoulders.

"Duncan, hold on – calm down – what happened?" Trevor asked. "Where is he?"

"Look." Duncan pointed behind him, to Alex's blonde head just visible under a blanket covering his body. Food and gear were strewn about, like something had sliced into their packs and thrown it around. "I didn't know what to do; his chest is ripped up and I don't know what happened and – I left for a while to wash in the creek, then I came back and found him here, all bloody. I covered him up."

"Wait, no," Viv choked out, as they crept toward their friend's body. "This can't be him. This can't be happening." Her throat was closing up as she got closer to the body on the blanket. "Let me see his face."

"I can't look at him again." Duncan turned his head away. "It looks like a bear tore his whole stomach out."

"Holy shit." Trevor started trembling. "We have to call the cops."

Later, back in Mammoth, Chief Ranger Randy Walsh summoned Alex, Trevor, and Viv to meet with him and his deputy rangers in the Yellowstone Justice Center. A large, imposing man, Chief Walsh looked like he was made for the job with his thick gray mustache, square jaw flanked by long sideburns, turquoise bolo tie, and dark brown Stetson. His ranger uniform looked brand new, and his badge gleamed. Walsh spoke in the even manner of someone with compassion but who didn't tolerate duplicity.

"Okay, kids, let's start from the beginning," he said to them. "Tell me exactly what happened, from the time you set off on this excursion."

Duncan, who had gathered himself but was still noticeably

distraught, began. "Alex and I left two days ago to hike Ramshorn Peak. We've been planning it for months, since way before we got here. Trevor here drove us to the trailhead, dropped us off at about 8 a.m., and we started the hike."

"You notice anything unusual?" Walsh asked. "Any of you? Smells, weather, wildlife, other hikers?"

"No," said Duncan. "We only saw a couple guys that first day, on their way down, and they just told us it was a great climb and kept going. The weather was normal, hot – we saw some elk and a bald eagle. That second day, we saw two mountain goats from far away."

"I wasn't really paying much attention," Trevor added. "It was kind of early, so I was a little out of it. I just remember thinking it was beautiful out there and I wished I could join them, but I had to work. After work, I just hiked around the Terraces for a while, taking pictures."

"These other hikers," said Walsh, "any idea where they might have been from? Wouldn't hurt for us to talk to them," he told one of his deputies.

Duncan shook his head. "They looked pretty much like us – our age, look like they're outside a lot...but no, we didn't ask."

The deputy made some notes and mumbled something about trying to track them down. Shifting uncomfortably in her chair, Viv asked to be excused to use the bathroom. As she went down the long hall to the restrooms, she passed an office on the right with the door slightly ajar, a pale yellow light emanating from the crack.

"...little bastards. Every year, there's just more and more of them." It was a woman's voice, and Viv recognized it as Flo's. *What could she be talking about?* Viv thought uneasily, pausing outside the door.

"Here I've been busting my ass for 20 years, with no pay increase, and I'm expected to oversee these ungrateful little urchins. None of them are reliable; I can't expect any of them to finish out the season. If only I could stop the Park Service from hiring the ones who flake out. All they care about is playing in the great outdoors – none of them actually want to work."

Holding her breath, Viv tiptoed on down the hall. She didn't know who Flo was talking to, but she didn't want to hear any more. It was jarring to hear Flo being so negative. But she must just be venting, having a moment. *Everyone is human,* Viv told herself, *even Mrs. Claus.*

Back in the conference room, both Viv and Trevor shared their minimal observations, and Duncan finished his story of their uneventful hike, camping, and descent. "But when we got to the bottom, I went off to wash in the creek. A while later when I came back, I found him like that – his torso was literally shredded. He was dead."

"There's always lots of griz activity in the Tom Miner," Chief Walsh said, casting his eyes northward toward the area. "It's the risk you take out here. We've also been having problems with poachers. I wouldn't put it past those sons of bitches to rough up anyone who threatens their livelihood. We'll see what the autopsy says, but it looks like a bear attack to me." He paused, then seemed to remember something. "Either of you boys carrying any weapons?"

Duncan stared at Walsh. "I always have my hunting knife on me; just a habit from working in the backcountry last summer. I was a tracker and a guide."

"I need to ask you to turn that over to me, son," Walsh told him. "Just to cross it off the list."

"Sure," said Duncan, pulling the large, shiny blade in its leather sheath out of his side pocket and sliding it across the table by its antler handle. He hesitated, then said, seemingly to himself, "I never should have left him alone. I just don't understand how I didn't hear it."

By late August, Viv refused to recreate outside at all.

The temperature was starting to drop in Mammoth with the approach of fall. The large cottonwoods interspersed with the buildings were starting to shed their leaves, and the familiar taste of a nearby forest fire was in everybody's mouth. The elk rut had begun early, and bugling bulls kept the employees and guests awake at night with their strange, guttural calls.

The mood in the village was at once depressing yet phony; everyone knew what had happened, but the management acted like everything was normal. Chuck Barrett greeted employees in passing with the same happy-go-lucky grin he'd worn since the beginning of the season. Flo walked around muttering to herself, a bitter expression clouding her face, only to snap up and paste on a wide, forced smile whenever someone approached her. Even Victor didn't seem like his usual friendly self.

Staff had been strictly instructed not to talk about the tragedies with visitors. The concessionaire service was worried that sales would go down if tourists thought there was a rabid bear on the loose, and they were right. Despite the consistent population of morons who got too close to wildlife – a Spokane, Washington, man had recently been gored by a bull bison near Norris – the majority of tourists was cautious, and Park numbers had slightly decreased as news of the two unsolved deaths spread.

"Got your note, babe." Viv was at Trevor's door, holding the note he'd left for her in the housekeeping office. Her gray eyes surveyed the room as she pulled off her work boots.

Trevor was gathering his backpack and some clothes, stepping cautiously around Alex's now-vacant bunk, while Duncan, who had the evening off, sat staring at an unfinished jigsaw puzzle on the desk in front of him. Ever since Alex's death, everyone but Viv and their friends looked at Duncan with suspicion, and he'd had to sit through a second interrogation with Chief Walsh. It was starting to wear him down.

"Yeah, I wanted you to come with me," Trevor said, pulling on his sheepskin coat and zipping up his pack. "It's sort of chilly out; how about a soak before dinner?"

"Are you crazy?"

"No, I'm not. There's never bear activity down there. Besides, maybe it wasn't a bear. We don't know for sure."

Viv raised her voice. "Trevor, the Boiling River is just as wild as anyplace around here. I'm not taking any chances."

Duncan, suddenly alert, met Viv's eyes. "I don't think you should go."

"Well, I'm not going to, and neither are you," Viv told Trevor. "I'd like us to live to see our twenty-first birthdays."

"Vivian, you're being ridiculous. It's broad daylight."

"How does that help? Alex got killed in broad daylight."

"But he was alone," Trevor argued. "The Spanish dudes are already down there. Miguel said he'll wait until we show up. It's fine – I promise we'll be safe."

"My love, you can't promise anything." Viv's head hurt. She wished she could rewind time to when everyone was alive. "I can't stop you, but I'm telling you I don't want you to go."

Trevor shook his head firmly, slipping on his backpack. "I'm not going to stop living, just because people can die in nature. And you can't avoid life by hiding inside all the time. It's not healthy. I'm going." He took Viv in his arms, gave her a kiss, hugged Duncan, and marched out the door.

Five hours later, Viv was reliving the night Nancy disappeared. Trevor wasn't back. She stared out the rickety dorm window into the darkness. The Spaniards, who had returned from the river around 7 p.m., verified that Trevor had indeed shown up and joined them in the hot springs. They had hung out soaking together for a while, and when they'd exhausted their alcohol supply, Miguel and the rest of that crew trudged back up to the EDR for some food, leaving Trevor alone. Then they'd gone down to the bars in Gardiner, with Duncan.

"It's nine o'clock," Viv said to Sasha, who now spent all her waking hours in Viv's and Carrie's room. "I doubt he'd drink enough to pass out, and he knows I'm too scared to go searching for him. I'm freaking out."

"I'm sure he's just hanging out with other people down there," Sasha answered, pulling on a pair of faded yellow sweatpants and closing the window. "Brrrrrr. You know how social he can get."

"Unless..." Carried started to speak, then clamped her mouth shut.

"What?" Viv prompted.

"Well...I know how he likes to walk the boardwalks around the Terraces," Carrie said slowly. "It's getting kind of dark; an elk could have spooked him and –"

"God, Carrie, what are you saying? That he fell into the springs?" Sasha barked. "Don't be insane."

Carrie looked down. "I'm sorry. I'm just thinking out loud. Anything seems possible at this point."

Viv's heart was starting to pound. "I'm going to call Victor. I don't know what else to do."

As it turned out, there were policies in place to deal with missing employees. Usually searches weren't initiated when someone was gone for just a few hours, but under the circumstances, Chief Walsh was called in, and Viv and her friends were told to go back to their rooms and wait for any news.

The next morning, after a sleepless night of wrestling with potential horror scenes, Viv alone was personally summoned to Flo's office, where she was met by Chief Walsh, Chuck Barrett, Victor, and Flo. The room smelled of bleach and Windex, and Viv noticed the paint peeling on the room's one small window frame. Walsh told everyone to sit down at the battered wooden table, which was littered with Flo's files and loose papers. Viv felt her eyes well up before anyone spoke.

"Vivian," Walsh began, "I'm afraid we have some bad news." He took off his hat and paused, nodding at Chuck before looking around the table at three frozen, terrified faces. Flo was gripping Victor's hand on one side and Viv's on the other, her usually-cheery face fighting to stay strong. The room was silent, except for Victor gnawing on a pencil and tapping his foot nervously, and Viv's heart was thumping so hard she was sure everyone could hear it.

"Trevor Connelley was found unresponsive in the Boiling River at around 2 a.m. this morning. He was pronounced dead at the scene."

"No – no!" screamed Viv. She began sobbing uncontrollably, keeling forward over the table, her black hair falling over her face. She heard Victor inhale sharply and felt Flo's hand warm on her back.

Walsh took a breath and kept going. "The body was fairly gashed up – something got to him, and we don't think it was post-mortem. It looks like he may have been mauled and then bled out."

"Honey, I am so sorry." Tears spilled out of Flo's eyes as she took Viv in a huge, tender hug, her crown of white hair soft against Viv's cheek. "I know how close y'all were."

Chuck cleared his throat. "We've notified the next of kin; Mr. Connelley's parents are on their way here from Oregon now." He ran a hand across his forehead, then folded both together on the table in front of him and crossed his legs, as if he didn't know what to do with his limbs. "I'm so sorry for your loss, young lady. Chief Walsh here has bear traps set all around the area, and we're going to catch this son of a bitch grizzly. It'll be destroyed, I can promise you that."

Still weeping, Viv raised her head and asked, "Where's Trevor? Can I see him?"

"I'm sorry, that's not possible," Walsh replied briskly. "Mr. Connelley's body has already been transported to Bozeman, and is likely on the way to be processed up at Sunset Hills. You can reach out to his folks and see what their plans are – they might be able to get you in to see him. But I'm warning you, he'll look rough."

Viv wearily let her head drop again as her sobs slowed and she considered this. "What else can you tell me?" she asked. She blew her nose on the orange sleeve of her sweater, wondering how there were no tissues in a housekeeping office.

"Nothing at this time, other than the place and time of death," said Walsh.

"You found him *in* the river?"

"Yes, lying across some of the rocks that form the soaking pools," Walsh said carefully. "His legs were partially in the water, holding him there. It's lucky that whatever happened was within the pools. Otherwise the current would have swept him away."

"Was his backpack there?"

"It was. The only things inside were some clothes, a towel, and canteen of water."

Feeling suddenly exhausted, Viv said, "I need to go call my mom."

"Of course," Walsh answered. "Victor, can you escort Vivian back to Spruce?"

"Sure," Victor said quickly, putting his arm around Viv's shoulder's. "Come on, hon. It's going to be okay."

After they had left the room, Chuck turned to Flo. "There's something you should know," he said in a low voice. "We don't want it getting out, but in your capacity we thought it best to keep you fully informed. A hunting knife was found at the scene."

Flo froze. "What? A hunting knife?"

"Unfortunately, yes," Walsh said, his face grim. "It was just lying there, on the river's edge, not far from the victim's backpack. And it was bloody. We have reason to believe it didn't belong to him. We're sending it off to the lab to check it for fingerprints."

"Good God," breathed Flo, clutching her chest. "Who would do such a thing? And why? I can't..." Flo made an odd yelping sound, and then suddenly dabbed at her eyes, as if an afterthought. "In all my years here in the Park, I've never seen anything like this."

"Neither have I, and I've been a ranger for 27 years." Chief Walsh stood up, putting his Stetson back on. "We still suspect the same bear, but now we have to consider the possibility that these deaths are homicides."

A few days later, Viv and her friends were preparing to leave. Golden bars of sunlight streamed through the dorm windows as they gathered trinkets from the shelves, took down posters, and stacked books. After many long, tearful phone calls to their parents and painful conversations with each other, the group decided to call it quits. Their Yellowstone summer was ruined; none of them felt safe at all anymore.

The women planned to drive to Bozeman with Duncan first thing in the morning, where Viv was going to see them off at the airport before driving back to her parents' house in Livingston.

"How you doing, Carrie?" Viv turned to look at her friends, who were packing their duffels with clothes and camping gear. "Did you remember all your bathroom stuff?"

"I got it, thanks," Carrie answered. "Where do we turn in our uniforms, do you know?"

"Victor said we can just leave them on Flo's desk," said Sasha. "I feel bad. I can tell we're leaving them kind of high and dry."

"I think they understand," Viv told them. "I'm sure they've had people quit early before."

Around six, the women met Duncan and Miguel for one last dinner in the EDR. "I'm going to miss these soggy cucumbers and over-salty hotdogs," Duncan tried to joke, as they sat down. "This is so much better than the cafeteria at Lewis & Clark."

They all started to laugh, but at the mention of their college, they thought of Trevor, Nancy, and Alex. Viv, for one, hadn't given any thought yet to the coming fall semester in Portland; she couldn't think that far ahead. All she knew was that she wasn't sure she could stand to be there without them.

They ate silently for a while, before Miguel, who would be returning to Spain in late September, asked, "Do I still get to play poker with you all tonight?"

"I've got a better idea," said Viv. "How about a final walk around the Terraces before we go? In honor of Trevor?"

"That's a great idea." Carrie took Viv's hand across the table. "We should change first; there's still mosquitoes out there. I need sleeves."

After they'd all put on pants and long sleeves, Viv, Carrie, Sasha, Duncan, and Miguel reconvened in front of the sprawling old hotel. Duncan had brought them each a can of Miller Lite, which they opened and clinked together.

"To Nancy." Viv wiped tears away. "To Alex and Trevor. To you guys. I love you, and I'll always love them."

Everyone took a swallow, impeded by the sobs in their throats.

"They'll always be here," Carrie said quietly. "Their spirits will stay here, with the most beautiful land on earth."

"Dangerous, but beautiful," Sasha added, unable to shed her pessimism.

"Let's go." Vivian knocked back the rest of her beer, tossed the can in the brown, bear-proof trash bin, and started up the path toward the travertine of Opal Terrace.

In the dark, the group walked single-file up the boardwalk, following the route that Trevor had so often taken. Nobody spoke. The strong scent of sulfur was all around them, and they could hear coyotes yipping in the distance. The white layers of limestone gave off an eerie, glowing appearance as they approached the towering Angel Terrace. Then, a high-pitched cry pierced the cool air.

Viv whipped her head around, in time to see everyone else do the same – except Sasha. Sasha was gone.

"Sasha!" screamed Viv. "Sasha, where are you?"

"Did you guys see anything?" Duncan yelled, who was bringing up the rear.

"No!" shouted Miguel and Carrie, together.

Everyone spun around frantically, looking in all directions, but having a hard time seeing anything in the fading light.

"Check behind those bushes," Viv told them, pointing to some juniper stands. "I'm going behind these rocks." She carefully tiptoed off the boardwalk and slowly peered behind a large, lichen-covered boulder. Hearing a muffled sound, Viv's heart stopped. She took a few steps forward. "Sasha?"

There in the shadows, lying on her back and bleeding from the shoulder, was Sasha. She was holding her mouth and appeared unable to speak, and when she saw Viv, she removed her hand from her face, revealing swollen and bleeding lips.

"Sasha," Viv whispered, suddenly feeling the pressure of eyes watching her. She had to fight the urge to rush to Sasha's side and help her up, as it sunk in that they were all in imminent danger. With difficulty, Sasha gestured with her head to the wooded area behind them. Viv started to creep that way, her eyes darting between Sasha and the darkness ahead. Sasha nodded.

Viv approached a hulking sagebrush, so tall it was almost a tree. The hair on the back of her neck was standing; she could feel adrenaline rushing through her veins. She heard a low growl as she pushed back a wall of sage. And there, looking back at her were not the dull pupils of a rabid grizzly, but the beady eyes of a plump woman with white hair, crouching down low, a large hunting knife in her hand.

"*Flo.*" Viv halted mid-step, willing her body to keep moving. But she was too petrified to move. Suddenly, Flo lunged at Viv, the knife raised above her head, screaming, "You're next, you little harlot!" But before she could plunge her weapon forward, Duncan and Miguel jumped Flo – they tackled her and pinned her to the ground, causing her to drop the knife. Carrie grabbed it and ran to Viv, who was shaking but no longer immobilized.

Viv walked slowly toward Flo, who was squirming under the weight of the young men, and said, "Don't worry, Flo. We'll be going home tomorrow. And I think we all know where you're going."

KATIE THOMAS GREW UP NEAR YELLOWSTONE NATIONAL PARK, IN Bozeman, Montana. Family visits, field trips, and friends' birthday parties within the Park were a regular part of her life. She later attended Western Washington University, where she earned a double degree in Linguistics and English while living in a cabin at the base of Mount Baker. She spent her summers working in Yellowstone. The town of Gardiner, Mammoth Hot Springs, and the now-extinct Boiling River were especially influential in her life.

After exploring the San Juan Islands of Washington state, Katie returned to Bozeman where she now works as a freelance writer, writing about people, food, and the outdoors for *Edible Bozeman, Western Home Journal, Outside Bozeman, Montana Fly Fishing Magazine, Bozeman City Lifestyle,* and others. When not writing, Katie enjoys cooking, hot-springing, gardening, skiing, and hiking with her husband and their black Lab.

12

High Wide and Heinous
Lise McClendon

By the time the Federal Bureau of Investigation was called, the death was nearly three days old. It rankled Special Agent Lucy Arnold but it wasn't the first time law enforcement agents of the Park Service thought the FBI's services were unnecessary. They considered the death an unfortunate accident. But the more they dug into the case, the more confused they got. Thus, she got the call.

Not that she minded the long drive into Yellowstone National Park, or the majestic old lodge. Not a bit. The Old Faithful Inn made an iconic setting for a death. She wondered, stepping through the red doors into the vast lobby, crisscrossed with ancient, gnarled logs and centered with the massive stone fireplace, whether the man intended to send a message when he fell off the high balcony.

She craned her neck, wondering which balcony he had chosen for his—*pardon*—swan song. It might have been suicide but she doubted it as did the ISB.

The agent from the Park Service's Investigative Services Branch, her second on this job, pointed high up.

"There. The crow's nest. That's where he was working," Ned Reynolds said in his youthful baritone.

Lucy squinted. The crow's nest was some sort of tree house, a small structure four stories up from the lobby. "Way up there? Why?"

"I'm not sure. He told people he was writing a book about the Inn. Doing research. The PR guy said he liked to hold court, sign books, in sight but inaccessible."

That's weird, Lucy thought. "He's a famous author? Was?"

"Oh, yeah. Haven't you heard of him? Hiram Whyte? He's from Montana."

So was she, born and bred. She'd come back to the state a couple years ago after assignments around the country. "No. Was he a big deal?" That always made things more difficult. "Fans around? Paparazzi?"

"Not so much. Some fans were here for the book signing but they left. Just the PR guy now. His name is Riley Davis. He was helping Mr. Whyte with the signing earlier that day. It was over there, in the bar." He pointed to a room beyond the fireplace.

"Is Mr. Davis still here? I need to speak to him as soon as possible."

Reynolds promised to get the man to the police headquarters. They had set up a small command center in one of the local law enforcement offices across the parking lot.

"But first show me where it all took place."

After they walked the wooden stairs up to the third balcony, they continued along to the last set of stairs up to the crow's nest where they inspected the two chairs and tiny table wedged into a small space. They looked down at the lobby, a precipitous drop, and returned to the ground floor. Lucy asked to be pointed to HQ. Three days had gone by. The crime scene near the stone fireplace, taped off for a few hours until the body was removed, was thoroughly contaminated by now. A thousand tourists later? Nothing to see here, folks.

As she walked across the vast parking lot, stuffed to the gills with RVs, cars, and campers, she reviewed what she'd been told about the case:

- Smoke billows out of fireplace at seven-thirty in the evening, causing fire alarms to blare.
- Pandemonium breaks out. Screams heard from the gift shop.
- Visitors rush for exits.
- Hotel staff hits the panic button, alerting staff and everyone in guest rooms to evacuate.
- Cameras obscured by smoke.
- Man up in the crow's nest, famous author apparently, falls to lobby floor and breaks his neck.
- Quick-thinking bus boy throws a bucket of water in the fireplace.

Something bothered her but she couldn't pinpoint what it was. And it angered her that she hadn't been called earlier. But she had to put that behind her and concentrate. A smoky fire in mid-July? It did get cool here, even in summer. "Do they have closed circuit cameras?" she asked. Ned pointed out a solitary security camera for the entire lobby, obviously inadequate for police work, but there you go.

The balcony floors were varnished to a high gloss. Had they been cleaned recently? Who was in charge of that? Who was the last person Hiram Whyte had talked to up there?

Maybe this Riley Davis had some answers.

THE PUBLIC RELATIONS MAN WAS THIRTYISH WITH NONDESCRIPT brown hair, a couple days of beard, and the kind of glasses you'd see on librarians in the past, or perhaps John Lennon. He wore a neat button-down shirt, cargo pants, and hiking boots, and fidgeted in the chair in the outer office. Agent Arnold opened her door, paused to look him over, then called him inside.

He sat on the edge of the wooden chair and clasped his hands in his lap. She smiled and tried to get him to relax. "Mr. Davis. May I call you Riley?" He nodded stonily. "Can you tell me, did Mr. Whyte have any odd encounters during his days here in Yellowstone?"

"Odd encounters? No, I don't think so. I wasn't with him all the time though. I just helped him set up the book signing." He glanced at her. "And fetched him whiskies as needed."

"Was that often?" He shrugged. "How many drinks would you say Mr. Whyte had the night of the accident?"

He pursed his lips. "Four maybe?"

"Whiskey? Gin? Beer?"

"Whiskey."

"Tell me about the book signing." She held up Hiram Whyte's latest release, given to her by the ISB, a dark western hardcover called 'Six Ways from Sunday.' It featured a leather-clad man who looked half cowboy, half biker, holding a lariat arranged as a noose, against a fiery sunset.

"He was really popular. The publisher said he always sold tons of books at signings because he was so charming." He shook his head. "I liked him. But he didn't sell that many on Wednesday."

"Why was that?"

He shrugged again, blinking hard. "He wasn't so charming, I guess."

"Was there a big crowd?"

Riley shook his head. "He was mad about it. Blamed me. He was kind of a shouter."

"Were you angry about that—the blame, the shouts?"

"It goes with the territory."

"So there were unsold books. What happened to them?"

"Back in his room, I guess. I took them there after the signing." He looked up again as if considering what to say. "He brought them himself so I wasn't taking them with me."

"I was told he was famous. Is that true?"

Riley gave yet another shrug.

"Let's go look at his room, shall we?" Lucy rose and gestured to Riley. "A short walk will do us good."

BACK IN THE OLD FAITHFUL INN THEY DETOURED TO LOOK IN THE BAR where the signing had taken place. Almost deserted, it bore no traces of books or authors, just a long bar and round tables near windows looking out toward the geyser. They walked down a side wing to a room on a dim hall lined with red carpet. She unlocked the door and waved Riley inside.

The ISB had already searched the room and discovered nothing of consequence. The man took several prescription drugs, for cholesterol, high blood pressure, and the like. Typical for a man his age. The bottles had been taken into evidence, in case they were tainted. His clothes still hung in the closet. A suitcase lay open on a luggage rack. And piles of 'Six Ways from Sunday' sat on the small desk in the corner.

"You've been in here, right? Anything missing? Out of place?" She looked under the bed, threw back the covers, checked drawers, pawed through his suitcase.

"I'm not sure. I don't think so."

As she searched the room she kept up the questions. "Did he have family in the area?" No. "Where did he live?" On a remote ranch in the Big Open, a vast grassland in eastern Montana. "Wife or girlfriend? Kids?" Riley didn't know. The ISB had already told her he was single, long divorced, and childless. "Who will inherit his ranch, do you think?" A distant relative, Riley guessed. A sister was mentioned. Or maybe a cousin. Inheritance was always a motive. She made a note to dig deeper for an heir.

"Have you met any sister or cousin while you worked with Hiram? Did he ever arrive with a woman or a friend to one of his signings?"

"No, ma'am."

There was a framed photograph of the man himself, on a night stand. Who takes a picture of themself on business trips? He looked not that different from the man on the cover of his book, a leather jacket, chaps, black hat, standing in front of buff-colored horse, maybe a palomino. He had a black beard, going salt-and-pepper. He held the reins in one hand and glared menacingly at the camera. Quite the bad ass. Or so he'd like the public to believe.

She picked up a copy of his new book and leafed through it before setting it back on the pile. There was another book on the night stand. 'High Wide and Heinous' was the title. She'd read a Montana history tome in college with a similar name, only 'Handsome' not 'Heinous.' The author of this one was Leon Stands Alone. On the back cover was a photograph of the author, taken from the back so that you could not see the author's face. An Indian blanket over the shoulders, a cowboy hat, and one long black braid—no other identifying features. So maybe Leon Stands Alone was a pen name.

"You know this book? Was he reading it?"

Riley frowned. "Maybe."

"You do know the book though?"

"I've heard some talk. Some kind of scandal."

"Is it porn or something?" Lucy rifled through the pages, pausing on a chapter named 'An Embarrassment of Richard.'

"I can't remember, honestly."

She skimmed the preface. The book was a collection of essays written over twenty-plus years, apparently all about authors and their books. From the titles, they were not complimentary.

"Do you mind if I take this? He won't be reading it, will he?" It was rhetorical. Hiram was dead and Riley Davis had no authority here.

As they walked back to the lobby Lucy asked Riley where he was when the smoke filled the room. He explained he had been sent to the bar by Hiram for a whiskey and was just heading back upstairs with it when the alarms sounded.

"I turned and ran back down, dumped the drink, and ran outside with everyone else."

"Who else was up there with Hiram that evening?"

"Nobody."

"What's your theory? He panicked and slipped?"

Another shrug. "I guess." As Lucy turned to go back to the office he asked, "Can I go back to work now? I have a big signing next week in Helena, and the next day in Missoula."

She smiled and touched his arm. "Give us another day, Riley. We really appreciate your help."

REYNOLDS WAS WAITING WHEN SHE RETURNED. HE HAD A SANDWICH and a cup of coffee for her but more importantly, he had the CCTV tape queued up. They sat side-by-side in the outer office and he hit 'play' on his laptop.

"This is a minute or so before the alarms sounded." Ned

pointed at a man walking across the lobby. "That's your PR man, Davis."

"He told me he was getting a drink for Whyte, in the bar."

He did appear to be carrying a tumbler. He paused, halfway across the lobby, looked behind him, and continued out of the shot.

At least they could see the fireplace, she thought, squinting at the grainy, black-and-white video. A trickle of smoke appeared, skimming across the hearth. Then more, heavier smoke. A small child ran by and the smoke scattered, rising. A big puff of smoke appeared. There was no sound on the video but apparently somebody yelled 'Fire.' People started running across the screen. Most were headed for the main doors but with a building like this, there were many exits.

"Here's where the alarms went off."

The panic intensified, as did the smoke. In a short time there was nothing to see on the video, just smoke. They watched the blank whiteness then Ned shut it off.

"So no view of the fall," Lucy said.

"No."

She thought of the lobby she'd just walked through. "What started the fire?"

"It seemed to start from the ashes."

"Was there a fire laid in there that day?"

"The night before, they say. So maybe it smoldered."

Lucy sat back in her chair. "I was just over there. There was a mild smoky smell around the fireplace but nothing else."

Ned frowned. "You mean—what do you mean?"

"Wouldn't that much smoke leave a heavy odor for days? Or a bluish haze up in the rafters?" Lucy stood up. "Can you email me that tape? I have to make a call." She turned back. "Oh, who inherits his ranch?"

"We haven't seen a will yet," Ned said.

"Well, get on it."

In the office she picked up the post-mortem, already completed by the Teton County coroner in Jackson. Hiram had definitely broken his neck. But what was his blood alcohol? She ran a finger down the lab report. His BAC was 1.8%, well over the legal limit for driving. So it was a reasonable assumption that he could have lost his balance and tipped over the railing on his own.

It just seemed so convenient for it to happen while the smoke filled the lobby. Was he rushing down the stairs and slipped? She shook her head. No way was it a coincidence. She didn't believe in them.

She opened her email and found the video clip that Ned had just sent her. She attached it to a new email addressed to a friend who was an arson investigator. She wanted his opinion on the fire. She didn't tell him her suspicions. He knew what to look for.

Lucy drummed her fingers on the two books on her desk, Hiram's latest, the cowboy fantasy, and the book found in his room. She spent about thirty seconds doing an internet search for Leon Stands Alone. Not much there, some speculation but no revelations as to the real identity. On Hiram Whyte there was plenty. She skimmed his Wikipedia page, his publisher's page, his website. He'd been publishing for years, since his twenties and he was seventy-five when he broke his neck. His early work was championed by some big names in western literature. Even Lucy had heard of them, though she didn't read that kind of thing. He appeared to ride that glow for years, through extended droughts, like the ten years in the '90s when he published nothing.

Ah, she noted with a smile, he had attended her alma mater, the University of Montana. Quickly she texted one of her college friends who had stayed on at the University. Stella

Winsome—her real name even though it made her sound like a romance author—taught English literature.

'Urgent. Sort of. Can you zoom?'

Ten minutes later she was staring at her friend's pretty face, her red hair still curling around her freckled cheeks, just like in college.

"What's up, copper?" Stella asked with a smile.

"It's not exactly urgent," Lucy said, apologizing. "But I need some English Lit info. Do you know this writer, Hiram Whyte?"

"Yeah, I do. I did. He died, right?"

"I'm in Yellowstone, on the case, but keep that on the down-low. What do you know about him?"

"He got a Master's here when he was about thirty, I think. Way before my time."

"So what's the scuttlebutt? Was he a nice guy? Famous? Drinker? Womanizer? Plagiarizer?"

"He used to be famous. Now, drinker."

Lucy knew that already. What was she missing? She stared down at the two book covers. She held up Hiram's book. "Have you seen his new one?"

"Yeah. Maybe he posed for it."

"Good scowler?"

"Word was he had a terrible temper. But that he'd mellowed over the years."

"Anything weird in the rumors? Fraud, kiddie porn, gambling, axe murderer?"

Stella stifled a laugh. "Not that I heard."

"Okay." Lucy picked up the other book. "This was in his room. I assume he was reading it before he died."

Stella's eyebrows jumped. "Everybody's been talking about that. You know about it, right?"

"Tell me."

"Okay. For about, oh, twenty-five or thirty years, a parody story or a vicious essay would be published in some obscure magazine, usually about a Montana author. Every time, anonymously. All sorts of stories flew around about who was writing the essays, because they were really harsh. Like several well-known authors that 'Anonymous' skewered tried to sue him or her. Probably a man, by the way. Lots of misogynistic stuff, pretty vile."

"What magazine?" Lucy asked.

"I can't remember the first one. They got sued by one of the targets of an essay and folded. So Anonymous found a new magazine. Um, called *Hi-Line Whispers*, I think. Out of Sidney or somewhere."

Lucy was scribbling all this down. "So then the book collects them all and re-publishes them under this Leon Stands Alone name?"

"Right. So we all thought, okay, that's who Anonymous is. But who is this Leon character? Nobody's heard of him. There was an article in the college newspaper about the hunt for him last month when the book came out. I'll send you a link." Stella looked thoughtful. "The thing is, he was careful. He always changed the name of the author he targeted, just enough so he wouldn't get sued. Of course he got sued anyway for that one parody, which was awful. Suggestions of devil worship and weird sex. I'm not surprised the magazine went under."

"So what's your department's pool saying—on who he is?"

"There was a lot of talk about it being one of our own, maybe Russell Victoire. There was a clever parody of his western novel done by Anonymous around 2000. It was a funny one, not too harsh, and people thought he wrote it to distract from the attacks on other writers. I knew him, he could do it. Brilliant man."

"Russell Victoire," Lucy repeated, writing his name in her notebook. "What was the conclusion by the faculty?"

"Well, he died about seven years later and the pieces kept coming, like every two years. So it wasn't him."

"Okay, if I read you the names in this book can you tell me who they are slamming?"

Lucy began to skim each piece, picking out the names. There were fifteen essays or short stories but finding the fake name was always easy, right in the first paragraph. Stella rattled off the real people: Richard Wheeler, Edna St. John, James Crumley, Dorothy Johnson, Tindley Lamar, James Welch, Russell Victoire, and on through the fifteen pieces. Lucy wrote the names on a new sheet of paper, tore it off, and told her friend a million thanks before signing off. She walked to the outer office and handed Ned Reynolds the list.

"See if you can get basic biographical info on these people. Birth, death, marriages, publications. They're all writers."

"Sure thing. Oh, we got the will. He left everything to his horses. He wanted the ranch set up as a horse rescue operation. His sister lives on Park Avenue in New York and has no interest in the ranch. But he did make her executor of his literary estate, for what that's worth."

"Would that be a lot of money?" Lucy wondered.

"He had investments of about five-thousand dollars and a couple hundred in his checking account. His last advance was less than a thousand. So probably not."

No motive there. She frowned, sitting behind the desk again. There had to be something, some clue, some lead. There always was if you dug deep enough. These two books. They had to be key to this case. Hiram was reading 'High Wide and Heinous.' What if Hiram Whyte himself was Leon Stands Alone? One of those writers he savaged might have figured out who he was and was angry enough to do him harm.

She looked on the copyright page of Hiram's western. The publisher was Stardance Books out of Helena. She called the office. It rang at least ten times. She almost hung up when a breathy voice said, "Hello. Stardance Books."

Agent Arnold introduced herself. "I am leading the investigation into the death of your writer, Hiram Whyte. My condolences. Whom I speaking with?"

Her name was Amanda Jensen, assistant publisher. The head man was her husband, Randy, out of office.

"Tell me about Hiram, Amanda. What was he like to work with?"

"Oh, I don't like to speak ill of the dead."

"I'll remember to be good then. But how about you tell the truth about Hiram? For the FBI?"

"Oh. Ah." She gulped. "In that case I can tell you he was a pain in the ass. He never liked what we did for him, always complained. The covers weren't right. The books were late. We didn't advertise. Always some excuse why he didn't sell."

"Did you mention the writing as a factor?"

"Randy did. But, well, you see—Hiram was an investor. He sort of keeps—kept us afloat." She muttered, "Not sure what we'll do now."

"Did he publish under pseudonyms, Amanda?"

"What? I don't think so."

"Did he have other publishers?"

"I never asked."

"Did he use the name Leon Stands Alone?"

"What?"

Lucy stared at the other book cover, flipping it over to the so-called author photo. "You folks didn't publish the book 'High Wide and Heinous?'"

"Goodness no. I've heard terrible things about that book. Nasty things."

Lucy gave Amanda her phone number and asked her to call if she or Randy remembered anything that might help with the investigation.

The agent opened the first pages of Leon's book. The copyright was listed as Stands Alone PLLC, and the publisher was Gold Nugget Press. She did an internet search for the publisher and came up empty. Same with Leon Stands Alone. Only some sales pages for the book. No bio. No Wiki. No website.

In her inbox was the email from Stella. Lucy downloaded the attached article titled, 'Who Is Leon Stands Alone?' The gist of it was that the college reporters had looked high and low for this person, possibly a Native American, maybe living on one of Montana's seven reservations or nearby in Wyoming or Idaho. Or possibly a failed writer with a grudge—but there were so many of those that any search would take months.

Nobody knew anything about Leon. The article mentioned that no one had ever outed 'Anonymous,' the original author of the essays. Speculation in the last paragraph was that Leon was a pen name and that the vicious nature of his writing had made Fake Leon afraid for his safety. Or at least his reputation.

So, no help there. Her phone pinged. A text from Gary, the arson investigator.

'Was there smoke residue on furniture? Lingering woodfire smell?'

Lucy replied, 'not much.'

'Looks like a smoke bomb. The kind photographers and magicians use. Not real wood smoke.'

He sent a link to an internet store. She imagined some kind of fireworks of the cherry bomb variety but quickly realized she was mistaken. These were hand-held gadgets that made smoke from little canisters of liquid dry ice for incense imitations, Halloween gags, romantic portraits, and so on. Would the canisters make enough smoke to fill a six-story lobby? She watched a video on the site. The smoke crept across a tabletop exactly like the smoke had slithered over the hearth in the surveillance video.

"Dammit." She was next to Ned again. "Did you search the fireplace?"

He looked startled at her tone. "We sifted through the ashes. They were gummy from the water but there was nothing in there."

"So you searched only the bottom of the fire box?"

He frowned. "Did we miss something?"

"Come on. Bring your flashlight."

Fifteen minutes later Lucy had commandeered a bed sheet from Housekeeping and laid it over the remains of ashes in the fireplace. Ned had balked at lying down in the filthy fire box with its decades of ash and black. What a wuss. Lucy pulled on gloves and climbed into the cavernous fireplace. She turned on her back, scooting back to the deep recesses of the stone structure. She flicked on the flashlight.

Ash drifted down on her face. She blinked to clear her vision. Maybe Ned had the right idea. This was a disgusting job. But when she pointed the flashlight into the corners of the firebox, where the stone lined it, she knew she was right. In one corner something stuck out, a black tube. She tugged on it gently and wiggled it until it came loose. Out came a length of black tubing attached to a cylinder about eight inches long. A smoke bomb.

She set it on her chest and pointed the flashlight at the other nooks and crannies. It was hard to discern dark tubing among the blackened stones. But there—what was that? She poked at a crevice, glad she'd worn latex gloves. A chunk of creosote fell on her shoulder. She tugged on the object. Slowly it gave way, gray with soot. Another smoke bomb.

"Here." She handed it to Ned.

Were there more? The amount of smoke in the lobby suggested there might be. She kept prodding. The last contraption emerged from the right upper corner, hidden behind a protruding stone. Lucy inched out of the fireplace and sat up, holding the other two smoke bombs, her upper body black with ash.

She held out her hand and Ned passed her the third one. "Who's in charge of fireplace maintenance? Get them in my office. Now."

Ned peered at her. "Ah, you might need a shower first, ma'am."

When Lucy Arnold emerged from the rest room, patting her face with paper towels after a quick, inadequate wash, a middle-aged man in a brown janitorial uniform sat in the outer office. He stood, looking nervous, his graying hair a mess and his hands grimy.

Ned piped up. "This is Freddy Fairweather. He's in charge of the fireplace most days."

Lucy waved him into her office where he sat on the wooden chair, holding a knit cap. She rounded the desk and sat down. "Freddy. There have been some foreign objects found in the fireplace and we need to know what you had to do with them."

"Foreign ob—" He frowned. "Ma'am?"

"Bring one in, Ned," Lucy called. The ISB agent laid one of the smoke bombs in a plastic bag on her desk. "Smoke bombs, Freddy. Did you place them in the fireplace?"

His eyes widened as he stared at the gadget. "No, ma'am."

"Did you work on the eighteenth? That was Wednesday." He shook his head. His day off, he said. "What about Tuesday? Did you build a fire in the fireplace on Tuesday?"

He glanced at the corner of the ceiling. "Let me see. Yes, I did. It was a special request by that writer."

"Hiram Whyte?"

"That's the one. He wanted atmosphere for his party."

Lucy looked at her notes. "His event was on Wednesday. Not Tuesday." She frowned at Freddy. "Who exactly did you speak to about the fire, and when?"

"Mr. Whyte. That young fella."

"Mr. Whyte was over seventy. Did this young fella have little spectacles and brown hair, five-nine, around thirty?"

"That's the one. He found me on Tuesday, about noon. I was cleaning out the ashes. We don't usually have fires in the summer. But sometimes."

After Freddy left, Lucy sat, wondering what Riley Davis was up to. Why had he passed himself off as Hiram Whyte? Had Freddy mistaken the day of the signing? Why would Riley want a fire? What did that have to do with the smoke bombs?

She walked out to Ned's desk. "Find the CCTV for the night before the death. Was anyone screwing around in the fireplace? And get those smoke bombs to the lab."

"How are they triggered? Remotely?" Ned asked. She nodded. He continued, "We searched the trash cans in the public areas and found a small remote."

"Send it to the lab too. What did you find out about those writers?"

Ned grabbed his list. "Out of fifteen, twelve are deceased. Of the other three, two live on the East Coast. The last one is in a nursing home in Billings." He handed her the sheet. "Not much help, I'm afraid."

At her desk she stared at the names of the writers still alive. She flipped open Leon's book and read the Tindley Lamar entry, a parody of a romance novel, all throbbing bits and sweaty groping—pretty rank stuff but not insulting. Tindley was the one in the nursing home. The other two living writers, the only ones with a chance of not having an alibi, were in their 80s and subjects of weak parody as well. If these pieces angered them enough to commit murder, they had thin skins. Lucy sighed. Maybe she was on the wrong track.

Her stomach rumbled. Eight o'clock already. She grabbed her jacket and went to find food. After a quick dinner she collapsed in her room in Snow Lodge, exhausted. Her mind refused to shut off so she read a few more entries in Leon's book. How immature—how petty—do you have to be to collect all your hate pieces like a sixth-grade slam book?

At ten o'clock she texted Ned: 'Did anyone do a background check on Riley Davis? Need complete bio.'

THE LEGENDARY GEYSER WAS SHOOTING OFF AS SHE PICKED HER WAY across the parking lot to the command center early the next morning. *Old Faithful: the tourist attraction that never sleeps.* Sleep, for Lucy, had been uneasy. Too many unanswered questions. Sometimes her subconscious spewed out an answer but not today. The poisonous words of Leon Stands Alone, whoever he was, rattled in her head. But his identity was cloaked in that fake smoke.

Ned was already behind his desk in the outer office. He looked a little rough this morning but he had put the coffee on at least.

"Davis background check?" She muttered as she poured the inky liquid into her mug.

"On your desk."

She turned, grimacing at the taste of the coffee then putting on a smile. "Thanks. I hope you got some sleep."

He sighed. "A little."

"We're closing in, Ned. I can feel it."

He grunted as she pulled her door shut. She needed to figure this out, and *now*. Two sheets of printer paper sat in the center of the blotter. She leaned over them and read quickly. Then she popped up again and leaned out the door.

"I need more than a criminal sheet, Ned. I need his parents, sisters and brothers, grandparents, colleges, hometown, everything. Can you get me that?"

Time to cut to the chase. Back at her desk she called the Inn's reception manager and asked for the room number for Riley Davis.

"It's B-205, ma'am. But he checked out. Just dropped the key here before six."

Dammit. "I need to get into his room. Send a guard. Don't let Housekeeping touch anything. I'll be there in five." Lucy grabbed latex gloves and stepped out. "Coming with me, Ned? Davis has flown. We need to search his room."

"I've got the CCTV ready for you," he said, standing.

She handed him gloves. "Search first."

ROOM B-205 STOOD OPEN WITH A SECURITY GUARD STANDING AT THE door. Lucy nodded to him as she flashed her badge. Inside it was apparent that Riley Davis was one tidy dude. The bathroom was immaculate. His room looked barely used. The search was quick but thorough. Ned and Lucy had almost decided to bag it when Ned reached a long arm behind the night stand. "Got it."

Lucy took the small white bottle. On the label it read '60 ML Fog Machine Vegetable Glycol - Propylene Glycol Non-toxic Smoke.' She smiled at Ned. "Bingo."

She called in the APB on Riley Davis. Wanted for questioning at this point. Hopefully they could catch him before he left the park. If not, somewhere in Montana. She gave Ned a high-five as they slipped the bottle into an evidence bag and stripped off their gloves.

Back in the office they watched the CCTV from the night before the accident. A janitor in a knit cap and dark uniform rolled a garbage can in and began working on the fireplace at the strange hour of one in the morning. The lobby was shadowy and dim. There were still a few people around but nobody paid him any attention as he disappeared halfway inside the fireplace for long minutes. His face was obscured, never toward the camera, but Lucy thought she saw a reflection of eyeglasses as he dumped the ashes in the can and left the scene.

Stella Winsome, her professor friend, called minutes later. "Have you seen the news? Somebody outed Leon Stands Alone. He was your victim, Lucy. Hiram Whyte. That cagey bastard."

"Who outed him?" Lucy said while she googled his name. *The Missoulian* newspaper popped up: 'Mystery author who defamed others revealed.'

"It says 'credible source.'"

"That's hardly definitive." Lucy paused, reading the article as it refreshed itself. "Wait, there's an update."

Stella gasped. "His sister! He told her about his fake Indian name and she put it together. She said, 'He always was an incorrigible brat.'"

Lucy said thanks and hung up. She didn't have time to gossip. Where was Riley Davis? She paced her office, caressing her cell phone, willing it to ring. She waited two hours before Davis was picked up by the Montana Highway Patrol near Livingston. He had been slowed by a bear jam near Norris Junction then pulled over for speeding in Paradise Valley and arrested.

The bottle found in his room tied him to the smoke. But

what tied him to the murder, if in fact it was a murder? It was still circumstantial, even if they could prove he set off the smoke bombs. The smoke was non-toxic so that was likely a misdemeanor for malicious mischief. He did have opportunity going for him, on those stairs. It couldn't have been difficult to nudge a drunk over the balcony. In the smoke and panic no one would be the wiser.

After the arrest Ned finally finished the biographical report on Davis and rushed it in to her. "His grandmother was Edna St. John. From the list." He pointed breathlessly at the family chart. "She died about twenty years ago."

"How did she die?"

"It just says 'nervous breakdown.' But you know what that means."

Twenty years ago. Lucy picked up 'High Wide and Heinous' and leafed through to the essay with the character named 'Edie Saint-James,' originally published in 2002. This was the piece that got him in trouble. It was no wonder Hiram got sued. He barely obscured her identity. An essay so vicious and hateful that the magazine folded rather than defend Mr. Anonymous.

Lucy held a finger on the title. 'Smoke and Mirrors: Edie Picks Up a Pen.' She showed it to Ned then closed the book, staring at the cover.

"'Heinous' is the only honest word he ever wrote."

RILEY DAVIS KEPT HIS COOL DURING HIS INTERROGATION—FOR ABOUT twenty-four hours. Then the anger and bile that had built up in him over his grandmother's passing spewed out of him. He had visited Hiram Whyte at his ranch as part of his job and discovered the original manuscripts for the hate pieces. Then he had planned a grandson's revenge in the most sensational way he could imagine.

"Edna had a flair for the dramatic," he said proudly, at the end of his confession. "She would have liked it."

Lise McClendon is the author of over 30 novels of mystery and crime, including the Bennett Sisters Mysteries and the Jackson Hole series featuring art dealer Alix Thorssen. She has published a number of short stories including one in the prize-winning anthology, *The Obama Inheritance*. She has served on the national boards of Mystery Writers of America and International Crime Writers/North America, and on the faculty of the Jackson Hole Writers Conference.

She lives in Montana near Yellowstone National Park, her inspiration for this book. Learn more at lisemcclendon.com

13

YELLOWSTONE AWAKENING:
A LEGEND ARISES
CHERYL FALLIN

An icy wind, laden with the whispers of forgotten souls, swept through the skeletal branches of the beetle ravaged pine grove. As the last of the day's sunlight disappeared, the full moon peeked over the snowcapped sentinels of Yellowstone National Park, enshrouding the wilderness in an eerie pallor.

Dr. Erica Starlight shivered. From the moment she was born, Yellowstone had enveloped her in its magic and wonder. But something was off in this vast wilderness. For the past five years working as a geologist for the Department of the Interior, she had faithfully recorded the predictable geothermal heartbeat of Yellowstone. Suddenly, over the past month, new geysers erupted daily, spewing their steaming fury and consuming visitor boardwalks.

Old Faithful, once a steadfast feature of the park, had transmuted into something ominous. Its scalding water and billowing steam rose with an increasing and unpredictable frequency. Spectral images danced in the spray of each eruption as though counting down to some supernatural reckoning.

Erica patted Timber, a wolf with snow white fur and her loyal companion. "I'm glad you're with me tonight."

Growing up exploring Yellowstone with Timber had been one fun adventure after another. It was only in the last few years that Erica realized having a six-foot long and four-foot-tall wolf as a companion could make for a fairly lonely existence. The simple fact was that people feared Timber. Despite her reassurance he was a gentle giant, whom her grandmother had raised from a pup, nobody but her boyfriend and colleague, Dr. Justin Andrews, dared approach him. Normally Timber stayed at the lab when she ventured out to collect samples, but the park had closed to visitors a week ago after six new geysers destroyed the majority of the boardwalks around Old Faithful and three tourists got burned.

Erica bent and took a sample of the runoff from Old Faithful's latest eruption. She shook it and deposited it into her field test kit. The small analyzer whirred to life and ran the sample through a battery of tests.

The comm on her wrist vibrated. Erica flipped it on and Justin appeared on the video screen.

"Erica, there's something weird going on here. I finished collecting the Fairy Falls samples. You're right, the iodine level in the river is rising."

Erica's analyzer beeped. She shook her head. "The sulfur levels in the runoff from Old Faithful's last eruption are sky high, just like the levels in Grand Prismatic Pool and Castle Geyser. Even the air feels off." She took a deep breath and glanced at the night sky. "It's like the old legend Grandma used to tell around the campfire."

"Ooh, I heard some of those. Which one? The story of the

headless bride haunting visitors of Old Faithful Inn or the one about the Sirens playing music across Yellowstone Lake?"

"Neither. I'm talking about the legend of the evil that lurks under the geysers of Yellowstone."

"I haven't heard that one." Justin wrinkled his nose, scrunched his forehead and chuckled. "I don't put much stock in those old ghost stories."

"I don't know. They used to scare the heck out of me." A heaviness fell over Erica even as the hairs on the back of her neck tingled. She missed Grandma and her stories. It had been a year since Grandma had passed away but that didn't make the hurt any less. "Maybe I'm letting my imagination get the better of me, but something weird is going on in the park. Something from which legends are made."

Justin laughed again. "Legends maybe, but there's a scientific reason for everything. We just need to find it."

"You're right but some days I wish we had ancient spirit warriors to make the geothermal activity chill, and get our park back to normal."

"No spirits. Just us." Justin smiled and peered off into the distance. "I noticed a new geyser shoot up about fifteen minutes ago. I'm going to check it out."

An uneasiness fell over Erica. "I don't think you should go alone. Give me a few minutes. Timber and I will come with you."

"Erica, don't be ridiculous. It will only take two seconds. Pick me up in the jeep at the trailhead. I'll meet you there after I record the activity and get the evidence we need." Justin cut their communication.

Erica packed up her equipment, slung her backpack over her shoulder and headed to the parking lot. "I'm almost starting to believe those old legends." She patted Timber as he trotted next to her. "What about you, old boy?"

He woofed.

Grandma's voice resonated in Erica's head as she and Timber made their way to the Jeep. *The Guardians of Yellowstone trapped an Evil in the Caldera many years ago. It has simmered in anger ever since, venting through geysers and mud pots. It swore one day it would take its revenge on all those who inhabit these lands.*

Erica tapped her forehead with her open palm. "Stop thinking about the legends and focus on the science, Erica." She opened the door of the Jeep.

Timber leaped in and perched in the passenger seat. Erica climbed into the driver's seat, turned on the car, and backed out.

The moon's wicked glow crept across the desolate parking lot, engulfing the emptiness in a haunting light. Grandma's legends, ghost stories and bedtime tales jumbled in Erica's head as she drove to the trailhead. *The stars will lead the way.* She couldn't remember the rest of that story, something about spirits or ancestors. Her comm beeped.

Justin's face appeared. "Erica, how close are you?"

"Pulling into the parking lot. Where are you?"

"Nearly to the geyser. It was a lot farther than I thought. I had to go off trail and through an open field I didn't even know existed."

Erica parked the car next to the trailhead.

A panicked expression crossed over Justin's face. "Holy crap! You won't believe this. You gotta see—" The sound of an erupting geyser drowned out the last of Justin's words as he turned the comm away from him.

Mesmerizing mist swirled on the comm picture.

Erica rubbed her eyes as the eruption transformed into what appeared to be huge octopus tentacles.

Justin screamed.

With a loud crack, the picture on the comm shattered as if someone had stepped on it.

"Justin! What's going on?" Erica yelled into the comm, even though her brain told her she wouldn't get an answer. "Let's go, Timber."

She hopped out of the jeep, clicked on her flashlight and rushed down the trail. Timber stayed close on her heels. They raced past Fairy Falls and over an enormous tree trunk that crossed the river. With each step, a rush of adrenaline coursed through her veins. What had happened to Justin?

They came to a fork in the trail. There was nothing to indicate which direction Justin had gone. "Which way Timber?"

Timber sniffed the ground and bolted down the left fork through a large aspen grove. Fallen leaves, wet from the first October snow, coated the ground and tree roots intertwined like snakes in front of them, making the trail treacherous and slow going.

The light from the flashlight faded and died. With only the soft glow of the moon and the twinkling stars to guide her, Erica slowed her pace. "Maybe this is what Grandma meant by 'the stars will show you the way'."

Timber howled and yanked on her winter coat, stopping her forward progression as a new mud pot oozed from the ground.

Erica sucked in a breath, realizing how close she was to danger.

The mud slithered toward her as if imbued with a sinister life-force. Acid rose in her throat.

The hackles on Timber's back stood on guard. He snarled.

The mud recoiled as if afraid of him. Erica grabbed the nape of Timber's neck and dragged him around the mud and deeper into the woods.

Shadows cast by the moon skirted through the trees, taunting Erica as she and Timber continued their quest.

She halted at the edge of the forest. In front of her, geysers erupted across an expansive open field. The sound of rushing water filled the still of the night.

Timber nuzzled her hand and growled.

"It's okay. I feel it too." She offered a reassuring pat on Timber's head as electricity coursed up her spine.

A sudden belch of steam burst through the earth, five feet to their left. Hot water in the cool air generated vapors that swirled through the moonlit woods, creating a haunting spectacle of dancing shadows.

Timber snarled, white teeth glaring, and moved between Erica and the geyser.

Erica's heart pounded. "What is it, boy?" Her voice quivered as she unsheathed the hunter's knife she carried and scanned her surroundings.

Nothing moved.

A heavy silence descended, like a suffocating wet blanket.

Erica gasped for breath.

The ground shook, and the geyser ahead huffed.

Silence.

The still air exploded as fiery fingers at the end of a glowing arm of water burst from the geyser and pitched Timber to the side before seizing Erica's leg.

She screamed. Shooting pain surged through her calf as tentacle fingers burned the flesh under her pants. The arm yanked her off her feet and dragged her toward the epicenter of the geyser. Erica kicked with her other foot, struggling to break free.

Timber lunged and bit into the nightmarish hand, jaws snapping with watery smacks. The hairs on his snout singed in the heat.

A blood-curdling screech from the geyser-being pierced the thick air.

It released its grip on Erica.

She scrambled to her feet, ready to run. The geyser transformed into a malevolent steam bear, wispy and scalding.

It hurtled toward her, its sharp teeth gnashing as it charged.

Timber raced under Erica's legs, launching her over his head onto his back.

She righted herself, leaned forward and wrapped her arms around his neck.

He charged away from the monstrous bear.

Erica clung tightly, her heart pounding as they rushed through the aspen and pine forests, heading toward the river. She glanced back. The fiery bear flew after them. Scorched aspens fell in its wake.

Timber paused at the river's edge before wading in and bracing against the cold current. The bear writhed and retreated into the dark forest. Erica glanced over her shoulder again as Timber stepped up onto the bank. A vague mist stood where the bear had been.

Timber raced forward with an unnatural speed until they came to the edge of the Grand Canyon of Yellowstone.

Erica only had a moment to be shocked at how far they had come in such a short time before Timber's giant paws tore through the yellow pitchstone scree as he descended into the canyon's depths.

Spray from the river soaked them. Erica dug her fingers deep into his coat to hang on, letting the warmth of his body soothe the fear in her heart.

Timber barged through a powerful waterfall curtain and landed on a moss-covered ledge.

Erica dismounted from his back and reached out to the

mossy rocks dripping with rivulets. Her fingers glided over the rough contours until she found a crevice and reached in.

The smooth rocks, weathered from years of rushing water, parted, revealing a concealed door. She typed into a keypad and the door opened. Timber and Erica stepped into the secret chamber. The shelf to the right proudly displayed Erica's cherished childhood toys. To the left a silver metal table held laboratory equipment. Encompassing the entire back wall was a large analyzer. This was her sanctuary. A place known only to her, Timber, Grandma and more recently, Justin.

Erica secured the inner lab door as the outer rocks scraped shut. "Are you okay, boy?" She applied Devil's Club salve to her leg and Timber's nose. Amazingly, the inside of Timber's mouth had been spared from any injury.

Erica shook her head. "I'm dreaming. This is all a horrible nightmare. Justin's going to come in the door any minute now." She pinched her hand and winced from the pain.

Ghostly whispers floated through the air.

Timber raised his hackles and laid his ears back.

A woman's withered voice emanated through the lab. "You're not dreaming."

"Grandma?" Erica threw her hand over her mouth. She shook her head to remove the cobwebs.

Timber turned in a circle, gave a friendly woof, and wagged his tail.

"How am I hearing you?" Erica slumped into a chair. "I hit my head. That's it. I'm hallucinating. There's no way this is happening."

"Look around you, child. The changes to the park. The monsters. The burns on your leg. The legends are real. We are the Guardians of Yellowstone. The Evil is awakening and growing stronger by the second," Grandma said.

"That bear—" Erica clutched her chest. "—those fingers."

She squeezed her temples. "Evil? Coming to Life? It can't be real."

"We don't have time for your disbelief. You must defeat the Evil," Grandma said.

"How?" Erica's mind raced. "I don't know where Justin is. I don't have his evidence. I don't even know if he's okay."

"Everything will be fine. Remember the stories," Grandma said.

Erica stood. "I need to run more tests with better equipment than my field analyzer." She opened her backpack and extracted the test tubes with the evidence from the mud pots she had collected earlier and inserted them into the large analyzer. "Without these tests, I won't know how to destroy the Evil."

Alarms sounded through the room. Erica flipped a switch on the side of the door. The video feeds she used to observe the park's main geologic features lit up the walls of the laboratory. Glowing blue-green water creatures emerged from Morning Glory and Grand Prismatic Pools. Mud golems resembling buffalos glopped out of Fountain and Painted Mud Pots.

Erica screamed. "What the hell are those?"

An enormous dragon took flight from Dragon's Mouth Spring. It opened its mouth and released a blazing inferno, incinerating the boardwalks and trees in its path.

"And so it begins," Grandma said grimly. "The Evil has reached its full power. You don't need any more tests. Remember our family legends. You can do this. I cannot stay. I must—" Grandma's voice was cut off by the rattling of the analyzer. Ghostly vapor rose into the air and disappeared.

The analyzer exploded, releasing a torrent of expanding mud that oozed over the table and up the walls.

Panic gripped Erica as the mud encroached across the room toward her. She frantically pushed the buttons to open the door, while trying to recall the other tales her grandma had told her. "Why did I not pay more attention when she talked?"

The door opened. Cool droplets of river water from the falls blew in, hitting the mud monster now inches from Erica.

The mud creature writhed and retreated. Its shrill screech sent vibrations down Erica's spine.

As a child, Erica had never understood Grandma's admonition that the sacred waters of the river were a gift and a weapon. "But now—the river water in Yellowstone has increased iodine levels. The sulfur levels are rising in the geysers and mud pots. What if—?" The gears in her head spun. "If the Evil is composed of sulfur and heat, could the iodine neutralize it?"

Grabbing a bucket off the floor next to the door, she filled it with the sacred cascading water. As the mud continued to advance, she flung the water at it. The mud hissed, shrunk and disappeared in a whiff of smoke.

She gathered three gallons of water into two Camelbaks, set one of the wearable water bags in her backpack and strapped the other across her chest.

Emergency alarms rang out across the park. She glanced at the camera feeds on the walls. Northern lights lit up the sky and the earth below. Animals and park rangers were locked in a desperate battle against glowing monsters and mud creatures. An elk bellowed as its hair caught fire from a steaming dart flung by a geyser bear. More otherworldly organisms descended the hillside toward her hiding spot.

Determined, Erica slipped out the door of her chamber, Timber close by her side. They scooted around the waterfall and climbed upward along the treacherous moss-covered perforated-steel steps of Uncle Tom's Stairs, long ago closed to visitors.

A glowing green and blue moss creature, half-coyote, half-mountain goat, descended toward her, baring its sharp fangs.

Timber charged.

Erica squeezed the mouthpiece at the end of the tubing from her Camelbak and shot the creature with water.

The monster whimpered and twisted into a tornado wind tunnel before disappearing.

They continued their ascent. Timber charged at four mud creatures. Erica shot water at them.

They evaporated.

The Big Dipper commanded the dark sky. The stars of the handle gleamed with unparalleled clarity, pointing toward Fairy Falls.

The mystery of the legends unraveled in her mind. At that moment, Erica knew what she had to do. She whistled to Timber. "I need to get back to the geyser with that nasty bear."

He lowered his head in understanding.

Erica mounted his back. They raced away from the Grand Canyon of Yellowstone and across the wilderness. A few feet from the tentacle-geyser, the monstrous, glowing bear that had chased them earlier lunged from behind a tree, knocking Timber to the ground and throwing Erica clear.

The fiery hand at the end of the water-arm snatched her, its heat penetrating into her skin. This time she didn't struggle, allowing it to drag her into its epicenter.

The hand dropped her onto the cold ground of a murky cave. To her right, in a cage with bars made of fire, Justin stood and stammered. "Erica? What? How? What are you doing here?"

"Justin." Relief swept over Erica as she saw him alive. She raced forward, determined to free him. A geyser burst between her and Justin's fiery prison cell, stopping her from getting any closer.

Six humanoid heads, each with wretched burn scars, five eyes and a mouth, appeared from the geyser. The middle two heads opened their mouths and spoke in a baritone voice. "Your ancestors have held us captive for long enough."

The sides of the cave magically displayed the video feeds from the park's cameras. The cave reverberated with anguished cries of humans and animals as they fought a losing battle against the geyser monsters and mud creatures, outnumbering them five to one.

The two heads on the right of the monster turned and sneered at her before speaking in a gravelly high-pitched voice. "You and your kind cannot win this battle."

A shock raced up Erica's spine as she tried to concentrate on the task at hand and not on the videos.

The Evil focused all six heads on her. This time, all the mouths spoke in unison. They assumed the voice of a poacher who had attempted to kill Timber a few years ago. "Watch as I massacre the ones you love." The monster glided to the side as blue and white flames engulfed the prison holding Justin.

Justin's body twisted as he screamed in pain.

The camera feed focused on the glowing geyser bear. It sank its teeth into Timber's hindquarters. Timber howled in agony and wrenched away.

Erica's heart clenched. With a warrior's yell, she sprinted toward the six-headed monstrosity, spraying the rest of the water from the bag on her chest.

The beast screeched, dodged the water and latched onto Erica, pinning her arms to her side and squeezing her savagely.

Erica screamed and twisted, attempting to free her arm as the geyser exploded up and out of the cave, carrying her with it. Desperation gripped her as she struggled to breathe. *Grandma, I need you.*

Ethereal images of her grandmother and her ancestors

manifested in the steamy mist. They swirled around the monster's heads. The mouths snapped at the ghostly images. The necks intertwined, forming a tightly braided knot.

Erica took a deep breath, wrenched her arm free, grabbed her hunter's knife, and sliced the remaining water bag, drenching herself and her captor.

All six mouths emitted a deafening wail that echoed to the highest peaks.

The hand released Erica, who plummeted to the ground, landing hard in a pile of fallen aspen leaves.

Glowing creatures from across the park lit up the night sky as the monster swallowed them into its mouths. In a whirlwind, the six-headed creature twirled back into the depths from which it came, leaving only a steaming vent in its place.

The damp leaves against her skin provided a cool relief as Erica pushed herself up and gently massaged her bruised hip. Her arms, legs and abdomen stung where the Evil had left its burns. She pulled salve out of her backpack and applied it.

The wind whispered. Her ancestors floated above her and smiled before evaporating into the starlit night.

Erica hobbled over to Timber, who licked his wounds.

She wrapped her arms around his neck and sobbed. "Justin." Tears flowed freely down her cheeks.

Timber nudged her and freed himself. He raced to a grove of trees near the geyser vent and barked.

Underneath the quaking aspen, curled in a ball, lay Justin. Burned flesh was visible through his torn clothes.

Timber licked him.

Justin rubbed the wolf slobber off his face, uncurled and patted himself. "I don't understand. The fire. How did I escape?"

Erica sat next to him, pulled out her salve and applied it to the burns on his face, arms and legs. "It's got to be the magic of my ancestors."

Justin shook his head. "So, spirit warriors saved us in the end."

Erica shrugged. "Them, legends, and science." She helped him to his feet. They looked out over the vast moonlit caldera. The Big Dipper moved higher in the sky. Timber trotted up next to them and leaned against Erica's leg.

An icy wind, heavy with the whispers of ancient souls, blew through the skeletal branches of the aspen grove.

Erica shivered. Like her ancestors before, she was a Guardian of Yellowstone. A place filled with magic, danger and mystery.

CHERYL FALLIN M.D. IS A PEDIATRICIAN, AUTHOR, AND MOTHER OF two amazing children, Andrew and Emily. She lives in rural Wyoming with her husband Chad and border collie Stella. Her novel, SERAPH, a soon-to-be-released near-future medical thriller, is a Colorado Gold Rush Literary Award Winner. Her previously published works include poems, newsletter articles, two short stories in Speculative Fiction Writer anthologies and a newspaper column titled *What's up Doc.* When not writing or working she loves adventure traveling with her husband and family.

**READ MORE GREAT FICTION
FROM THALIA PRESS**

Discover novels and anthologies at ThaliaPress.com

Printed in Great Britain
by Amazon